The Cellar Beneath the Cellar

Lee Duigon

STOREHOUSE
PRESS

VALLECITO, CALIFORNIA

Published by Storehouse Press

P.O. Box 158, Vallecito, CA 95251

Storehouse Press is the registered trademark of Chalcedon, Inc.

This book is a work of fiction. Names, characters, businesses, organizations, places, events, and incidents either are the product of the author's imagination or used fictitiously. Any resemblance to actual persons, living or dead, events, or locales is entirely coincidental.

Book design by Kirk DouPonce (www.DogEaredDesign.com)

Printed in the United States of America

First Edition

Library of Congress Catalog Card Number: 2010936270

ISBN-13: 978-1-891375-55-2

ISBN-10: 1-891375-55-5

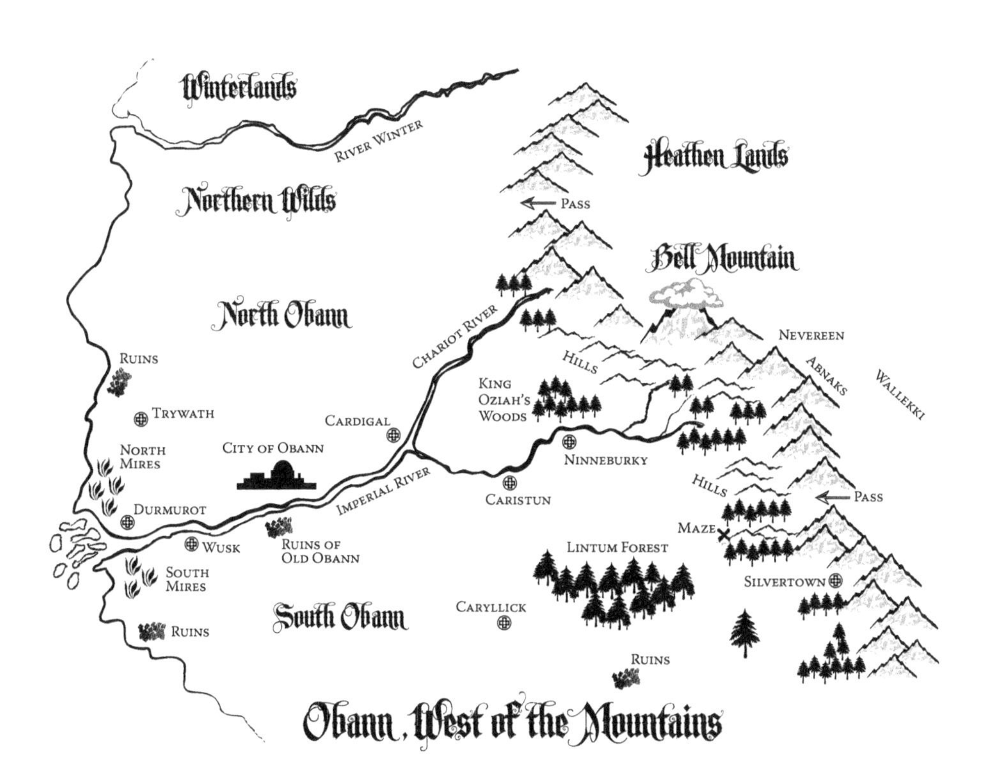
Winterlands
River Winter
Heathen Lands
Northern Wilds
Pass
Bell Mountain
North Obann
Chariot River
Nevereen
Hills
Abnaks
Wallekki
Ruins
King Oziah's Woods
Trywath
Cardigal
North Mires
City of Obann
Ninneburky
Imperial River
Caristun
Hills
Pass
Durmurot
Maze
Wusk
Ruins of Old Obann
Lintum Forest
South Mires
Silvertown
Caryllick
Ruins
South Obann
Ruins
Obann, West of the Mountains

CHAPTER 1

Down from the Mountain

If you have read the story of how Jack and Ellayne climbed Bell Mountain and rang the bell that King Ozias put there, you may have wondered what happened to them next.

Jack fully expected the world to end as soon as the bell stopped ringing. He did not know how it would end, he was not even sure he understood what "the end of the world" meant, and he was afraid it would be loud and painful. But what choice had he? God had sent him dreams about the bell, and those dreams were commands. Something even worse than the end of the world would happen if those commands were not obeyed. Besides, God would just find someone else to ring it.

You can imagine his feelings when the clouds blew away and he and Ellayne were still there. The ancient wooden frame that had supported the bell for centuries had collapsed into a pile of splinters; the bell itself was broken in pieces. But the world was still there. He let out a long, deep sigh.

"I'm cold," he said.

"The bell's broken, so I guess that's that," Ellayne said. "Where did all the fog go?"

They might have stood there some time longer if they hadn't noticed a man lying facedown on the trail, maybe half a stone's throw from them. Jack remembered the man coming out of the mist just as they'd grabbed the chain to ring the bell, and waving at them and hollering. But they couldn't hear him over the pealing of the bell.

"Who could that be?" Jack said. And because it was too cold on the mountaintop to be just standing there, he went to have a closer look at the man. Ellayne followed; Jack heard her teeth chattering.

"I wonder if he's dead," she said. "Whatever you do, don't touch him."

But the man wasn't dead. As they stood over him, he rolled onto his back and let out a groan. His eyes fluttered open. He stared at them.

"Who are you?" Jack said. "What are you doing here?"

"Are you sick?" Ellayne asked.

Martis opened his eyes. When the bell rang, he'd had the sensation of falling headfirst into a black pit, falling and falling forever. Now he lay on solid ground, and there were children looking down at him and asking him questions. When he pushed himself up on his hands, he saw that the bell was down, broken, its supporting framework ruined.

He'd failed in his mission. The children had rung the bell, and it would never ring again. He'd failed to stop them. If he ever returned to Obann, Lord Reesh would have a new assassin waiting for him.

He stood up with a sigh, his whole body aching.

"Who are you?" the boy demanded.

Martis laughed; but he didn't like the way his own laugh sounded.

"You don't know what you're asking me, young sir!" the man said. "But to answer you briefly, the Temple sent me to make sure you didn't ring the bell. I was sent to kill you. But you needn't reach for your knife. I won't hurt you now—or ever."

Ellayne recognized the Temple insignia on his torn, stained coat. His beard was white but his hair was brown, which she thought very odd. He told them a story about how he'd followed them all the way from Ninneburky and found Obst dying in a shelter on the mountain; and Obst had told him how to follow them the rest of the way up. The children listened for a while, but now they wanted to see Obst again. He deserved a decent burial, at least.

"We have to go back down," Jack said. "It's too cold to stay up here. We need a fire and food. You'd better come back to our camp with us."

The man agreed, and slowly, together, they proceeded down the trail.

Martis spoke no more. He could barely think. He remembered coming up the mountain, hurrying after the children, toiling in a blinding cloud, unable to see more than a step or two ahead, in a fog thick enough to force its way under your clothes. Now, coming down, they fared in the full light of the morning sun. Every pebble on the trail, every scratch on every boulder, stood out bright and clear. The neighboring peaks, glistening with streaks of ice and snow, looked like you could reach out and touch them, pick them up and take them with you.

He was cold, a deep-down cold that went all the way to the core of his mind, freezing thoughts before they could take shape as words. And yet with every faltering step he took, the sun caressed his face and each step was just a little stronger. He could not remember the last time anything had felt as good as that sun on his face.

They hustled down the mountain as fast as they could, anxious to reach camp before nightfall. No one felt like talking. There was too much to think about, and too much to see. Bell Mountain's cloak of clouds was gone.

No one had ever seen the peak; clouds had always shrouded it. Down below, growing up in Ninneburky, Jack looked up at the mountains every day of his life; and on every one of those days, Bell Mountain's peak hid under that bank of clouds. What were people thinking down there now that the cloud was gone? What did the mountain look like now? Jack wished he could see it.

But even more on his mind was the question of when the world would begin to end and what that would be like. He couldn't put those thoughts into words: they were too big. More than anything else, he wanted to sit down by a fire and have something to eat. He was terribly tired.

And in good time, there it was, their camp, with Ham the donkey still there and little, hairy Wytt, no bigger than a rat, hopping up and down and chittering to greet them. There was a horse hobbled, too.

"Is that your horse?" Ellayne asked the man from the Temple.

"Yes."

"Let's get a campfire started!" Jack said. He was shivering all over.

Their camp was just a wide spot in the trail, with some huge boulders well-placed for shelter from the wind and the firewood they'd brought up with them; but it felt like coming home. Jack got busy right away, making a fire. If he used up the last of his matches, he didn't care; and anyhow, Ellayne knew how to start a fire without matches (Jack had never gotten the hang of it). She passed out drinks of water, and the man sat down and sighed.

Wytt stood in front of him, chattering, brandishing his little sharp stick. The man stared at him.

"Jack! Wytt's talking to us!" Ellayne said.

He paused. She was right—it was a kind of talking, not just scolding like a squirrel in a tree. It wasn't words, like human speech. Nevertheless, Jack understood it.

"Wytt's met this man before," he said. How Jack knew that, he couldn't have said; he just knew. "Well, of course he has. That's how the horse got here."

"He's telling us this man is all right," Ellayne said. "That's funny! We never used to understand him. But that man in the forest, that Helki—he said he could talk with the little hairy folk. And I always thought Wytt understood most of what we said to him."

"He's been with us long enough. We ought to understand him by now," Jack said. He was too tired for a miracle, just now. He got the fire started, finally, then looked up at the man. "You haven't told us your name, mister."

"My name is Martis. I'm a servant of the Temple."

With the fire going, and food in their bellies, and Wytt cuddled in Ellayne's arms, they finally got the man to talk.

And he had much to say.

"I've been following you for a long time," he said. "Lord Reesh himself, the First Prester, assigned the mission to me. He wanted me to see if you could find the bell. He wanted to know if there really was a bell. But I was not to let you ring it. I was to kill you."

It would be the easiest thing in the world for a grown man to kill a pair of children. Jack knew that. There was nothing to stop this man from killing them now.

"Don't be afraid!" Martis said. "Everything's changed. I wouldn't hurt you now, not for anything."

"But the First Prester!" Ellayne cried. "He's a great lord, and a man of God! Why would he—?"

"Because he was afraid. Afraid of you, afraid of the bell. Most of all, he was afraid God might be real, after all. I understand that now."

Martis shook his head. He looked desperately sad, Jack thought.

"I never thought Lord Reesh believed in God. He always said there was no God; or if there was, it didn't matter. He said the only things that matter are order and progress: wise men moving the world forward, he always said.

"Was everything he taught me just a lie? Everything? He must have known it was a lie, or he never would have sent me to stop you from ringing the bell. He must have believed God would hear it, just like the Scripture says. He must have feared God would bring the world to an end. He had dreams about it."

"But how could the First Prester not believe in God?" Ellayne said. She was more upset about it than Jack was, being much better educated. "I mean, he is the First Prester!

He's holy."

Martis laughed quietly, a kind of laugh with a lot of pain in it.

"I was the servant of that holy man," he said. "He took me off the streets and taught me everything I know. And can you guess how I served my holy master?

"I killed the people that he wanted killed, and found false witnesses to speak against persons that he wanted cast into prison or hanged, although they'd committed no crime. I stole the things he ordered me to steal. I doubt I could tell you half the crimes that I've committed—but I did them all by his command."

"Then you must be a very wicked man!" Ellayne said. "You must be as bad as he is, or worse."

"That can't be denied," Martis said.

"But it really doesn't matter," Jack said, "seeing as how the world is going to end." That silenced them all for some moments, until Ellayne spoke up.

"But it doesn't feel like the world's about to end," she said. "Instead, it feels more like everything is just about to start. It all feels *new*."

Jack was about to say that that was just about the stupidest thing he'd ever heard—but was it? Even in this washed-out mountain landscape, weren't the colors somehow brighter than they were the day before? It was late afternoon; the sun had already gone down behind the mountain peaks, and it was getting dark—but look how bright those first stars shone!

"Oh, what do you know about it!" he grumbled. "I guess Obst knew a hundred times better than you do, and he always said that after we rang the bell, God would end the world. I guess he must've known what he was talking about."

"Poor Obst! I wonder if he heard it when we rang the bell," Ellayne said. "I wonder what he thought of it before he died." She wiped away a tear. Just like a girl, Jack thought, ignoring the tear trickling down his own cheek.

"He was still alive when I left him," Martis said, "very weak, but in good spirits. That was, I think, two days ago." He shook his head. "I'm not sure of how much time has passed, lately."

"I wonder if there's a chance he's still alive," Jack said. "Maybe tomorrow, if we hurry ..." He turned to Martis. "But how do we know you won't kill us?"

The assassin shrugged. "You don't."

"But Obst was going to kill us, too, at first—he even said so," Ellayne said. "And then he changed his mind and helped us. We couldn't have got here without him."

"But Obst is a good man!" Jack said. "And this is a bad one. He told us so. How can we trust a bad man?"

"I don't ask you to trust me," Martis said. "I don't ask anything of you. But I'll protect you if I can. I know Lord Reesh. He will stop at nothing to have you brought before him, in secret; and then he will have you killed, in secret. He'll find another assassin to do his bidding."

"So you're going to turn against him? I thought he was your master," Jack said.

Martis sighed. "Up there on the mountaintop," he said, "I found another master. I think I came very close to dying. I doubt I would have come back to my senses, if you hadn't spoken to me."

"Another master?" said Ellayne.

"One to whom I owe my life—what's left of it. And to you and Jack, too, I find myself in debt. I wouldn't know how to turn into a good man," Martis said, "but perhaps my wickedness can be put to some constructive use.

"One thing I do know now that I didn't know this morning: God is truly God, and God protects you. He will not let me harm you, and I would be a fool to try. I hope I've never been as big a fool as that."

CHAPTER 2

Where Is Obst?

The following morning—cold, but bright and sunny, without a wisp of cloud—they hurried down the trail, making for the camp where they'd left Obst dying. He'd insisted they go the rest of the way without him. Otherwise there would've been no point to their journey.

Two things had changed. It was much easier to see, and hence they could travel faster (not to mention the advantage of going downhill instead of up); and Martis was strong.

"It must be the mountain air: it's so clean," he said. "I feel rejuvenated."

"The world hasn't ended yet," Ellayne said.

"Oh, maybe it did, and we just didn't notice."

"That's a stupid joke, Jack."

"Is it?" Martis said.

"Well, I certainly think it is."

"I'm not so sure. Maybe Jack has hit on something. It's too bad Lord Reesh didn't give me more instruction in theology. There might be some hidden sense in what you've said."

"What's theology?" Jack asked. Ellayne thought that was funny, but it turned out she didn't really know, either.

"It's the systematic study of God," Martis explained.

"We'd need Obst for that," Jack said. "He was a hermit for a long, long time, and he was always studying, and reading the Old Books, and meditating and praying. When he prays, you could light a fire under him and he'd never know it. He says God speaks to him."

They made excellent time, so much so that toward the end of the afternoon, Martis mounted his horse and went on ahead to reconnoiter. Ellayne sighed when he disappeared around a bend in the trail. "I wish we could trust him," she said.

Riding atop the pack on Ham's back, Wytt chattered.

"Wytt's not afraid of him," Jack said. And to Wytt, "Have you always understood everything we say?"

The little hairy man whistled. It meant, "Not always, but I do now."

"And we understand you," Ellayne said. "I don't see how that can be; it's not like we can speak your language." Wytt clicked his tongue to say it didn't matter.

Jack would not shrug off Wytt's opinion. They'd met one man on their travels who really would have harmed them, a tinker who drugged them and tied them up so he could sell them into slavery. Wytt killed him: stabbed him through the eye when he lay down to sleep.

"Why aren't you afraid of Martis, Wytt?" Jack asked.

A long stream of chattering and chittering, punctuated by clicks and chirps, delivered the message: "He is not like he was. He had something very bad in him when he came up the mountain. Now he doesn't. And he is afraid of you."

They heard the clatter of hooves on the stony trail, and then Martis reappeared. He swung gracefully out of the saddle.

"I've been to the camp, but Obst is not there," he said. "I searched, and found signs that indicate he left under his own power. I would have thought that was impossible, but that's how it looks to me. I do have some skill in tracking."

"But where would he go?" Ellayne said.

"He didn't come after us, or we would've met him on the way. This is the only trail up to the top, and we're on it," Jack said. "So he must have gone back down."

"Without us?"

"I guess so. But you'd think he would've waited for us."

"I wouldn't have said he had the strength to crawl ten feet," Martis said. "He seemed very near the end when I parted from him. Nevertheless, he seems to have walked away. He took food with him."

"But he's too sick to go anywhere alone," Ellayne said. "He wouldn't get far."

"It'll be dark soon. We ought to make camp," Martis said. "Maybe we can pick up his trail in the morning." He pointed to Wytt. "Maybe your little friend can find his scent."

Wytt showed his teeth and growled. "He'll try," Jack said.

Yes, Obst was dying when they left him. He didn't mind much. He was an old man, and he was proud he'd come that far up the mountain. Besides, the bell would ring very soon now, and he didn't suppose the world would outlive him by very much.

After Martis left him, he drifted into a kind of dreamless sleep from which he was surprised to wake up still alive.

It was dark. He was thirsty, but he couldn't remember where the water was and hardly had the strength to reach for it. He thought he must be pretty near the end.

As he lay there, thirsting, the darkness gradually lightened. It occurred to him that he couldn't feel anything from the knees down: dying by inches, he thought. God is merciful.

He had just begun to pray when he heard the bell.

What else could it be? The music came rolling down from the top of the mountain; it was the most beautiful sound he'd ever heard. His feet suddenly prickled, but he hardly noticed. He thought, if you could ring the stars, they'd sound like that. He felt his heart throb forcefully with every peal of the bell. He felt a pressure inside his head that made it uncomfortable to be lying on his back.

So he sat up.

By the time the bell stopped ringing, it was light enough to see and Obst wasn't dying anymore. He didn't think anyone would die that day, anywhere in the whole world. He could not remember the last time he'd felt so strong. He picked up the waterskin and took a good, long drink. It was delicious! Then he crawled out of the shelter, stood up easily, and stretched.

"Lord," he asked aloud, "why have you restored my life on the last day of the world? But nevertheless I thank you. It does feel good!"

As Obst understood Scripture—and he'd studied it all his life—the bell would ring, God would hear it, and God would unmake the world. It would be the ultimate punishment of man's wickedness; every prophet warned of it. God had given to each prophet a different way to say the same thing. Abgar, who lived a thousand years before King Ozias, had it: "As a rush of waters, a clash of mighty waters, the wrath of God shall drown the nations." A thousand years after Abgar, the prophetess Phobeth said, "Burn, burn, saith the Lord, in the great burning from which there is no deliverance." And other prophets spoke of plague and pestilence, earthquakes, ice, and all-devouring swarms of locusts with venom in their tails. So there was really no guessing what form the end of the world would take. It might be any one of those, or all of them.

"But what to do now?" Obst said to himself. As a hermit, he had long had the habit of talking to himself.

He had an unaccountable urge to hurry down the mountain as fast as his legs would carry him. It would be too bad not to see Jack and Ellayne anymore, but Obst was sure they were already in Heaven. God would have taken them up as soon as they'd rung the bell.

"I can't just stay here," he said. "It may be that the Lord will grant a period of grace, so that souls may be called to repentance before He carries out the destruction.

"Yes—that's why you have given me a little extra life, Lord, isn't it? So I can warn the people that the end is close at hand. It has been decreed. Any day now, really! One last chance to repent, and then the end."

Snatching up the waterskin and a satchel with some dried meat in it, Obst began his trek down from the mountain, back to the inhabited lands below. God had given him one more mission, and he was eager to begin.

So he was long gone when Jack and Ellayne returned to the camp, and they didn't know what to make of it. Tomorrow they would try to find his trail.

Over the campfire and the last of their food, Martis had a word of caution for them.

"The First Prester will have his servants combing the country for you," he said. "He will realize that I failed him; he may believe I met with some mischance. But I think he'll probably be looking for me, too. If any of us fall into his hands, we'll never emerge from them alive. So we'll need a safe place to hide, and for a long time. Or until the world ends."

"Lintum Forest, where King Ozias' mother hid," said Jack. "That's where we ought to go. They'll never find us there."

"I've already thought of that. But Lintum's full of outlaws. Any one of them might sell us to the Temple. And you can be sure the First Prester will devote his full attention to the forest."

Ellayne looked like she might cry. "But I thought we could go home!" she said.

"As if we could get home before the world ends," Jack said. "We probably won't even get off the mountain."

"We must proceed as if the world were not going to come to an end," Martis said. "I know little of theology, and you know less. It'd be foolish for us to try to make a judgment one way or the other.

"If I had only my own life to save, I'd go back to Obann, to the city. It's a great city, and I daresay I know it as well as anyone, and better than most. And there's the Old City across the river, too—what's left of it.

"A man who knows the city as I do could hide there for a very long time. Many do. Obann is full of men with prices on their heads. Some of them have dodged the hangman for many a year, without ever setting foot outside the city.

"There are sewers, abandoned buildings—even buried buildings. Dry wells and hollow places in the city walls. There are fugitives living on the rooftops. There are whole city blocks where neither the day watch nor the night watch ever go."

And—but this he didn't mention to the children—there were ways for a skilled assassin to get close to Lord Reesh: close enough to kill him.

Treason? But I'm already a traitor to my master, Martis thought, and surely he's a traitor to his God. I'm already condemned to the pit of lost souls; but if these children live, I'll have one good deed to my name—not to mention the last laugh on Lord Reesh.

"Do you think we could all hide in Obann?" Ellayne said. "Wytt, too?"

"We can think about it while we journey down the mountain. We don't have to decide tonight," Martis said. "The Old City might be the best place for you. And I have friends, as it were, in both cities, of whom the First Prester knows nothing.

"Besides all that, it's the last place he'll look."

CHAPTER 3

Of War and Prophecy

We need now to visit Obann ourselves, where Lord Reesh is attending a meeting of the High Council of the Oligarchy.

The chief councilor of every stone-walled town in Obann has a seat among the oligarchs; but only half a dozen lords sit on the High Council. These are the men who truly rule Obann.

They were gathered today in the First Prester's great audience chamber in the Temple, with its high, vaulted ceiling, tall stained-glass windows, and jewel-like mosaics of the great kings and prophets of Obann's long history. These, with their wide, solemn eyes, looked down from the ceiling and lent an air of gravity to the proceedings. The six lords sat at a round oak table, highly polished, that had room for sixty.

Chairing the meeting was Lord Ruffin, the governor-general, elected by his peers, a small man with dark, piercing eyes and a long, sharp nose. At his left sat burly, black-bearded Lord Gwyll, responsible for the management of Obann's armies; then Lord Chutt, Taxes and Revenue; Lord Davensay, Commerce; Judge Tombo, Civil Administration; and to the governor-general's right, representing the Temple, Lord Reesh himself.

Fat, his face wrinkled like an old apple left in a closet, his hair white and stringy, his eyes a pale and filmy blue, Lord Reesh sat blinking impatiently as Lord Gwyll went on and on about his preparations for the coming war. It was Reesh who had suggested calling this meeting; but the governor-general first wanted to hear from Gwyll. Thankfully, the general was almost finished.

"If we can just supply the major cities," he said, "so that they can stand like great rocks awash in the wave, they'll still be standing when this wave recedes, as it inevitably must. These Heathen confederacies never last for long. Come the winter, they'll head back home."

"Meanwhile, Lord Gwyll, it'll be a bit hard on those of our people who don't live behind fortifications, won't it?" the governor-general said. "It sounds as if you're giving up a whole year's crops for lost."

"We'll come out of the walled cities and hit the enemy hard, every chance we get," growled Gwyll. "I'm sorry if you don't like a defensive strategy, Lord Ruffin. I don't either! But by all accounts, this is going to be one big, nasty invasion—worse than anything we've seen in our lifetimes. We shall do well just to hold on to our cities till the winter."

"It's always bad when the Heathen unite behind a holy man," Lord Davensay said. He didn't look especially worried about it; but then he never looked worried.

Wearily, Lord Reesh held up a hand. Ruffin nodded to him.

"My lords," said Ruffin, "the First Prester wishes to speak."

"Thank you, my lord," said Reesh. He looked at each of the five great lords. He was finding it difficult to begin, although he'd been brooding for hours over what he was going to say. Might as well begin, he thought. The words will come to me.

"My lords, there is no longer a cloud over the top of Bell Mountain. The Heathen have gathered in unprecedented numbers to attack us.

"In our thinly populated regions, strange beasts have been seen, creatures for which we have no names. Strange fish have appeared in our waters. I am sure some of you saw that enormous lobster-thing that some yokels carted in from the coast the other day.

"Here in our own city of Obann, hysterics run to and fro, babbling about their dreams and visions. Right here in the Temple, we've had kitchen-maids, scullions, and old washerwomen going out of their heads and speaking nonsense. Old wrecks who never learned to read or write, who never listened to a sermon in their lives, now speak words that sound very like passages of Scripture. I doubt there's a great house in Obann that hasn't heard this moonshine from its servants."

The other lords nodded. Reesh was telling them nothing that they didn't know already; but this was the first time anyone would speak of it.

"You are well aware, my lords, that seven days ago, just as dawn was breaking, the pealing of a great bell was heard throughout the city. We have, of course, many bells in Obann; but it was none of them. Furthermore, we know now that the same thing happened elsewhere, at precisely the same time. Even in towns that haven't any bells! I think we may just assume that this bell was heard everywhere in Obann.

"By now, you have all been reminded of the Scripture in which King Ozias, going into exile for life, announced his intention to erect a bell on the summit of Mount Yul, which most of us call Bell Mountain. Someday, the king said, someone would climb the mountain and ring the bell; and it was the king's hope God would hear it. To which the prophet Penda replied, 'Yea, God will surely hear it.'

"It is my belief that the mysterious tolling we all heard at dawn a week ago was the ringing of that bell."

Lord Chutt, Taxes and Revenue, laughed out loud, a harsh and unbelieving laugh.

"My lord First Prester—you, of all people! You're talking rot, pure rot. Medieval superstition. You don't even believe in God. We all know it."

Reesh silenced him with a look.

"I am an old man, my lord, the oldest man in this room," Reesh said. "I don't have time for fantasy. I don't have time to push the facts away until I'm forced to swallow them.

"The fact is that we heard the bell, and it wasn't any bell of ours. The fact is that they heard it in every city, every town, every farming village, and every logging camp that has reported in so far.

"The fact is that the cloud that hid the summit of Bell Mountain for uncounted generations has disappeared, and it disappeared the day we heard the bell.

"And the fact is that the Scriptures speak of this. The old and the young shall dream dreams, the prophet Ika said, and see visions. And Prophet Asara said, 'The lowliest among you shall be as prophets to you.'

"This is exactly what has happened, and it is a fact. It cannot be ignored.

"I have devoted all my life to laboring for Obann, toiling to lift it back to those heights of glory and greatness that it enjoyed a thousand years ago under the Empire. I take no pleasure in these facts that I have enumerated to you."

"Of course not—but burn it all, what do they mean?" Lord Gwyll roared. "Another fact is that we're about to have a war—a war such as none of us has ever seen in all our lives. We can't be chauntering on about bells and prophecies at a time like this! There'll be precious little time for pondering Scripture, if the Heathen get over our walls."

They nodded at that speech, too. Reesh could hardly blame them. Until the day the bell rang, he, too, would have dismissed it all as medieval superstition.

"My lords, my friends," he said, spreading his wrinkled hands on the cool, smooth surface of the table. "It is popularly believed that the ringing of the bell on Bell Mountain presages the destruction of the world. A few country presters who should have known better have already said so in their sermons.

"This belief is spreading like a fire in a dried-out cornfield. We have to do something about it. Who's going to fight if he thinks the world's about to end? Who's going to work? Unless we find an effective answer to it, we will not win this war. We shall be unable to defend our cities; and then, whether God ends the world or not, it'll be all over with us."

Judge Tombo, fatter than Lord Reesh by fifty pounds, and twenty years younger, remained after the meeting was over and the others had gone.

"They don't believe you," he said.

They had adjourned to Lord Reesh's private drawing room and ordered wine. The judge was the First Prester's best friend. Between them, Tombo liked to joke, they'd buried a whole cemetery's worth of men who would never be missed.

"This has to be stopped, and I don't know how to stop it," Reesh said. He noticed his hands were trembling: a bad sign. But his mind continued to grapple with the problem, nonstop.

"I agree," Tombo said. "You alarm me, Reesh. If there really is a God, and the Scriptures tell the truth about Him, then you and I are in serious trouble—notwithstanding everything we've done was for the good of our country."

"And ourselves!" snapped Reesh. "I'm old enough to be honest."

"There doesn't seem to be much we can do about God deciding to end the world."

Reesh waved those words away. "Bah!" he said. "All the Scripture says is that God will *hear* the bell when someone rings it. It doesn't say what He will *do*. All those prophecies about the end of the world were fulfilled when the Empire was destroyed. That was a thousand years ago, and we still haven't struggled but a part of the way back to where we were when it happened."

Tombo grinned at him. "But then you weren't chosen First Prester for your attainments as a theologian, were you?" he said.

"I was chosen because I made it my business to be chosen. I never had time for all the holy books and commentaries. I did what I could to make religion a force for order and stability. Now I realize I should have done more. But it's too late: every half-wit in Obann is prophesying these days. I underestimated the power of superstition, and its persistence."

"I can't tell my people to arrest everyone who prophesies," Tombo said. "That'll only make it worse. And yet we can't ignore it, either."

"You can help me find out who rang the bell, and take them into custody," Reesh said. "I had a report of two children from somewhere up the river. They dreamed dreams and ran away from home to climb the mountain. I put my best man on it—Martis—to find them, follow them, and stop them. It seems he failed."

"He never fails."

"Well, this time he did! Someone rang that bell, probably those two children. The whole nation heard it, which is supernatural in itself."

Tombo peered into his wine. "So we were wrong," he said. "Wrong about everything."

"Not everything! We were right to labor for order and progress. We were right to remove anyone who stood in the way. But now we are confronted with a supernatural event, one that threatens to demoralize the nation in a time of crisis. We must find those children and question them—exhaustively. The Temple doesn't have the manpower for that, so you must help me, Tombo."

"I will. I promise you that."

"My task will be even harder. The entire Temple must be mobilized. Every prester, every reciter, in every chamber house across the land, must preach against these wild prophecies. We cannot deny the event, so we'll have to dream up another explanation for it. We may even have to rewrite parts of Scripture. It won't be easy to get everyone to agree to that."

"Those who don't agree must be replaced," said the judge.

Reesh sighed. The wine had lost its taste for him. Even so, he relaxed in Tombo's company.

"I've been thinking very hard," he said, "and it may be that I have an idea, in very general terms, of what we must do.

"This Heathen confederacy is under one of their holy men from the Great Lakes. They say he works miracles. *We* will say he has a mission to destroy the Temple and all Obann with it; I don't think we'll be guilty of exaggerating.

"We will say that God Himself rang the bell to alert us to our peril and assure us of His aid, if only we do our part. We will say the world is not going to end, but our world, Obann, could end—if the people are not faithful to their Temple and their state, courageous in battle, and willing to endure grievous hardships.

"We will say this is a time of testing, the hardest test there ever was: so that through us God might show His power and His might. If we are worthy, we will emerge from the test renewed and blessed.

"This time, we shall say, the Heathen must be subdued forever, and all their filthy, false idolatries wiped out. We shall say God is angry because we have allowed the Heathen to flourish and let them alone on their side of the mountains. This time, we shall say, victory shall not be declared until our armies have crossed the mountains, thrown down all the Heathen idols, and planted our standards on the far shores of the lakes."

Reesh ran out of breath, and stopped. He was surprised to find Judge Tombo grinning at him.

"They were wise to choose you as First Prester," Tombo said. "We'll restore the Empire yet."

CHAPTER 4

How the Scouts Captured a Madman

Obst started down the mountain two days before his friends, and they were not fated to catch up to him.

He felt strong; he made good time. His legs felt twenty years younger, forty years stronger. If the path he followed hadn't been so steep, so twisty, so strewn with stones and tree roots, and so hemmed in on either side by briars and undergrowth, he would have skipped down the mountain.

Paying little attention to where he was going—as long as it was downhill, it couldn't matter much—Obst had but little idea of where he was. Feeling strong and fresh was a great distraction. He drank in the clean, cool air, reveled in the song of birds and the chattering of squirrels. A blue jay followed him for some distance, scolding raucously. Under his breath, he prayed.

"Thank you, God, for giving me one more piece of work to do! Thank you for revealing to me, once again, the beauty of this world you have created, and now must uncreate. I trust in you, O Lord: use me to save souls before it's too late."

So occupied, he almost rammed into two men who suddenly stepped out into the path ahead of him. He stopped just short of a collision.

They stared at him. He stared at them. He knew, of course, that they were Heathen, guessed they must be scouting the ways across the mountains. But that was all he knew about them. The one was short, powerful, with dark skin covered with interlaced tattoos, and a shaved head with a single hank of thick black hair hanging down one side. He wore buckskin leggings and a string of many-colored beads around his neck, nothing more. The other was taller, without tattoos, dressed in brightly patterned woolen garments, bearded, with long hawk-feathers woven into his hair. Both clutched weapons in their hands: the tattooed man a hatchet, the feathered man a short spear.

"Excuse me, friends!" Obst said. "I didn't see you until it was almost too late."

"Who are you?" demanded the one with the feathers. "Who are you, westman who speaks the language of the Wallekki?"

The other glared at his companion. "Wallekki? Nay, he spoke Abnak!"

But Obst had spoken in the only language he knew, besides the archaic language of the Scriptures, the everyday speech of Obann. It amazed him to hear these Heathen speaking it, too.

He knew the Wallekki and the Abnaks were two different Heathen nations. There were many more, each with its own language or dialect, each with its own set of idols and distinctive way of life. He also knew they'd invented a common language, called Tribe-talk, with which the different nations could communicate. But what he heard from these two was Obannese, pure and simple.

The Wallekki menaced him with the spear. "Speak up, old man! Who are you, and what are you doing on the mountain, and how did you learn to speak Wallekki?"

"Abnak!" said the other. "Tell us, or you die here."

"Warriors, there's no call to be angry with me," Obst said. "I'm nobody special—just an ordinary servant of God coming down from the top of the mountain. Well, almost the top. Didn't you hear the bell when it rang two days ago?"

The two Heathen exchanged worried glances. "Aye, we heard it," said the Abnak. "Even as I hear you speaking Abnak as if you were born to it."

"A bell, you say?" exclaimed the other. "There is no bell here."

"But surely you know the name we give the mountain," Obst said. "I don't know what name you have for it, but we call it Bell Mountain. That's because there is a bell on top of it, erected two thousand years ago by King Ozias. He hung it there so that, someday, someone would come along and ring it, and God would hear it. That was the bell you heard. Someone has rung it, and God has heard it."

It was not surprising that these Heathen men knew nothing of King Ozias' bell.

"This is madness," said the spearman. "When he speaks, I hear every word of it in Wallekki; and yet you hear it in Abnak. But he can't speak two languages at once."

"And when you speak," Obst said, "I hear only the language of Obann!"

"We speak to each other in Tribe-talk," said the Abnak. "I know not one word of your silly westmen talk."

"Nor I," the Wallekki said.

Obst understood, then, what had happened. It was all he could do, not to leap on the men and embrace them: but that would have been dangerous.

"Oh, it's wonderful!" he cried. His feet felt like dancing. "You wouldn't know this, my friends, but it's all in Holy Scripture: God has given me the means to talk to you and to understand you when you speak to me. It's not my doing, but God's. For I assure you that I can't speak a word of any of your languages, no more than you can speak mine. Nevertheless we understand each other! It is a gift from God."

"We had better take him back with us alive," the Wallekki said to the Abnak. "We have a proverb, 'Leave the fighting to the men, and the gods to the priests.' If we kill him here, the priests will ask us questions we can't answer."

"It's bad luck to kill a madman," said the Abnak, "and this old man is surely mad. Or else he is a shaman among his own kind. But it's bad luck to kill a shaman, too."

"I'm only too happy to go with you fellows," Obst said. "God has given me a message to deliver to your people. If you heard the bell, you need to hear the message, too.

"My name is Obst, by the way. I don't think I'm mad, and I know I'm not a shaman. For most of my life I've been a hermit. My home was in Lintum Forest, a long way from here."

"We know where Lintum Forest is," growled the Abnak. But the Wallekki introduced himself: "My name is Sharak, son of Ahal, the son of Eebra ..." He went on for an impressive number of generations, while his companion scowled.

"And I am Hooq, the son of no one in particular," the tattooed man said. "But I have washed my hatchet many times in the blood of Abnak's enemies."

"Of which I am not one," said Obst.

CHAPTER 5

Obst Becomes a Missionary

Wytt's keen senses—not to mention his being so close to the ground—soon picked up Obst's trail.

"How did you come to have him as a traveling companion?" Martis asked the children, as they all followed the little hairy man. Martis had a scab on his hand where Wytt stabbed him the first time they met. He had not yet told the children about that meeting.

"Oh, we met him when we camped in some ruins one night," Ellayne said. "There must have been hundreds of them on that hilltop, but you would never know they were there. Anyhow, we gave Wytt some of our food, and he just befriended us."

"They're in the Old Books, you know," Jack said. "They're Omah, which means 'hairy ones.' Obst told us all about it. God says, 'I shall give your cities to the hairy ones.'"

Martis knew that verse, and others. The tiny man, the size of a large rat, completely covered with brown fur—the sight of it still made him uneasy.

Commentators didn't even know what the ancients meant by "hairy ones." Some sort of mythological creature,

Lord Reesh would have said, like a dragon or a unicorn. "Scripture is full of folklore and mythology," he used to say. He believed hardly a word of it. And yet here it is, Martis thought, a mythological creature, right before my eyes. Just like the bell on Bell Mountain.

The thought that the Scripture might be true, cover to cover, he found a dreadful one. Some of it was true, no doubt; but the rest of it was only stories. The Children of Geb escaping from the Deluge on stepping-stones across the sea, which God raised up for them, sinking each one as the fugitives passed over; the wicked King of Kesh, whose sorcerers built him a golden colossus that could talk; the Hundred Mighty Men who were slain by treachery, but whom God raised up again—surely these and all the rest were only stories. Every scholar said so.

But at least in respect to the existence of the hairy ones, it seemed the scholars were all wrong. And where, Martis wondered, does that leave us?

In this frame of mind he toiled down the mountain, leading his horse, Dulayl, and the children's donkey, Ham, while Jack and Ellayne raced ahead after their little hairy friend.

"It beats me how Obst could have come so far," Jack said. "He was so sick, and he was sure he was going to die."

"Well, he must've gotten better," Ellayne said. "Maybe hearing the bell made him better."

"I don't see how hearing a bell could make anybody well again. Especially a bell that's supposed to mean the world is coming to an end."

Ellayne spun around and glared at him. "I'm sick of your saying that!" she cried. "The world hasn't come to an end, has it? But what do you know? You're just a carter's brat; you've never been to school. You just say it because you heard Obst say it, and poor old Ashrof, back home. And maybe they were wrong! Why should God need someone like you to ring a bell so He can end the world? He could end it anytime He wanted to!"

Martis intervened. "Ellayne—shush! I strongly advise both of you not to raise your voices. There are Heathen scouting parties on this mountain."

Ellayne then remembered the murdered men they'd found on their way up, trappers killed by savages, and fell silent instantly.

"I can't help it that my father died and my mother married a fool who drives a cart for the town council," Jack said. "That doesn't make me stupid."

"It doesn't make you smart, either."

Much of the afternoon went by before the two were speaking to each other again. Then they had to stop and gather nuts and mushrooms for a meager supper, and the camp they made on the trail had little to offer in the way of comfort.

In the morning Wytt picked up Obst's trail again, and they followed it for most of the day until Wytt stopped and jabbed the stony ground with his stick, squealing and clicking.

"What's he saying?" Martis asked. How the children could understand the Omah was beyond him.

Jack shook his head. "He's saying Obst met somebody here, two men, and went off with them."

"Let me have a look."

Martis knelt. His eyes were not as keen as Wytt's, and his nose was no help to him; but he had experience enough to see in the earth and foliage ample proof that Wytt was right.

"Obst has been captured by the Heathen," he said. "Look here: the Heathen sew their moccasins together, and they don't use nails, as we do; so there are no marks of nails in the earth. No sign of a struggle, either. He went with them peacefully."

"What will they do to him?" Ellayne said.

Martis shrugged. They would probably kill him; what use would they have for an old man? But he didn't tell the children that.

"The Heathen are spying out the ways across the mountains. There's going to be a war," he said. "So anyone they meet, they won't let go again."

"Then people have to be warned!" Jack said.

"The Temple already knows, Jack. This war has been brewing for some time. On their side of the mountains, the Heathen have been coming together, making treaties, swearing oaths, preparing armies. It's going to be a big war. You can be sure the oligarchs are doing everything they can to make ready for it."

Jack was astounded. For how long had the Temple known? Why hadn't the rulers of Obann said anything to the people? But Ellayne said, "What about Obst, though? We ought to try to rescue him."

"They'd only capture us, too," Martis said. "And then, war or no war, they would probably sell you to the Temple—if they didn't sell you away out East, as slaves.

"We have to get off this mountain as fast as we can and find a safe place to hide. Lord Reesh will not forget you. And the war will not spare you, if you get in its way."

"But we can't just leave Obst with the Heathen!"

"Ellayne, would he want you to come to grief on his account?" Martis answered her. "But be comforted by this. I know the Heathen. I've spent some time with them. I count a few of them among my friends. It was a Heathen tribesman who gave me this horse, after my own was devoured by a giant bird.

"They are not all bad. They understand, as well as we do, such things as generosity, hospitality, and honor. They might be gentler with Obst than you expect."

And they might be much more savage with him, too, he thought. But he didn't say it to the children.

Obst's captors took him to a camp farther down the mountain. A dozen scouts were there, mostly tattooed Abnaks, with a tall Wallekki in command. This man agreed that Sharak and Hooq must take their prisoner all the way down to the big camp, where war-bands were gathering to come over the mountains.

"Take him down first thing in the morning," said the captain of the scouting party.

"Why don't we just lift his scalp here and now?" said one of the Abnaks. "Why should they have all the fun down below?"

"If anyone's scalp is lifted, it'll be yours!" Hooq answered him. "This is our prisoner, no one else's. And if you weren't such a fool, you would see he is a rare kind of shaman who speaks all languages."

"It's not hard to learn our language," said another scout. "There are many westmen traders and trappers who have learned it."

Hooq flourished his hatchet. "I tell you," he said, "this old man speaks even the speech of birds and knows the thoughts of trees!"

No one but Obst found this statement very remarkable. Had he known the Heathen customs better, he would have known that the Abnaks, poorest of all the Heathen peoples in lands and possessions, were the most richly endowed in the gift of the imagination. All the other nations knew this, and knew better than to put much stock in anything an Abnak said, once he was excited. But no one would call an Abnak man a liar, unless he wanted a fight to the death.

"I know a language he can't speak!" said a man with a tattoo of a snake slithering over his eyebrows. "My mother was a slave, and she was sold many times, each time farther east. So I was born in the land of Chardzhu, on the far shore of the Lake of Islands."

He stepped up to Obst and addressed him—in words that Obst heard in simple Obannese. "I think you're a fraud, old man, lying to save your worthless skin. If you can understand me, answer me in the language of Chardzhu. But I don't think you can."

Obst spread his hands helplessly. "How can I explain it, except as a gift from God? I have understood every word you've said; but to my ears, you have spoken in the speech we use west of the mountains. And that's the only language I know. That each of you hears my words in his own tongue is a miracle of God."

The man's jaw dropped; but they were all amazed.

"By all the holy serpents, he spoke Chardzhu!" the snake-man swore. "And yet he claims he doesn't!"

"I told you he's a shaman," Hooq said.

Poor Obst wasn't even sure what a shaman was: some kind of witch, perhaps.

"What's this god he speaks of?" a scout demanded. "There are as many gods as there are acorns in the forest. Which one gives him the power to speak all tongues?"

"But, my friends, hear me!" Obst said. He was the tallest man there, and when he raised his arms over his head, he towered over them. "It's not a question of which god; for there is only One. The One God, the True God, has chosen me to speak to you.

"You all heard the bell on Bell Mountain. It rang two days ago. And you were meant to hear it.

"God, who made the world, has decided to unmake it. But before He does, He wishes for all men to know Him, and to save the souls of all who might be saved. That bell rang for you, my friends. It was telling you to turn to God, to acknowledge Him the one and only God, so that you may inherit the new world He creates in place of this one. But the time is short! That's what the bell was telling you."

The Heathen stared at Obst and at each other.

"What's a soul?" asked one of the Abnaks.

"It must be shaman talk," said another.

"Now you can all see why he must be taken down below," said the Wallekki who commanded them. This time all the men agreed.

And so Obst, who wanted only to be a hermit living all alone in Lintum Forest, became a missionary to the Heathen.

CHAPTER 6

A Horse for Wytt

Coming down from the mountain, even with Martis to help them, took Jack and Ellayne several days. They had to stop, too, to gather food. Jack was lucky enough to bag a squirrel with his slingshot, and in one of their snares they caught an animal the likes of which none of them had ever seen before.

It was about the size of a small dog, the color of a fawn, but with white stripes instead of spots, and feet with little toes instead of hooves. Along the top of its neck stood a stiff mane of bristly black hair; and it had large, liquid eyes. Ellayne had to turn away when Martis killed it.

"I've been in these mountains before," he said, "but I've never seen one of these."

Wytt stood over it and chattered. "He thinks it's a horse," Jack said. "Well, it'd be about the right size horse for him. Maybe if we could catch one alive, he could learn to ride it."

"What do the Scriptures say about all these new kinds of animals coming along?" Ellayne said. "Remember the knuckle-bears!"

"And the giant bird I saw that night," Jack said, "and that great beast that ate a knuckle-bear."

"I've seen the birds, too," Martis said. He was thinking

of the monster bird that killed his horse and devoured it, and the birds that chased him and Dulayl across the plain and nearly caught them: only the Heathen horse's speed saved them.

He had never been so afraid of anything in all his life. But now, coming down from the mountain, those creatures seemed less fearsome. The black, mind-paralyzing terror that had almost unseated his reason—he'd lost that. He didn't think he would ever be afraid like that again.

"I don't know the Old Books much better than you do," he said. "I can't think of any verse or fascicle that speaks of such things."

"It doesn't make much sense for God to bring a lot of new animals into the world if He's going to destroy it soon," Ellayne said. It was all very confusing, Jack thought.

They had the striped animal for supper, and found its meat sweet and succulent.

"I think we'd be wise to make for Lintum Forest and get there as fast as we can," Martis said. "We can keep to the fringes of the forest if we decide to go on to Obann. We don't know when the war will break out, and we don't want to be caught on the open plains when it does."

"My father was in the militia," Jack said. "He fought the Heathen."

Jack's father died right after Jack was born, so Jack had never known him. He envied Ellayne her family: her father and mother were still alive, and she had brothers. That they lived in a fine big house, and her father was chief councilor of Ninneburky, he didn't envy. But he supposed that was why Ellayne refused to believe the world was soon to end: it must have been a very happy world for her.

And yet she'd left it all behind to journey to Bell Mountain with him. No one else would have.

"Martis," Ellayne said, "there's something I've been wanting to ask you. I hope you don't mind. How old are you? You have a young man's face, but your beard is as white as snow. Was it always white?"

Martis' hand went involuntarily to his chin. "White? My beard is white?" he said. "But it should be brown, like the hair on my head."

"It's white now," Jack said.

Well, how long had it been since he'd looked into a mirror? Martis shrugged. "It was brown when I went up the mountain," he said.

"Abombalbap once met a young prince whose hair turned snow-white after he spent a night in the Accursed Tower," Ellayne said. The old stories of Abombalbap were her chief source of knowledge concerning adventures.

"Never mind," Martis said. "This'll make it harder for Lord Reesh's new assassin to recognize me if he sees me."

But things were afoot in the world that Jack and his companions knew nothing of.

Helki the Rod had returned to Lintum Forest with a strange little girl in his care, whom he'd found wandering all alone on the plains. Her name was Jandra; her family must have lived in the wooded foothills below Bell Mountain, until Heathen raiders killed them—at least that was what Helki thought must have happened. She was a tiny blonde thing, barely old enough to walk and talk. Helki hoped to give her to a family of settlers in the forest who would take proper care of her. With his giant frame, wild hair, and clothes that were mostly patches of all kinds of different fabrics and colors, they made an odd pair.

What was strange about Jandra was that sometimes her eyes went all glassy and she said things that she could never remember saying, and which to Helki made no sense. He supposed that the destruction of her family had addled her mind.

"There is a book missing," was one of those things she said, and others, equally obscure, like, "Restore, restore the throne of Ozias." What in the world did it mean, any of it?

He had not been gone but a few days, but Helki found the forest in an uproar. The first cabin he visited was deserted, the family up and left, with no sign of a struggle or a robbery: friends of his, and he could not tell what had happened to them. And various outlaw bands were on the move, which forced him to remain in hiding for much of the time. He doubted this activity was on his account, albeit Latt Squint-eye, the richest and most murderous of all the outlaw chiefs, had sworn to kill him.

Helki had a nice, dry cave he used from time to time as quarters. Its location was a secret known only to him. There he set up a temporary home for Jandra, intending to stay there with her until he knew the cause of all the uproar. He made her a bed of fresh ferns.

"Now, little one, you mustn't go outside when I'm not here," he told her. "It isn't safe. But there's a nice spring of clear water nearby, and I'll find us all kinds of nice things to eat. The forest is a good place to live, as long as you know how to live in it."

"You be my daddy?" asked the child.

"Yes, my peeper, I'll be your daddy—at least until we can find you a real daddy, with a mommy, too, and other tykes for you to play with. I've been a daddy to baby birds and baby squirrels, and little fawns, so I reckon I can be a daddy to a good little girl like you, if needs must. Only promise me you won't set foot outside this cave unless I'm with you."

"Bad mens?"

"Bad enough, and plenty of them—but I'll see to them, never you fear."

And then her eyes went funny—Obst's eyes used to get like that when he was meditating, Helki recalled—and she said, "You shall be the flail of the Lord," and then fell fast asleep on her bed of ferns. Helki sighed and ran thick fingers through his tangled hair.

"Flail of the Lord, is it?" he said. "And what might that be? Burned if I know!"

There was uproar in the city of Obann, too, but of a different kind.

With a loud and measured tramp that filled the space between the buildings, companies of spearmen marched, their captains on horseback, their boots ringing on the cobbles, the people lining the streets to watch and cheer. Lord Gwyll's officers had raised the levies of the coast and along both banks of the Imperial River, all the way down from the city to the sea, and marched them here for mustering into brigades. Now they were being sent east, to firm up strong points and make ready for the invasion of the Heathen.

Lord Reesh watched from the roof of his own house,

with Judge Tombo by his side. They watched intently.

Tombo pointed down to the street. "There!" he said. "Watch."

Reesh leaned forward, squinting, his hands braced on the marble parapet. "Down there by the bootmaker's shop," said the judge.

Reesh saw her then, a scrawny old woman capering along the cobblestones. She was shouting something that they couldn't hear over the rattle and thud of marching feet. As Reesh watched, two burly men emerged from the crowd, each seized her by an elbow, and before you knew it, all three were gone. The people watching the parade glanced around uneasily for a moment, then gave their attention back to the troops.

"Very nicely done," Reesh said.

"We can't grab them all, of course," Tombo said. "But I think we'll do well just to take them when we can, without my making any official statement about it whatsoever. As you saw, my men were out of uniform. Soon enough, people will understand that now is not a good time to play at being a prophet. It won't stop the fanatics, but it might prompt others to avoid them instead of standing around listening to them."

Reesh nodded his assent.

"I've sent out agents to look for those two children you're so worried about," Tombo said. "They'll try to find out what happened to your man Martis, too. It'll be a difficult task in wartime, but we'll do our best. Then again, if the world suddenly comes to an end, it won't matter."

What was there to be done, Reesh wondered, about religious delusions that affected even nonbelievers like Judge Tombo?

"Don't worry about me, Reesh. I don't listen to the prophets."

"The Old Books are obscure, my lord judge," said Reesh. "No one knows what half the verses mean, or if they mean anything at all. If there is a God, He delights in mystifying us.

"But the past mystifies us, too! So little is left of it. Just enough to tantalize! Men talking to each other miles apart; crossing the sea in great ships; even flying through the air in conveyances too fabulous to imagine; destroying enemy cities in the blink of an eye ... and nothing left of it but tantalizing fragments. Little scraps of rusted metal.

"And yet the muddled story these tell must be true. Men did do all those things, once upon a time. They were so infinitely wiser than we, so infinitely more powerful."

"Infinitely more wicked, too, from what I've heard," said the judge.

Reesh waved the words away. "Rubbish," he said.

"But isn't that why God destroyed the Empire? Isn't that what the Temple teaches? You only have to look across the river to see the ruins of Old Obann. And those are thousand-year-old ruins. Imagine how much greater a city it was than ours! The ruins of the Old Temple alone are half as big as our entire city."

"But they were great!" Reesh said, suddenly gripping the parapet so hard his knuckles whitened. "And their greatness is our birthright, if we have but the endurance and the courage to pursue it.

"People were no more wicked in those days than they are today. Human nature doesn't change. Who knows what destroyed the Empire? Maybe it destroyed itself.

"But I refuse to believe in a God who speaks to us in parables and riddles in the mouths of lunatics, who remains aloof for ages, and then, when the spirit moves Him, wrecks our world. I cannot know what will happen now that the bell on Bell Mountain has been rung. Scripture doesn't say what will happen. All we can do is to go on as we have done, to pursue what we have always pursued, and let our achievements speak for us."

"Always providing that we win the war," said Tombo.

CHAPTER 7

The Mardar and a Boy Named Gik

The big camp on the east side of the mountains was a mass of Heathen of all nations, a sprawling jumble of conical tents, round felt yurts, the low black tents of Wallekki chieftains, and the rickety lean-tos of the Abnaks. It covered a great area, and Obst couldn't guess how many fighting men were there. Along with their women, slaves, and camp followers, he supposed there were enough to populate a good-sized city.

"Why aren't you scared?" Hooq demanded, as they covered the last mile to the encampment.

"Why should I be?" said Obst.

"Don't you know what our people do to westmen prisoners? Sometimes we roast them slowly in a fire, alive. Sometimes we throw them to wild dogs and watch them get torn to pieces. And if you think that's bad"—he jerked a thumb at Sharak, the Wallekki—"his lot do worse."

"No worse than the westmen do to us when they take one of us alive," Sharak said.

"The human heart is cruel, ours no less than yours," Obst said. "From it come all wars, murders, and the boiling evils of this world."

"That's a funny way to talk," Hooq said.

They walked right into the encampment, there being no barricade, no sentries posted. Its air was heavy with a mixed reek of horse and cattle dung, cooking fires, and the sweat of men. The warriors for the most part ignored them, but a few inquisitive ones formed a small procession after them.

There was a great black tent in the midst of the camp, rising as high as a house and surrounded by tribal standards fixed on poles: skulls of men and animals, ox and horse tails waving in the breeze, round leather shields fringed with human scalps, and long red socks billowing in the wind. In front of the big tent was a stone altar, not unlike the ones described in the Old Books. At the entrance to the tent stood a pair of spearmen.

"We've brought a prisoner," Sharak announced. "He is an unusual man, who speaks all languages, yet claims to know only his own. Our chief thought the mardar would wish to see him."

"Wait here," said a guard, and the other went into the tent.

He returned a minute later with a most outlandish figure of a man. Feathers of every kind and color imaginable crowned his head, and some kind of sharp white bone pierced his nose. A necklace of human teeth added to the natural fierceness of his expression—that, and the fact that half his face was painted red and the other half a ghastly blue. He wore a feather cloak of red and purple, and boots and garments of deer hide with the furry side out.

"O Mardar," Sharak said, "we found this old man wandering alone upon the mountain. He has the rare gift of being able to speak any language known to man. He says a god gave it to him."

The mardar, whatever a mardar was, came up for a closer look. He smelled of rancid animal fat. He looked as if he would be just as pleased to eat a prisoner as question him.

"The gods do the bidding of the Great Man, who has power over them," the mardar said. "The westmen's god shall also be made subject to him." He glared at Obst. "What have you to say to that?"

It was blasphemy, of course: no two ways about it. But you could hardly expect a Heathen medicine man to have a right notion of God, Obst thought.

"Who is the Great Man, sir?" he asked. "I'm ignorant; I've never heard of him."

"You understand my language and speak it well enough," the mardar said. "But look around you! Do you see all this warlike host? The Great Man called it into being, and it is only one of many armies that obey him.

"The Great Man bears the sword of the War God, which the god threw down from Heaven in obedience to his will. With it he shall subdue the world. He bears on his breast the mark that proclaims him the One Who Lives Forever. King Thunder is his name."

Obst wondered how he was to preach against such twaddle. Time enough for that by and by, he thought. If the truth be told, the mardar frightened him a little.

"Sir, I know nothing of these things," he said.

"Can you speak Ro-Ko?"

"Sir, I have never heard of Ro-Ko."

"And yet you answer me in Ro-Ko!" said the mardar. "It

cannot be that any westman should know a single word of it: it is the secret language of the priests, among the Mighty People." He turned to Sharak and Hooq. "Take him away and keep him safe for now. I must devote some thought to this."

Sharak had an extra tent, small, much patched, and probably leaky, and a slave boy to go with it.

"You, Gik," the Wallekki said, addressing the boy. "This man is our prisoner. The mardar has seen him and will want to see him again. I place him in your keeping. He will sleep in your tent. See to it that he has food and drink. Don't let him out of your sight."

The boy bowed and said, "Yes, master."

"Don't try to escape," Sharak said to Obst. "You'll be killed if you try, and they won't kill you quickly. Hooq and I will have to rejoin our scouting party, but we shall stay here for another day or two to see what the mardar does with you. Who knows? He might send you on to the Great Man."

Hooq laughed, but not merrily. "Better you than me!" he said.

The two scouts walked away, leaving Obst alone with the boy. He was the dirtiest and scrawniest boy Obst had ever seen, with arms and legs like twigs and a head that seemed too big for his bony body. He wore only rags, and stood on bare, black feet. His hair was too dirty to be assigned a definite color. His only promising feature was his large, brown eyes.

"My name is Obst," the hermit said, "but Gik is no name for a boy." For the word meant something very foul in the Wallekki language.

"That's all they ever call me," said the boy. "I know what it means—what of it?"

"But surely you have another name?"

"If I do, no one ever told me what it was. I was born a slave in the household of Sharak's father. They sold my mother after she weaned me. No one knows who my father was. Sharak says it was a dog."

There was no slavery in Obann—except, of course, if you fell into debt and could not pay. But all the Heathen peoples practiced it, and sometimes bought Western children from outlaws. People living under the shadow of the mountains knew much about slavery.

"If you're going to take care of me," Obst said, "I can't call you Gik. It wouldn't be right. Isn't there anything else you would like me to call you?"

The boy made a face, shook his head.

"Well, then," Obst said, "since you leave it up to me, I shall call you Ryons, after a boy who lived a long, long time ago. He was an orphan, too; but God did not forget him."

"They said you've been to see the mardar," the boy said.

"Yes—and he has seen me. Tell me, what is he? *Mardar* means 'chief of servants' where he comes from, but he didn't seem like much of a servant to me."

The boy who didn't seem to care what you called him sat down by the low entrance to the tent. Obst joined him.

"The mardar is here to make sure that everyone obeys King Thunder," the boy said. "He makes sacrifices to the Great Man, and they're all afraid of him. He can sacrifice a chief of chiefs, if he likes. He can do anything he pleases, and no one tries to stop him. He'll probably have you cooked, and eat your heart."

"There wouldn't be much gain to him in that; my heart is old and all worn-out," Obst said. Ryons laughed; he seemed to find that very funny. Obst let him go on for a few moments.

"Tell me about the Great Man, this King Thunder, whom the mardar serves," Obst said. "Is he a man who claims to be a god?"

Ryons answered in a harsh whisper. "Don't even talk about him! It's dangerous even to mention him. They don't let us talk about him."

"Why not?"

"Because he's stronger than the gods! They all have to do what he says. He's already captured a whole army of gods and put them in prison in his castle out beyond the lakes. That's why the nations all have to obey him. If they don't, he'll call down fire on them and burn them up."

Obst had never heard of such a thing, outside of Scripture. There were heathens in ancient times, too, with heathen gods of wood and stone, and priests who pretended to make miracles. But he realized he would have to be careful of what he said.

"Well, Ryons, I know nothing of these things, but if you're afraid to speak of them, we won't," he said. "Do you think I might have a drink of water? And after that, we can talk of anything you please. I think we might as well be friends. Don't you?"

Ryons frowned, and went to fetch some water.

CHAPTER 8

Budric the Bluejay

"How green it is!" Ellayne said, when they emerged from the wooded skirts of the mountain and saw the rolling plains.

True, Jack thought. On their way out from Ninneburky, the plains were a dreary grayish-yellow. Had they really been up on the mountain that long, or was spring just coming on fast?

"I've never seen it so lush," Martis said. "As if the world were going to go out in one last blaze of glory. But let's not get into a theological discussion! The important thing is to get to Lintum Forest in a hurry. I think we'll be marching straight across the main invasion route."

Jack wondered how the Heathen came to be heathen, and why they so often made war on Obann. That went back a long, long way—all the way back to Scripture days.

"You say you know about the Heathen, Martis," he said. "What are they like? Why are they so fierce? Why do they make war on us?"

"They're like us, Jack—just people. Some live in cities. Others roam about and live in tents. There are many different nations. The only thing they have in common is, they're not us. They don't worship our God, and they don't hold allegiance to the Temple. And they attack us because we are richer than they are and we have things that they want."

"But our God *is* God, isn't He?" Jack said. "Ashrof says their gods are just make-believe gods. They must be very silly people, to worship make-believe gods."

"They don't think they're make-believe," Martis said.

"Tell us about them," said Ellayne. "It's dull, just walking on and on all day."

"I couldn't possibly tell you about all the Heathen gods. There must be tens of thousands of them," Martis said. "The people who gave me Dulayl"—his horse—"worship horses and the moon. And because their country is an arid land, they also worship rain and springs.

"There's one nation that has a different god for each day of the year. The Abnaks say their gods live inside the trunks of trees. Many of the nations make idols out of wood or stone or brass and worship them as gods. And I've heard of a people far out beyond the Great Lakes who say their god is a gigantic disembodied head at the bottom of Lake Sarmeen who dreams perpetually; and the people are his dreams. If the head ever wakes up, they'll all cease to exist. So their priests have to sing lullabies to it day and night, all year round."

Jack laughed. "How could anyone believe a thing like that!"

"They would say the same about us," Martis answered.

With the children riding Dulayl and Martis leading him, it took them three days to cross the plain and reach the fringe of Lintum Forest. Several times they passed families on foot or with ox-drawn wagons, fleeing the mountains.

"We all know there's going to be a big war," said a grey-bearded man whose wife and three spinster daughters rode in a wagon. "We don't want to be around when those murdering Heathen come across the mountains. They're already lifting scalps, burning people out of their homes. Cusset Abnaks are the worst—but then they always were."

These people were making for the river, hopefully to find refuge in a walled town before it was too late. The lean, long-nosed daughters only fidgeted, but the plump wife had some choice words for Martis.

"Now is no time to be traipsing around with small children," she said, "and here is not the place for it! What can you be thinking of?"

"We'll be safe in Lintum Forest."

"Hah! You'll find more robbers than honest folk in Lintum Forest." And she might have had even more to say, had Wytt not stayed in hiding under Ellayne's coat.

They went their separate ways. "I wonder if they'll be all right," Jack said.

"As long as they don't run into a Heathen raiding party," Martis said.

They were relieved when the great green mass of the forest loomed up in the south, and even more relieved when they actually entered it. Only Ellayne voiced some misgivings.

"I don't like to think about all the outlaws in this country," she said. "I felt safe with Obst: most of the outlaws were his friends. But what are we going to do if we run into a gang of them?"

"Some of them might show respect for a servant of the Temple," Martis said. His clothes had suffered badly during his travels, but he still bore his Temple insignia. "Of course, they might show more respect for weapons."

With his dagger as his only tool, he spent some hours fashioning weapons. He sharpened some nicely balanced sticks for throwing and shaped a stout staff for closer fighting.

"Have you killed a lot of people?" Jack asked.

"More than would please God, Jack. I killed because my master commanded it. Now I'll kill only to protect the two of you."

Ellayne wondered about it. Her hero, Abombalbap, slew robber knights and werewolves, giants, witches, and evil barons. But it was all so different when it happened in a story! Remembering the outlaw Wytt killed, and how he lay sprawled under the stars, she shuddered.

The forest was greener than they'd left it and alive with birdsong. Their first night in camp under the trees, they were almost deafened by another kind of music.

"Ho! The peeper-frogs are out in force already," Jack said. "There must be thousands of them. Hop-toads, too."

"I don't see how we're going to be able to sleep with all that racket," Ellayne said.

"Shh!"

Martis jumped up, staff in hand, and waved them to silence. Their campfire crackled. Jack hadn't heard anything but that and the frogs.

"Whoever you are," Martis called into the night, "if you come in peace, show yourself!"

Jack was about to ask what all the fuss was about, when there was a noise in the underbrush and a man stepped out of the shadows into the firelight: a small, fidgety man in ragged clothes, with burrs and leaf-litter stuck to his hair. He held up empty hands.

"I mean you no harm," he said. "It's just that I saw your fire, and I hoped it might be honest folk."

"What are you doing, walking around at night?" Martis demanded.

"Just trying to save my skin—that's all, I swear. I won't do you any harm. I'm all alone. If I might come and sit down ... and if you have a bit of food to spare ..."

The only weapon he had was an ordinary woodsman's knife in a sheath on his belt. Martis nodded, and he joined them at the fire, holding out his hands to it to get them warm. Wytt picked up his sharp stick and slunk behind Ellayne, making not even the ghost of a noise. The newcomer never spotted him.

"Give him those scraps of squirrel we have left over, Jack," Martis said. The man wolfed them down as soon as he took them from Jack's hands. "Now tell us about yourself, stranger."

"Not much to tell," said the man, as he gulped down the last morsel of meat. "The whole forest's all topsy-turvy, isn't it? I'm not the only one running for his life."

"Running from whom?" Martis asked; and Jack was suddenly glad Martis was with them. He, too, remembered the man who'd tried to sell them into slavery.

"Latt Squint-eye has done some kind of a deal with the chiefs of the Heathen," the visitor said. "It's going to be a different kind of war, this one. They mean to go all the way to Obann—maybe all the way to the sea. But it seems they don't want to trouble themselves about Lintum Forest. They've got Latt for that. With him on the warpath in the forest, they won't have to worry about the government handing out pardons and raising some kind of army to bother them from this direction. I suppose he gets to be King of Lintum in return. But that's what he's always wanted, isn't it?"

"Why would a king chase you?" Martis asked.

"Oh, it's not just me. They're chasing everybody. A lot of the bands have joined up with Latt. Them as hasn't, he's putting out of business. Rousting all the settlers, too. It'll keep the oligarchs from raising any troops out here."

"Are you one of those he's putting out of business?"

"Only in a small way." The fugitive belched and sat up straighter. "Had my own band, though, didn't I? Budric's Bluejays. Not exactly the terrors of the forest, but we did all right: reiving, thieving, trading with the Abnaks now and then. And Budric, which is me, never would pay scot to Squint-eye. So now they're out to get poor Budric, who never did them any harm.

"But there's one thing Squint-eye didn't count on. A little something he left out of his big plans. And that little something is going to turn out to be a big something! Mark my words—"

Before anyone could mark his words, he fell forward, face-first into the campfire, with the feathered shaft of an arrow protruding from his back. Someone in the dark yelled, "Don't move, we've got you covered!"

But Jack did move because two little hairy hands seized his, and Wytt's voice chattered, "Hurry!" So Jack rolled off the log he was sitting on and bolted into the darkness, even as heavy feet crashed through the underbrush and harsh voices warned Martis not to make a fight of it.

CHAPTER 9

The Omah of the Forest

Jack couldn't see at all. He blundered into a sticker bush and just kept going, tearing his skin and almost putting out an eye. He tripped over a root and kept on crawling on his hands and knees. He crawled through a nasty puddle of cold water.

Behind him, around him, men's voices rang out. They were hunting him. They made quite a racket, crashing through the foliage, with here and there a spate of cursing.

But they weren't going to find him. Jack finally stopped when he blindly crawled under an arch of briars, into a deep hollow where they wouldn't find him in broad daylight. He had the good sense to stop there. Almost out of breath, he would have had to stop soon, anyhow.

What was he going to do, all alone? What was going to happen to Ellayne, and Martis? Martis couldn't fight off a whole gang of robbers by himself, no matter what his skills as an assassin.

Jack almost yelped out loud when Wytt suddenly tugged on his sleeve.

"Burn it, Wytt, don't do that!"

Wytt chattered softly. It was not speech as we know speech, but Jack understood what he was saying: "You're safe here. The men have already gone back. But they have

Ellayne, and White-face." That was Wytt's name for Martis.

"What'll they do to them?" Jack whispered.

"They'll stop at our camp for the night. They're glad they killed that man who sat with us."

"Well, we're in the worm-can now, all of us," Jack said. "I don't know how much you understand about people, Wytt; but this is bad. Those are very bad men. They'll kill Martis and make Ellayne a slave. And sooner or later—"

Wytt let out a shrill, high-pitched whistle that made Jack clap his hands over his ears. You wouldn't have thought someone so little could make so big a noise. Wytt went on and on with it.

"What in the world did you do that for?" Jack asked, when he finally stopped. "Do you want those outlaws to find us?" He wished he could see Wytt, but in that hollow under the briars, it was impossible to see anything.

"The men won't come," Wytt answered. "But Omah of the woods will come: plenty Omah."

"I thought all the Omah lived out on the plains, in the ruins."

"Many Omah in the forest, too. You'll see," Wytt said.

"So you were calling them?"

"They will come."

Jack wasn't sure he wanted to be trapped in a briar patch with scores of strange Omah; but Wytt hadn't given him a choice. "When will they come?" he asked.

"When they can. Rest now."

The outlaws were furious with themselves for letting Jack escape. But after they'd dragged the dead Budric out of the fire and built it back up to a roaring blaze, they began to calm down.

They tied Martis' wrists behind his back and tied Ellayne's ankles together. She became ill when one of the outlaws bent over and cut off Budric's scalp with a knife. He tucked it into his belt while two others tossed the corpse into the underbrush.

"Not a bad night's work!" said one. "The last of the Bluejays shot down, and two prisoners into the bargain. We've earned a drink, lads, and a good night's sleep."

"We shouldn't've let the boy get away," grumbled another.

"Yes, that was too bad," said the scalp-taker. "But we expected no prisoners, and we've got two, so there's little to complain about." He sat down next to Martis. "So who are you?" he asked.

"Fugitives from Mount Eagle," Martis said. "My name is Jace, and I was trying to take my niece and nephew to a town where they'll be safe. Heathen raiders killed their mother and father: that was my youngest brother, and I came out here to see him. I didn't know there was a war brewing. The whole family was going to come back with me, but the Heathen found us first. We three escaped; they killed all the others."

It was a good lie, Ellayne thought.

"Got any money?" asked the scalper.

"Spent it all," Martis said. Ellayne had money sewn into the lining of her coat, but Martis didn't know that. She prayed the outlaws wouldn't search her.

"Oh, well—we'll get some money when we sell you to the Heathen. Unless I decide to keep the girl myself! Tried to disguise her as a boy, didn't you?"

"I don't suppose it'd be any use imploring you to have mercy," Martis said. A few of the outlaws laughed. Ellayne had no idea men could be like this.

"What do you say, lads?" said the leader. "Should we let 'em go, and then go back to Latt and tell him what we did?"

"You tell him, not me!" said a scar-faced man.

"Sorry, Mister Jace—can't do it," the leader said. "But if you and the girl don't give us any trouble, we won't make it any harder for you than we have to. My name is Corris, and I'm as good as my word." This, too, earned a laugh from the others.

One of them produced an earthen jug, popped a cork out of it, took a swallow of its contents, and passed it around. Others had dried meat and nuts in their pouches. Corris let Martis have a drink, but Ellayne wasn't offered any—not that she wanted anything an outlaw drank.

She was glad Jack got away, but wished he were here. The thought that she might not ever see him again was one she pushed back down, as deep as it would go. And what would happen to him all by himself out there? She felt like crying, but didn't want to cry in front of these lawless men. She wished her father were here, with the town militia. They'd hang these murderers, and she'd like to see them do it—which made her surprised at herself.

Meanwhile, Martis got to talking with their captors.

"What's this I hear," he asked, "about one of your chieftains setting up as King of Lintum Forest? That man you shot mentioned it."

"That'd be our boss, Latt Squint-eye, the ugliest varmint in the forest," Corris said. "But also the fiercest, the strongest, and the smartest. He deserves to be a king."

Martis had already had a brush with some of Latt's men on his outward journey, before he'd caught up to the children. A few of them had captured him; and he expected to be murdered, for Latt was said to have a strong aversion to the Temple. But a lone man with a staff attacked the whole group, killed a few, put the rest to flight, and rescued Martis. Helki the Rod, that's what the fellow called himself; Martis remembered now.

He hoped his now-white beard would keep anyone in Latt's following from recognizing him. He wondered if Helki were still alive. For the time being, none of these outlaws seemed to have noticed the Temple insignia on his collar. Maybe his clothes had deteriorated more than he'd thought.

Martis decided to change the subject.

"A week or so ago," he asked, "did any of you happen to hear something that sounded like a bell?"

A couple of the outlaws sat up straighter and stopped munching food. One or two had fallen asleep. Corris frowned.

"Aye, we all heard it. Everybody heard it," he said. "It was just before sunrise. It woke up everyone who was sleeping. It woke up all the birds and made them crazy. It was hours before their noise died down."

"They say it was a bell on Bell Mountain," said another outlaw. "Some kind of curse!"

"I couldn't imagine what it was," Martis lied. "I thought one of you might know."

"Nobody knows!" Corris said, and poked Martis in the chest, hard. "No more than anybody knows about all the queer animals that've been popping up around these parts the last year or so. Nobody knows a cusset thing."

"I've seen some of those animals," Martis said. "Gigantic birds, for one."

"I think they must be coming up from the south," Corris said. "They've got to be coming from somewhere, eh? But why they've moved up here, who knows? Maybe something bad, real bad, happened away down south, and the animals had to come north. Nobody knows what happens in the southlands. Nobody goes much farther south than the edge of the forest."

"They say something bad's going to happen here, too," said one of the men.

"It already has!" Corris laughed. "Every Heathen fighting man from the mountains to the lakes is going to come this way, and soon. Just be thankful to Latt they're going to bypass us in Lintum Forest. There ain't no army on this earth can hold them back."

In spite of himself, Jack fell asleep in the briar patch. He woke when the black night gave way to grey predawn, and found himself stiff and sore all over, with his teeth chattering from the cold. For a moment he couldn't remember what he was doing there; it was as if he'd awakened from an evil dream. But as his eyes took in his surroundings, he realized where he was and that he was all alone. Wytt was nowhere to be seen.

"Oh, fine!" he muttered. "What do I do now?"

He could start by crawling out of the briar patch. He emerged into a fog-shrouded grove of ghostly birches, feeling like the only human being left in all the world. For all he knew, he was: God might have taken everyone else, but overlooked him in the briar patch.

Where could he go? He was no woodsman. Eventually the outlaws would get him, or some fierce animal.

But then Wytt called out to him from somewhere in the fog.

"Boy, boy! Be still, be quiet. We are here!"

Leaves rustled. From out of the fog, out of the underbrush, came Wytt with the Forest Omah following.

There were more of them than Jack could count. Wytt's fur was red, but these were grey, brown, with two or three coal-black ones. Their little eyes glittered. Most of them were even smaller than Wytt, but they all carried sharp little sticks. It would be quite easy to be afraid of them, Jack thought. They came silently, without chittering or chirping, and that made them more menacing. But there was nowhere to run, so Jack stood still.

In the little space in front of the briar patch, there wasn't room for all of them. Jack couldn't see them all, but he could sense them: a whole army of them.

"Omah will save Ellayne and White-face," Wytt said. "Evil men, we kill. You come, too. We are ready."

"Why do they do this for us, Wytt?"

If the little hairy man had understood a shrug, he would have shrugged. "We do this for you and for Ellayne. This we all know, this we must do. Come, the bad men are sleeping."

Jack followed the tiny warrior into the fog, making as little noise as possible. The host of Omah made hardly any noise at all.

The camp was much closer than he'd thought. The fire had gone out. Everyone was asleep, even the one sentry who should have been awake but had fallen asleep sitting up.

Jack had only a moment to take it all in. Wytt chirped once, and all the Omah charged the camp.

The men never had a chance. The Omah hit them like a swarm of bees, a river of rats. They stabbed the men's faces, necks, bare hands. Sharp sticks pierced sleeping eyes.

The stricken men screamed. It was terrible: the whole forest was full of their screams. Their bodies thrashed; Omah went flying, tumbled back to their feet, rushed back into the fray. The stronger men struggled to their feet, and those who didn't fall down again ran screaming into the woods in all directions.

It was over almost as soon as it started. Two men lay dead, with a third writhing in agony, covered with blood, his eyes stabbed out. A dozen Omah quickly finished him.

Ellayne and Martis, tied up to prevent escape, were sitting up, wide-eyed, ashen-faced, but unharmed, not a scratch. Jack breathed again. They startled when he burst out of cover.

"Jack!" Ellayne cried.

"Did they hurt you?" he said.

"We're both unharmed," Martis said. "But how did you accomplish … this?"

"Wytt did it. These are the Omah of the forest. He called them, and they came."

Wytt would not let them stay there. "Come with us," was his message, delivered in urgent squeaks and high-pitched barks. "Omah will take you to the big man."

"We have to go with him," Jack told Martis. "I think he knows a safe place for us."

They quickly collected their things, plus a few things the robbers left behind: pouches containing food. They unhobbled Ham and Dulayl. Amazingly, the horse and the donkey hadn't panicked when the Omah attacked.

"Did you talk to them, Wytt, and tell them not to be afraid?" Jack asked. "Can you make them understand you?"

"A little. Enough," Wytt said. "Hurry now!"

The day was just breaking. The Forest Omah had dispersed, melted into the woods without anyone seeing them go. A couple of the little grey ones stayed behind; they led the way. Others would follow after them and ruin the trail so no enemy could follow it, Wytt said.

The Omah led them along paths hidden by thick ferns, paths that just barely found a way through otherwise impenetrable sticker bushes. These were paths that animals knew and used, but not men.

"You came just in time," Ellayne told Jack. "They were going to sell us to the Heathen. And they scalped that man Budric! I didn't think there were any Obannese people who would do a thing like that."

"Where are we going?" Martis said.

"To see some big man, Wytt says. Don't ask me who," Jack said.

"Wytt wouldn't take us anywhere bad," Ellayne said. "Wytt, you saved us! I love you!"

She stooped over and held out her arms. Wytt hopped into them, and she picked him up and held him like a cat, and kissed him. He made a rapid clicking sound that meant he was gloriously happy. The grey Omah chattered at them.

"They want us to keep moving," Jack said. Ellayne put Wytt down, and they all got going again. She shocked Jack by yanking him close and planting a kiss on his cheek. "I thought I'd never see you again!" she said. "I was glad you got away, though."

It was on Jack's tongue to tell her to leave off the girl-stuff, but he couldn't get it out. Instead, he felt something he would have described as a warm, strong hand suddenly wrapped around his heart, cherishing him. It made him kiss her, too, right on the cheek. And of course that embarrassed him tremendously and made him blush. He threw a backward glance at Martis to see if the man was laughing at him, but Martis only looked a little sad.

"Don't get any funny ideas!" Jack said to Ellayne; and that made her laugh.

By midmorning they reached their destination, the mouth of a cave in a thickly wooded hillside. A man was waiting for them, someone whom they'd met before.

"Helki!" Ellayne cried.

"Helki the Rod!" Jack echoed.

There he was, a giant of a man in crazy rags that helped him blend into the leaves and shadows, with his deadly staff in his hand and a broad grin on his face.

"You made good time getting here," he said. "I'd have come for you, if I'd known you needed me. But I've only just this morning heard about it from the little folk.

"But I reckon there's a lot more for me to know. You went east with Obst and come back with this fellow from the Temple. That's twice you've been yanked out of Squint-eye's clutches, friend! Try to avoid going for a third time.

"Tell me all your tale—no secrets! But first I reckon you'll want a bite to eat and a good, long drink of water." He turned back toward the cave. "Peeper-baby!" he bellowed like a bull. "Come on out and meet Daddy Helki's friends."

Out of the cave came the last thing Jack, Ellayne, and Martis would ever have expected to see—a little girl.

And she carried a horrendous monster in her arms.

CHAPTER 10

Jandra Prophesies

Orth was the best preacher in Obann, in the First Prester's opinion. Even better, he eagerly preached whatever message the First Prester wished him to preach. This morning, in front of the crowd that packed the great chamber of the Temple, he was at the top of his form.

"I want you all to take a good look across the river today," he said, the high, curved ceiling of the hall amplifying his voice. "I want you to see the vast, shapeless pile of rubble that used to be the greatest city in the world.

"There was a Temple there, a much greater Temple than this one. When the Empire fell, a thousand years ago, and the entire city was destroyed, that great Temple was destroyed, too. You can see what's left of it, right across the river.

"But a thousand years before that, there was another destruction, of yet another Temple, on the same site as the greater one. This was the First Temple, the heart of the kingdom of Obann. The last king, Ozias, was the last of Obann's kings to worship there. Rebels drove him into exile; and then the Heathen came."

He paused for effect. He had a hard face, an iron-grey fringe of beard with a clean-shaved upper lip. Great lamps on thick gold chains hung over his head, concentrating light on him. From his throne at the right of the preacher's podium, Lord Reesh looked on him with approval.

"They came in numbers uncountable," Orth resumed. "They came like locusts, say the Scriptures: like a flood. They starved the city for a year; no one could get in or out. And then a traitor opened one of the sally ports to them. A handful of invaders entered the city by stealth, overwhelmed the guard at the Commerce Gate, and threw the doors open; and the Heathen host poured into the city. They slew with the sword until the streets were choked with corpses and the gutters ran with blood. They put the city to the torch. How it burned! Nor did they leave off until they had destroyed everything: the whole city had to be rebuilt.

"Now they are about to come again, in power and might and number greater than the world has ever seen. Their aim is to destroy this city and leave uninhabitable ruins on both sides of the river. That's why I want you to take a good look at what's left of the old city. That's what this city, your city, will look like, if the Heathen have their way. And they are coming—soon!"

He held the crowd in silence; they waited on his every word.

"By now you have all heard various people, supposedly imbued with the spirit of prophecy, claim that King Ozias' bell on Bell Mountain has rung out, proclaiming the imminent destruction of the world. And to be sure, the bell has rung; we all heard it. But very few have understood its message!"

Orth raised that mighty voice of his. It was like the tolling of an iron bell.

"Yes, it was a warning—a dire warning from God Himself, which we dare not ignore, on peril of our lives. But how can anyone be so blind as not to see what we are warned against? The danger we've been warned against is breathing down our necks! It is nothing less than the assembled nations of the Heathen, come together for our final and complete destruction.

"And what are the people of Obann, God's people, to do? Offer our throats to be cut, our cities to be burned? Bow down to Heathen idols?

"No, no, no! That bell was calling us to war, calling us to go forth and conquer. To put forth all the strength that God can give us, and once and for all, forever, destroy the Heathen and their idols! To drive them out of our land, and then to march beyond the mountains and ruin their cities, burn their idols!

"If we do not do this, if we do not obey the commandment of God, then that will be the end of us—the end of our world. For has not God commanded us, 'Ye shall surely destroy the Heathen'? But we have not destroyed them. We have not even tried.

"Now we have been warned. Ozias' bell has warned us. This is our last chance, the last time God will call on us to destroy the Heathen. If we do not, the Heathen will destroy us; and this time there will be no one to rebuild the Temple."

And that was that: a short speech, but certainly effective, Lord Reesh thought. Orth had written it himself; he'd be a good choice to be the next First Prester. But meanwhile, imitations of his sermon would be preached in every chamber house in Obann.

We can't silence all the crazy prophets, Reesh thought, but we can turn their fervor to our own uses.

Jack flinched, and Ellayne gasped and stepped back when she saw the thing the girl was carrying.

"Great powers, what is that?" Martis said.

"It's horrible! Take it away!" Ellayne cried.

It hissed at her, just like a snake. It had a scaly lizard face, with a mouthful of needle-sharp teeth and shiny red eyes; but the rest of it was covered with feathers, like a bird: dirty-looking, grey-blue feathers. It had clawed hands on its wings and a long, stiff, feathered tail. If it hadn't been only the size of a large crow, Ellayne would have thought it was a dragon. But maybe it was—a baby dragon.

"Don't be afraid," Helki said. "I'm burned if I know what it is, but it seems mighty fond of Jandra. She found it yesterday while she was playing in the bushes. It just hopped right into her arms and let itself be petted. Jandra, baby, these are Daddy's friends. Say hello."

"Hello." She'd be a sweet little girl, Ellayne thought, if it weren't for that monster she was holding.

The child looked up at Martis and smiled at him. "Nice man," she said. Martis looked away. He'd met Jandra on the plain before Helki found her, but she wandered away from him while he slept. Intent on his mission for Lord Reesh, he didn't try to follow her to protect her.

"She likes you," Helki said. Martis cringed. He'd given her food and water, nothing more, and left her behind. It was a miracle she wasn't dead.

"Who is she, Helki?" Jack said. "Don't tell me she's yours!"

"Only until I can find a proper home for her. I found her

on the plain, wandering around alone. I reckon the Heathen must've got her folks, and she escaped somehow. Peeper, these two kids are Jack and Ellayne. I'm sure they'll be nice to you. Why don't you put your bird down now, and let him find something to eat?"

Jandra released the creature. It strutted like a chicken, head bobbing as it walked, glaring at Ellayne. Helki picked up Jandra and invited his guests into the cave, where he fed them on fresh fish he'd caught with his bare hands in a nearby pool and some coarse little cakes he'd made by baking them on a flat stone. Only after they'd filled their bellies did he question them.

"Where's Obst?" he said. "Start by telling me that."

It took all day to tell their tale. Jack and Ellayne told him everything—Jack's dreams, their long journey to the summit of Bell Mountain, and their ringing of the bell. What Martis held back from his part of the story was his own affair.

"I wish you'd told me all that the first time we met," Helki said. "I'd have gone up the mountain with you. Obst should have trusted me; he'd've done better if he had. But then I reckon I wouldn't have been there to take care of Jandra."

"Can you help us get to Obann?" Jack asked.

"Never been there. It'll be a pretty good job just to get you through the forest, the way things are. Latt Squint-eye, King of Lintum Forest!" Helki threw back his head and laughed. "I'll crown him with my rod!"

Throughout the day Jandra played with Wytt, napped, and cuddled her hideous pet dragon, never venturing more than a few yards beyond the mouth of the cave. She sat on Helki's lap for a while, then puttered around the cave, humming a tuneless little song. She lay down on a bed of ferns for another nap, and they'd just about forgotten her—until she raised her voice in words that no toddler from the mountains should have known.

"The Temple is fallen; twice has the Temple fallen; but I will give the throne to Ozias, and my words to all the peoples of the earth.

"There is a Temple beneath the Temple, and a cellar beneath the cellar. *Ih wolbe c'heilet ander richteke-mann, an hehr wol Ih ophelten ...*" And with that she fell into a sound sleep.

"What in the world was that?" Ellayne whispered.

"It was a line of Scripture, in the language of the Old Books," said Martis. "It's from the prophet Ika: 'I will be honored by the righteous, and him will I uphold.' No reciter could have pronounced it better."

"But how could she recite Scripture?" Jack said. "How old is she? Two? Three?"

Helki shook his head. "She's always coming out with something I don't understand. If you say it's a verse from Scripture, that's more than I know. She talks about some book that's missing and tells me I'm the Flail of the Lord, whatever that is. The rest of the time, she's just an ordinary little girl. I wish Obst were here—he might understand it." He looked at Martis. "Too bad a servant of the Temple can't explain it to us!"

Martis spread his palms. "What can I say?" he answered. "Do you know how many thousands of men and women serve the Temple? We aren't all religious scholars!

"All I know is that these two children rang the bell on Bell Mountain, and what I suspect is that that changed everything. I don't know how; but I do know the First Prester, my master, was mortally afraid of it. He sent me out to stop them, and I failed—which is the one thing in my life I don't regret."

"Just get us as close to Obann as you can, Helki," Jack said. "I know everything is supposed to be ending, but it looks more like something else is beginning. Maybe," he turned to Ellayne, "you're right about that, after all."

CHAPTER 11

Obst Among the Heathen

Living out in the open in a leaky tent, surrounded by enemies, might have been the end of most old men; but not Obst. He felt stronger and healthier than he'd felt in many years.

He delighted in the company of the slave boy, Ryons, who soaked up friendship as rich soil soaks up rain. He could not have had much friendship in his life so far, Obst thought. Obst told him stories from the Scriptures, and stories of the forest and outlaws and hermits like himself; the poor child lapped it up. He especially liked the stories told of King Ozias as a boy, hiding in the forest from his implacable enemies, protected by his mother until he was old enough to outwit them on his own.

With no action forthcoming from the mardar, Sharak and Hooq returned to their scouting duties in the mountains. The Abnak surprised Obst with the friendliness of his farewell.

"I hope we meet again, old man," Hooq said. "I'm sorry I wanted to kill you on the spot, when first we met; I suppose it must be a bad habit. But you're as daft as a loon and as brave as a blackfly—just the kind of fellow we Abnaks like best. Just try not to fall afoul of the mardar!"

"What do you think they're going to do with me?" Obst asked Ryons, after Hooq left. "I'm beginning to think the mardar has forgotten me."

"You'd better hope he has," the boy said. "What he usually does to prisoners is to cut them open and read the future from their entrails. They're alive when he does it, tied down to the altar. He watches the way they squirm: that's supposed to tell him things about the future, too."

Which delivered Obst right to the doorstep of his dilemma—when was he to start preaching God's word to these people? And what would they do to him when he tried?

He knew the history of the prophets. Sychas the Mighty One, in his bearskin cloak, was a terror to the corrupt kings of ancient Obann, doing miracles by the power of God. Zaydabara, old and widowed, unable to walk without a cane: she never raised her voice, and yet her words called a nation to repentance. And there was Ika, himself of royal blood, who came out of his house unscathed after wicked King Meen's men burned it to the ground. These were God's servants, Obst reflected, and their Lord protected them.

But the Old Books of Scripture made mention of many other prophets who had not fared so well: prophets stoned to death by angry mobs, murdered by tyrants, or devoured by wild beasts let loose against them. Presumably their faithful souls had places reserved for them in Heaven. But the simple truth was, a prophet never knew if God was going to protect him in the flesh or not. As Prophet Menkawr said, when they were about to cut him down with swords, "At least I have obeyed my God."

"And where," Obst asked himself, "is my prophetic calling? How do I know God has really chosen me? It might be all my own imagination, after all."

"Eh?" said Ryons.

Obst startled. He'd forgotten he was not alone. Indeed, they were standing now beside the stream where Ryons went for water, and Obst could not remember walking there.

"Sorry, Ryons! I must have been talking to myself."

"What's all this about prophets and kings and some great god?"

Obst sighed. "Oh, I've been grappling with my cowardice. Of course God has sent me here to preach His word among the Heathen. Why else would He have given me the miraculous gift of understanding and speaking all the Heathen languages? It's just that when you got to talking about the mardar and telling me the things he does to people … I was afraid."

"Everyone's afraid of the mardar," Ryons said. "And everyone should be."

"So I've been hemming and hawing, and not getting started, and pretending I didn't know for sure what God wants me to do, just because I'm afraid. I wasn't afraid when Hooq and Sharak captured me, and I wasn't afraid when they brought me before the mardar. But now I am! Isn't that strange?"

He saw by the expression on Ryons' face that the boy was truly worried about him—this slave, who in all his life had probably never had the luxury of worrying about another human being because there was no one in the world who ever spared a thought for him. "Is that why I'm losing my courage?" Obst wondered. Was his love for this child reattaching him to this poor, doomed world? Had life suddenly become so sweet that he was afraid to part with it?

"Don't be afraid," Ryons said. "I'll keep you out of the mardar's way, and out of mind. The host is going to cross the mountains very soon: everybody's saying so. The chiefs are all as busy as ants, and I suppose the mardar must be busy, too. Once we start moving, they won't have any time for you. Just keeping the Abnaks from lifting everybody else's scalps and running back to their own women—that's enough, right there, to keep all the chieftains busy, every day. Maybe, once the host is on the move, you'll be able to run away and no one will even notice."

But Obst didn't run away, or even try to. The Heathen camp was like an anthill, and he felt like a slow and clumsy beetle in it.

Now that Ryons had mentioned it, he could see the army was just about ready to march. Horses were being examined, the weak and the unfit slaughtered and their meat smoked over slow fires so that it would keep. Drums of all kinds were being beaten, throbbing day and night. Riders clattered in with urgent messages. Warriors sharpened their weapons, mended their footwear.

And one day at noon, harsh horns blew, horns with the voices of devils; and when Ryons took a few steps forward to see what was the cause, two warriors came along and snatched him up, one by each arm, so that his feet were lifted from the ground.

"He'll do," said one.

Ryons screamed and struggled as they carried him off

toward the center of the camp. Obst, who had just emerged from a meditative daze, stared after them for a moment. Then he shot to his feet and gave chase for all he was worth.

"Stop, stop!" he cried. "What are you doing, where are you going with him? Put him down, I say!"

They halted, glared at him. Obst didn't know what nation they belonged to. They were tall, extremely swarthy men, with wolfskin caps and leggings.

"Who are you, old man?"

"Never mind him!" said the other. "Come on, the mardar's waiting for his sacrifice."

Obst tried to hold them back, but they pushed him to the ground. He got up and scrambled after them. A cramp in his leg made him hobble. Other warriors got in his way. He bumped into them, received more than a few abusive words, but kept on going. He just barely managed to keep Ryons' abductors in sight.

Warriors were flocking to the center of the camp, to the mardar's tent, and to the altar. They were intent on what they were going to see, and ignored Obst. He struggled past them like a man swimming against a heavy current. Drums boomed, and over their booming rose the shrill scream of a horse.

The crowding slowed Obst's progress. Over the men's shoulders he saw the top of the big black tent and the standards planted around it. He couldn't see Ryons anymore. His feet seemed to stick to the earth, as in a dream. He pushed on.

Through a solid wall of Heathen warriors, Obst fought. Someone struck him on the side of the head, making him see stars; but he didn't stop for that. And at last he broke through, ahead of the front line of men gathered before the altar.

Ryons was already tied to it, his single miserable garment torn away. The altar was already drenched with blood, and on the ground beside it lay the fresh carcass of a horse.

Chieftains in fantastic finery stood before the big tent, and before them stood the mardar, brandishing a bloody knife. He was bare-chested, spattered with blood; and all that host of Heathen men kept silence, and the beating of the drums died down.

"Hear me, ye gods, and obey!" the mardar roared. "Reveal to me the secrets of the heavens and the earth, the water and the fire: the Thunder King commands you. Drink deeply of the blood of sacrifice—"

And Obst said, "Stop!"

The mardar froze. That anyone would dare to interrupt him, let alone presume to command him, was more than he could take in all at once: the greatest chieftain in the army would not have dared to do so. His mouth hung open, but no words came out. The many-colored feathers in his hair trembled violently. His face was painted red and blue; his white eyes stared.

"Murderer, idolater, and servant of false gods, who are no gods!" Obst said. "The true God hates your sacrifices; they are an abomination to Him. Your Thunder King is but a man whose breath is in his nostrils, whose flesh shall wither like the grass. Every word in your mouth is lies and blasphemy. Don't you dare lay a filthy finger on that boy! The true God has seen your wickedness, and you shall do it no more."

No one lifted a finger to restrain Obst. No one spoke, not even a whisper. The only sound that could be heard, when Obst stopped to catch his breath, was the rustling of the tribal standards in the wind.

The mardar could not speak. His jaw trembled fitfully. Tics broke out on his body, on his face. His eyes rolled upward. He looked like a man choking on a windpipe-full of gristle.

His free hand reached for the base of his throat, but he toppled to the earth before it got there.

A tall, bearded chief with a gleaming golden breastplate stepped forward silently, stood over the fallen mardar. By and by he knelt, touched the body, rolled it onto its back. His hands felt for a pulse, a heartbeat. After a moment, he looked up.

"The mardar is dead," he said.

And Obst, who hadn't thought to pray for a miracle, and certainly hadn't expected one, fainted.

CHAPTER 12

Obst Among the Chieftains

When Obst came to, he found himself lying on his back with something tucked under his head for a pillow, looking up at a patch of sky framed by fierce, tattooed faces. Among them was another face that was not tattooed, just dirty.

"He's come back!" Ryons said. They must have untied him, let him off the altar, and given him back his ragged garment. "I told you he would."

Those were Abnak faces looking down at him, Obst thought. But where was the mardar? And what would happen now? Dread came flooding into his heart.

"Do you hear me, old man?" asked one of the Abnaks.

"Yes, I can hear you." Obst's own voice sounded cracked and hoarse. "If you'd just let me sit up ..."

Ryons helped him, and took the opportunity to whisper into his ear. "The mardar's dead. So be careful what you say!"

Dead? How could that be? They were still in front of the mardar's big black tent, on hard ground from which all the grass had been worn away, surrounded by chiefs from a dozen Heathen nations. But all the men clustered most closely around him, Obst observed, were Abnaks.

Ryons spoke to them. "See, my masters—it's just as Hooq said. This old man is a mighty shaman, and his god is a mighty god. You all saw how he struck down the mardar. None of your gods could do that."

"It's so," growled a burly Abnak with more tattoos than skin. "The old man is indeed a mighty shaman. The mardar should have obeyed him when he spoke." All the other Abnaks grunted their assent.

But not all the Heathen agreed. One of the chiefs in wolfskin caps spoke up: "Bah! What sorcery is this? The mardar was the servant of the Great Man. Through his eyes, King Thunder watched us; through his ears, King Thunder heard us. Now what are we to do? His wrath against us will be terrible!" And a great howl went up for that.

"They're upset," Ryons whispered to Obst. The boy raised his hands and begged leave to speak. More from curiosity than anything else, the chieftains made silence for the slave.

"Hear me, brave ones! You all know that this old man can speak in all your languages at once, so that each and every one of you can understand him, just as if he were only speaking in your own language. And he understands whatever any of you say to him. There's no one else in all the world who can do that. But he can, because his god gives him understanding and makes him understood.

"The mardar was a mighty man, but this old man's god made short work of him. It would be just as easy for this god to do the same to you! Be wise, therefore, and be instructed: your own eyes have seen it."

Obst startled: the boy had quoted Scripture, a line from one of the Sacred Songs. How could that be?

"Help me to stand," Obst said. And when Ryons had him back on his feet, "Hear me, you brave men of war. It was not of my own doing that I came to you. My God sent me, that is the true God who made the very earth you stand on. He sent me as His messenger to you.

"I have no power in myself. I'm only a man of flesh and blood, like you. But my God is God, and He intends that you should know Him better."

"The Great Man is greater than the gods!" shouted one of the Wallekki.

"Then how is it that his servant lies as dead as a rock?" answered one of the Abnaks.

The chieftains began to shout at one another. Fingers sought the hafts of weapons. "What do we care for any Thunder King beyond the lakes, where none of us has ever been?" an Abnak chieftain roared. Men of other nations roared back at him. Obst had been given the gift of understanding, but he had not been given the power to make himself heard over this din.

They might have come to blows, had not a squat, black-haired chief with black eyes hammered on a round brass shield with the pommel of his dagger. He clattered and clanged until the other chiefs subsided.

"You all know me," he said. "I am Szugetai, chief of horsemen, from the wide lands far beyond the lakes. My people, the Ghols, breed horses and camels second to none.

"We have come a long, long way, my men and I—farther than any of you. And we haven't come all this way to argue about a lot of foreign gods.

"No, my comrades—we came to get rich! By all the ghosts of all my ancestors, have you forgotten why this great host was assembled? Have you forgotten why the mardar was going to sacrifice that boy today?

"I don't care who's a shaman and who isn't. We've shamans aplenty in our own country, if it comes to that. I care about making war. I care about sacking cities, carrying off cartloads of plunder, and winning great fame that will never die. I care about crossing those mountains, just as we said we would.

"I don't care if we have to do it without the mardar. What does it matter if he's dead? We've been given a new holy man to take his place."

It took some moments for those words to sink in. The Abnaks were the first to cheer; they cheered uproariously. Then the others worked out Szugetai's meaning. One by one, it dawned on them; when it did, they cheered, too.

Ryons looked up at Obst and grinned. "You've done well, old man!" he said.

"But what have I done?" Obst said. He wished the chieftains would stop cheering; he couldn't hear himself think. "I don't understand."

"Well, I understand that I've just had the best good luck that ever I had in my life," said Ryons. "You're the mardar now, and it's my good luck to be your faithful servant."

CHAPTER 13

A Rescue Mission

Martis slept, dreaming strange dreams of new cities rising from the old ruins on the plains. They did not look like cities as he knew them. Slender buildings rose to impossible heights, and there were no walls. He startled when Helki woke him.

"Shh!" the big man said. "Don't wake the bairns. Come outside."

They crept out of the cave. It was still dark, with a sharp chill in the air.

"You're a man who knows how to use weapons, I think," Helki said. Martis nodded. "Well, then, we have some work on hand. Hope you're not squeamish."

"No one ever accused me of that," Martis said. "What's to do?"

"It's another one of Squint-eye's wolf-packs, eight men. They've kidnapped a couple of women, wives of honest settlers. They're holed up in an old stone tower that used to be someplace important. It's just a ruin now, but still safer for them than camping in the open. I aim to take those women away from them. Want to come?"

Martis smiled, imagining what Lord Reesh would think of this. He wondered what Helki would say if he knew he was enlisting the help of an assassin. He wondered what

God would think of it.

"I wouldn't have thought you needed any help against just eight of them," he said.

"Best to be careful," Helki said. "I don't want to take the chance of the women getting hurt."

Wytt popped out of the cave and chattered at them. Helki made some unintelligible noises, and the Omah went back in.

"You can speak with him?"

Helki nodded. "More or less. I told him to keep an eye on the kiddies. Come on, let's go. It'll be daybreak soon."

He led the way through the dark woods, Martis following as best he could. For such a massive man, Helki made barely a sound. Martis stepped on twigs that snapped, brushed against leaves that rustled, and stubbed his toe on roots. But Helki seemed to have eyes in his feet.

They crossed a stream from which wisps of vapor were beginning to rise. The sky showed a hint of grey—not that they could see much of it from underneath the trees. A stillness lay over the forest: too early for the morning birds, too late for the callers in the night. Everything in sight was shades of grey.

"How did you know about this?" Martis asked. "Did the Omah bring you tidings?"

"I have them scouting for me now, all around the neighborhood," Helki said. "Makes it hard for Squint-eye's men to take me by surprise. But don't talk. Sound carries far, this hour of the morning."

How far they hiked, Martis couldn't tell. They kept on going, and pale light spread over the sky, and subdued colors returned to the forest. Birds began to call. Martis guessed he and Helki had marched at least five miles. Once upon a time it would have been a hardship for him; but he'd gotten used to walking, by now.

Just as Martis resigned himself to hiking on till noon, Helki stopped. He drew Martis close and whispered in his ear.

"The tower's just ahead," he said. "The lads haven't started their breakfast yet, and their fire's gone out; otherwise, I'd smell smoke. I expect they're still asleep.

"We're going to get as close as we can, going as quiet as we can. When I give a holler, we rush right in. Use your knife on every man you can reach. Don't waste time making sure of a kill. We have to settle them before they hurt the women."

Helki crept forward in a crouch, quiet as a cat stalking a mouse. Martis followed closely, unable to imitate Helki's technique; and the little noise he made sounded like a racket to him. When it came to stalking a victim through the city by night, through streets crowded or deserted, Martis had no peer. But here in the forest, he was clumsy.

Overhead, a blue jay scolded them. Helki answered it, making a noise that sounded just like the bird's. The jay fell silent.

And there, just beyond a last screen of saplings, stood the tower, what was left of it. Once upon a time it must have dominated a clearing, maybe as a stronghold for a sheriff's woodsmen or a secret place of refuge for a rebel knight. It's five hundred years old, at least, guessed Martis. The clearing wasn't much of a clearing anymore, and the tower wasn't much of a tower. The top half of it was broken off, and all around it lay heaps of hewn stone, green with moss.

Over the years, outlaws must have cleared the rubble out of the inside of the tower so they could use what shelter it afforded. The stones that still stood formed a round wall. Even the ruin was as big as an oligarch's townhouse.

No one stood guard outside. The door was just a wide hole in the wall.

Shifting his grip on his staff, Helki crept across the last few yards to the doorway. Behind him, Martis drew his dagger. This would not be the kind of fight he was used to.

"Now!" roared Helki; he bellowed like a bull.

They charged into the undefended fort. The robbers must have been sleeping. Martis was only a step or two behind Helki, but one of the outlaws was already dead by the time he passed through the doorway.

The space inside was round, with plenty of room for eight men to give a good account of themselves against eight more; but Helki gave them no such opportunity. A man confronted him with a sword; the tip of Helki's rod shot out and jabbed him in the throat. Down he went, choking.

Martis saw two women tied with cords so they could hardly move. A robber with a knife was reaching for them. Martis launched himself at the man, who didn't see him coming, and brought him down, landing on top of him. A sharp strike to the head, with the pommel of the dagger, put him out of action.

Martis leaped to his feet, but the fight was already over. All the men were down but two.

"Drop your weapons and yield to me, and I'll do you no harm," Helki said. "Or you can fight and die." He made a threatening gesture with his staff, and a knife and a hatchet fell to the ground. "Up against that wall, face-first, with your hands up high. Don't move until I tell you to." The defeated men obeyed. "Friend, would you be so kind as to cut the lasses free of their bonds. Don't be afraid, goodwives—you're safe now."

They were just a couple of peasant women, plain and plainly terrified, faces streaked with tears and leaf mold, homespun dresses in disorder, and their hair in wild disarray.

"Sairy of the Dale, I'm glad to see you," Helki said. "Have they hurt you?"

"Not yet, God be praised," said the stouter of the two women, bracing herself not to flinch as Martis cut her bonds. "But they left my Davy lying sore hurt and like to die."

"I'll see if I can help him, after we get you to a place of safety."

Martis cut the last of the ropes and helped the woman to sit. She rubbed her wrists, wiped hair back from her face.

"This is my cousin, Soose, from out by the Eft-pond," she said, nodding at the other woman, whom Martis was now busy cutting loose.

"You must be Helki the Rod," said Soose. "I've heard of you. But what made you do this for us, and how did you know we were in need of you? But they do say you know everything that happens in the forest, end to end."

Helki laughed. "Lintum Forest is way too big for that, lass! But yes, I knew you were here, and I knew who brought you here. Now let me finish my business."

The two men up against the wall trembled, expecting to be killed.

"Turn around, you two," Helki said. "You both know who I am."

They nodded.

"You tell your boss, Latt Squint-eye, who wants to call himself the King of Lintum Forest, that the only crown he'll ever wear will be this." Helki spun his staff. "I'm a peaceable man, God knows, and I mind my own business. But I'll be burned if I let him turn this forest upside down.

"Tell him that if he wants to live much longer, he'd best clear out and go live with his Heathen friends. The day he sees my face, that'll be his last day on this earth. As for the likes of you, I reckon you'd best stop following Latt, because it won't be healthy. He may have a hundred men, or two hundred, at his beck and call, but they won't be able to protect him, and they're apt to get killed trying. Now go, and don't let me see you again."

The two outlaws looked at each other, stared once more at Helki, and then scuttled out of the tower. Martis heard them crashing through the underbrush.

"Goodwives, I hope you can walk a ways because we can't stay here," Helki said. "I have a place where you can be safe. And after we get there, Sairy, I'll go for Davy and see if there's anything I can do for him."

"What about this one?" Martis said, pointing to the man he'd knocked unconscious.

"Leave him be, we don't have time for him. You knocked his wits out but good, didn't you?"

"He'll thank me for it later, when he sees he's still alive," Martis said.

CHAPTER 14

The Chieftains' Council

The sudden death of the mardar threw the whole camp into confusion. As there were twelve nations represented in the army, the highest-ranking chiefs of all twelve met in the big black tent to decide what to do next.

The Abnaks placed Obst under their protection, in care of a subchief named Uduqu, who was the father of one of Hooq's wives, and, as he put it, "fond of the boy as if he was my own." Uduqu was the proud owner of a conical tent of cowhides sewn together and set over a frame of poles, twice as high and roomy as most of the others. There he kept Obst until the chieftains should summon him into their presence.

Their meeting started in the early afternoon and ran into the night. By then Obst had had an Abnak supper—roasted rabbit, wild onions, and a kind of bread made from acorns. He wondered how they cooked the bitter taste out of the acorns, but Uduqu couldn't tell him. He'd always had slaves or wives to do his cooking for him.

He was a squat, brawny man covered all over with tattoos and scars, with a rough knot on his forehead where someone had once clubbed him with a stone hatchet, and the wound hadn't healed neatly. But the man who'd done that was dead.

Having eaten his fill, and with sundown coming on, Uduqu relaxed. He lit the end of a long, brown bean—Obst didn't know what it was called—and sucked smoke into his mouth, blowing it out in rings. Obst had never seen anyone do such a thing before.

"I don't know what the big chiefs need to talk about," Uduqu said. "Either we're going to cross the mountains, or we aren't. But chiefs love to talk."

"Was the mardar your general, or just your priest?" Obst asked.

Uduqu didn't know what a priest was and had only a hazy notion of the function of a general. "The mardar was the eyes and ears of King Thunder, way out East," he said, "and his mouthpiece, too. That's how the Great Man commands his armies and knows if they obey. There's a mardar with each army, and even though King Thunder is weeks' and weeks' journey distant, a mardar can still hear his voice. Don't ask me how! But you're a shaman—you must know how those things are done."

"But I'm not a shaman," Obst said.

"Tell that to the mardar!" Uduqu laughed at his own joke. "But we won't shed any tears for him. Truth to tell, you'd have been burned at the stake already, except every man in this camp was scared silly of the mardar; and whether they'll say so or not, they're happy to be rid of him.

"But now they don't know what to think. They're glad he's dead, but they're afraid of what the Great Man will do about it. They're afraid of you, too, I guess. After all, it was you that killed him."

Obst shook his head. "Please understand: I haven't killed anyone. I never have, and I hope I never will. It was

God who struck down the mardar. Someday God will strike down King Thunder, too."

Sitting beside him as his servant, Ryons gasped.

"It's all true, brave one!" he blurted out. "Obst has been telling me about his god. That was the god's voice we all heard that was like a great bell ringing in the height of heaven."

Uduqu blew a puff of smoke at him. "Bah! What do we Abnaks care for the westman's god? It's just another god, when all is said and done."

"Try telling that do the mardar," Ryons said. Having his own joke turned on him made the subchief roar with laughter, until he coughed. He pressed his smoking bean to the ground to put it out.

"Right pert and sassy for a born slave, aren't you?" he said. "And to think you were all trussed up on the mardar's altar, just this morning. There's not many can say they lived through that. It's made you bold, boy—bold enough to speak just like an Abnak. I'll never blame you for that.

"Well, there may be something to what you say. I wouldn't mind if there was a god somewhere who didn't bow down to King Thunder. What have we Abnaks to do with some new god out beyond the lakes? Our own gods stay inside the trunks of trees where they belong. I never did like the idea of foreigners chopping down those trees and hauling them east to be put into a prison."

"The true God is not like that," said Obst; but before he could make a lesson of it, a tattooed warrior thrust his head into the tent and spoke to Uduqu.

"Bring the old man," he said. "The chiefs will see him now."

Ryons went along with them to the big tent. Obst wondered whether it was safe for the boy to go anywhere near that tent again, but he supposed Ryons knew the ways of the Heathen infinitely better than he did.

"Look how busy everybody is," Ryons said. "They aren't usually busy at night."

"The army's ready to move west," Uduqu said.

Men and boys were leading horses this way and that; women were snatching meat off drying frames; and children—most of them slaves—scurried about like ants, on a thousand different errands. Warriors sharpened their weapons.

Inside the big tent the air was thick with smoke and unusual odors. The light, provided by torches and braziers and fat-burning lamps, was feverish and fitful. Uduqu forced his way through a crowd of chiefs and subchiefs and halted before a group of heavily decorated chieftains sitting on stools. Obst recognized Szugetai, the chief of horsemen, and a clan chief of the Abnaks whose name was, simply, Spider.

"Here's the old man," said Uduqu, and the murmur of voices in the tent died away quickly. A tall, bearded Wallekki stood up from his stool.

"We, the high chiefs of this host, have taken counsel together," he said. "Each of us speaks for all his people in this camp. There are twelve of us. Together, from now on, we will consult for the good of the army. Whenever there is great need, we shall choose one of our number to be chief of chiefs until the need is past."

With stiff formality, each of the twelve rose and made a speech. Spider spoke last.

"I am Spider, son of Dloq; I speak for the Abnaks. If my people don't like what I say, they'll choose another speaker. We are here of our own free will. Now I will let Shaffur speak again."

That was the tall Wallekki chief, an imposing figure of a man, Obst thought; but of them all, Szugetai the horseman and Spider the Abnak struck him as the most dangerous.

"Tomorrow we go west," Shaffur said. "We have lost our mardar, but we will march without him. It is what we all came here to do, and the other armies expect it of us." He grinned. "They might get nasty if we don't do our part."

He pointed to Obst. "The mardar is dead because of this old man, who serves a powerful god. This god of his has not yet been subdued by King Thunder, so we'd be foolish to offend him.

"You, old man, shall speak to your god for us. Find out what sacrifices he desires, and we'll provide them. Ask him how he'd like us to pay him due respect. We shall treat you well, for we are going into your god's country. Ask him to help us to make wise decisions and to favor us in battle.

"But if you pray to him to curse us or if you try to run away from us, know that your manner of death shall be as unpleasant as we can make it. Is all this agreeable to you?"

Obst was speechless. The harder the chieftains glared at him, the harder it was to find words. Surely they had no inkling that what they proposed was outrageous beyond words.

"My chieftains, please be patient!" Ryons said. "My master even now is communing with his god, and he will answer you as soon as the god answers him."

One of the chieftains nodded to another and remarked, "Just like the mardar—only not so ugly."

Obst had to say something. Ryons was going to get himself roasted on a spit if he didn't learn to hold his peace. Didn't the fool boy realize he was playing with fire?

"Brave warlords," Obst stammered at last, "my God is Lord over the whole earth, from one end to another, and everything in it. He is not to be appeased by sacrifice. What can you give Him that He doesn't already own?

"God has heard every word you've spoken, all of you, from the time you were infants. Because He is all-powerful, He can afford to be all-merciful. He understands that you don't know Him. He sent me to you so that I might make Him known to you, according to my own poor knowledge.

"He will surely defend you from this false god, this blaspheming Thunder King, if you put yourselves under His protection. But it won't be in return for roasted bulls or horses. It won't be in return for gold or silver."

"What does he want, then?" asked Szugetai. "Women?" The other chiefs laughed, and it took all Obst's self-control to remember that the man was only a Heathen who didn't know any better.

He prayed they wouldn't kill him, or Ryons, for anything he said.

"No, my chieftain, that's not what He wants," Obst said. "From each and every one of us, He wants devotion—to Him and to His laws, which He laid down of old. He wants you to know Him and put your trust in Him: in Him alone."

"What are this god's laws, old man?" Shaffur asked.

Obst spread his palms. "How can I teach you, in a single night, the wisdom of the ages? His laws are many, and yet they come down to only two. You are to love Him and fear Him and honor Him as the only true God; and you are to observe all His laws in your dealings with one another, doing no evil, even as you wish no evil to be done unto you."

"That's all?" wondered a chief of a faraway people.

"It's a very big 'all,' warlord."

"Yet if we do these things you've mentioned," Shaffur said, "your god will protect us from the anger of the Thunder King?" Obst nodded, and the chieftains all stood up.

"I think we have our answer, comrades," Shaffur said. "The army moves tomorrow, so let us get what sleep we can."

CHAPTER 15

A Marvelous Material

To be invited into Lord Reesh's private study was a mark of singular favor. Reesh made sure Orth knew that before he had the preacher come up.

"It's my own little museum, Prester Orth," he said. "Look around, take your time. I'm interested to know what you think of it."

"I am honored, First Prester," Orth said.

It was a small room, with all four walls lined with shelves packed solidly with books and scrolls; a thick, felt carpet on the floor; and a single narrow window through which a shaft of afternoon sunlight slanted down at an angle. A wide table took up most of the floor space.

Upon this table Lord Reesh displayed his relics, his curiosities, collected from all over Obann, but most from in or near the city itself. Orth stood over the table, marveling at them. Reesh kept silence, letting the preacher's thoughts take wing.

Some of the artifacts, the really fragile ones, were under glass. Others simply lay on the table; Reesh had found them to be durable.

Finally Orth spoke. "My lord, what are these things?"

"Shards and fragments of a bygone age, prester. As to what they were—who knows?" Reesh moved closer to the table and picked up an object, displaying it in his hands. He offered it to Orth, who hesitated to touch it. "Don't be afraid, Orth. You couldn't break it if you wanted to."

At first glance it might have been a wheel, albeit a very small one. It had a hub, rounded on one surface and flat on the other, and only two thick spokes that connected seamlessly to the rim. Its color was a shiny dark blue, of a shade that few men had ever seen before, with an unreadable symbol in red and white inlaid in the center of the rounded surface of the hub. The whole was just a foot and a half in diameter. Orth handled it gingerly.

"What would you say it was made of, prester?"

That was a question no one had ever been able to answer; nor could Orth, although he examined it carefully, turning it over and over in his hands.

"My lord, I cannot tell," he said. "It's not any kind of metal, nor is it any kind of wood or stone, or leather. One might guess polished horn, but there's no grain to it. Nor does the blue color appear to have been painted on. There's a chip, right here, that shows you that the thing is blue all the way through. And it's not heavy."

"Try to bend it," Reesh said; and of course Orth couldn't.

"It's an exceedingly strong material, my lord. I suppose it might have been a wheel for some kind of small conveyance that had to bear a heavy load. I can't imagine what."

"We haven't even a word for this material, Orth. But it must have been in common use throughout the Empire. People are always finding pieces of it, digging in their gardens, tearing down an old house.

"As you can see, I have other relics made of the same material. It has been found in every color you can think of—and some you can't—and in all kinds of shapes. Look at this."

Reesh picked up a tiny figurine, a perfect little miniature horse with all four legs intact, although the tail was broken off. The little horse was a bright and cheerful pink, and where the tail used to be, you could see it was actually pink through and through. Orth's hands trembled as he studied it.

"Think of it," Reesh said. "These things are a thousand years old, at least, and they've been dug up from the ground. All that time they lay there, no effort being taken to protect them. And yet there's no pitting, no rot; and once you clean them off, the color is as fresh and bright as ever. The only thing that can hurt this material is fire. Then it melts.

"I have many more such specimens. I've had to set aside a separate storeroom for them. Some are obviously instruments of various kinds, although no one knows what use was made of them. Others are obviously pieces of something bigger and more complicated, now mostly lost.

"And of course there are all sorts of metal objects, more or less corroded, whose purposes I can't even guess, no matter how hard I study them. And I do study them—intently. For they have something important to tell me."

"What do they tell you, my lord?"

Reesh retreated to one of the two soft, padded chairs in the room, and sat down. At this point in his life, he couldn't stand for long. But Orth remained beside the table, captivated by the objects on it.

"Like any educated man, Orth, you know that certain

fragments of writing have survived from those days," Reesh said. "With great difficulty, we can read some of it. There are even scraps and shreds of printed paper.

"Plus there are traditions—some recorded in the New Books and the Commentaries, some just old wives' tales—that add to the picture. A determined scholar can amass a fair amount of information, using all these sources."

"Yes," Orth agreed, absentmindedly stroking the smooth surface of the wheel, which he had not yet put down. "Yes, I know my lord. It's said the men of those days traveled in coaches without horses, and spoke to one another over great distances, and called down fire from Heaven that could destroy an enemy city in an instant. It's said they knew how to fly through the air like birds and travel under the sea like fish.

"But it's also said they were abominable sinners, addicted to every kind of wickedness; and God wiped out their glory."

Reesh sighed. "That's as may be," he said. "Who can know the mind of God? I don't pretend to.

"But it's obvious from these few poor relics, and the traditions, that they were a great and glorious people indeed. Compared to them, we're savages."

"Yes, First Prester."

"Do you know what I believe our mission is upon this earth?" said Reesh; and his eyes grew hard and fierce. "It is nothing less than to make the steep, arduous, dangerous climb back up to the pinnacle of that glory, prester. To rekindle its flame. To be mighty, as the men of the Empire were mighty. To rediscover all their secrets, and make use of them!

"These days, a man is considered old if he lives to be sixty. A man is deemed to be well-off if he isn't starving and his roof doesn't leak. But it was not always so; nor will it always be so forever.

"Of course, if we are to climb any distance at all up the pinnacle of glory, we first have to survive this latest invasion of the Heathen. That's why you're here, Orth. Sit down."

Orth returned the wheel to its place and took the other chair. Reesh judged the man prepared for what was coming next.

"It goes without saying that the Temple must survive," he said. "Therefore, I wish you to compose some new Scripture to ensure that it survives. You're a strong scholar and the most eloquent man I know. Will you do it?"

Orth was shocked—but not as shocked as another man might have been. He forced a smile.

"Are you asking me to tamper with the holy Scriptures, First Prester? That might be construed as sacrilege. Perhaps even blasphemy."

"Hah! You're not a child, Orth. You know it wouldn't be the first time such a thing has been done. And it's in the greatest and noblest cause—Obann's survival."

"I am familiar with numerous verses of Scripture that are said to be interpolations," Orth replied. "Said to be, my lord, but not proved to be. The people, and the ordinary presters and reciters, accept them all as genuine. But in our own time, no one has dared to do this."

Reesh waved the objection aside. "Interpolations—bah! There are those who say the whole thing is an interpolation. That there never was a King Ozias; that various unidentified men, not he, wrote the sacred songs attributed to him; that the great prophets were schools of nameless prophets, each adding something of his own to another man's work. There are those who say all those things and more—wise, learned men, of unimpeachable integrity, the finest scholars in the land. No one but a peasant or a hermit, or some other kind of poor, ignorant creature, believes Scripture to be nothing but the pure and infallible Word of God."

"But there are many who believe that, my lord. Some of them are scholars, too."

"But you're not one of them, are you?"

"I've never considered it, my lord."

"Then consider this," Reesh said. "I'm an old man, and sooner more likely than later, I'll die. When I do, the Temple will need a new First Prester; and my recommendation will carry much weight with the presters, when they have to choose one. I thought I might recommend you, Prester Orth. But the First Prester's first duty is to see to the survival and advancement of the Temple. Do I make myself clear?"

"Very clear, my lord. And I am honored." Orth stood up and made obeisance. "But if we suddenly discover a hitherto-neglected piece of Scripture, won't these same wise scholars be suspicious?"

Reesh smiled. "You can leave them to me," he said.

Orth bowed again. "I am yours to command, my lord," he said.

CHAPTER 16

A Prophet Speaks to Jack

Helki found Sairy's husband, and there was enough life left in him to offer hope that he'd recover soon, under his wife's care. Ellayne watched, fascinated, as Sairy mashed leaves and roots, gathered by Helki, into a poultice that would dull pain and speed healing.

Before many days had passed, Helki found himself responsible for half a dozen more people who'd been run off their homesteads by the outlaws and were wandering helplessly in the forest. The group included two able-bodied men (a father and his seventeen-year-old son), three more women who'd been separated from their families, and an old woman who'd been living alone.

"What am I going to do with all of you?" Helki wondered. "There's not enough room in the cave for everybody, and there must be dozens more of you out in the woods."

"We'll build a fort," the man suggested.

"Latt will only burn it down," said Helki. "No—the only thing is to send you all deeper into the forest, much deeper. I know some good places where nobody goes. It won't be easy to get there—we'll have to carry Davy on a litter—but

I reckon we can make it. And then I'll come back here and see if I can't put a stop to Latt."

Jack had been hoping just to stay at Helki's cave for a while. Maybe he could learn to be a woodsman. But now no one would be staying at the cave.

"We'll set out first thing tomorrow morning," Helki said. "It'll take five days to get to where I want to go. You'd all better rest while you can."

"What do you think we should do?" Jack asked Martis, later in the day. "Should we go with Helki? Deep in the forest we'll be safe, he says."

They were sitting on a log together, some twenty paces from the cave. Nearby, Ellayne was playing with the little girl, Jandra: they were trying to make a doll's house with twigs. Jandra's hideous pet looked on, bobbing its head. Ellayne had gotten over her aversion to it. For all its hissing, it never bit anyone.

"It seems a better plan than anything I've thought of," Martis said. "But I had my heart set on Obann. What the forest is to Helki, the city is to me."

"They'd catch us there," said Jack, "sooner or later."

They were still talking it over when Jandra abruptly abandoned her game, stood up, and walked over to stop right in front of Jack. Her face had no expression on it, none at all.

"There is a book missing," she said, in that voice that wasn't her own.

"What book?" Jack said. "Burn it, that's what you say to Helki all the time, isn't it? Well, I wish you wouldn't say it to me."

She didn't hear him. She looked right into his eyes, not seeing him. Or maybe she saw something Jack didn't know was there.

"I have said the throne belongs to Ozias," she said. "Beneath the great cellar is a greater cellar. There you will find what is lost. There, in Obann: in the desolation of Obann."

Jack's short hairs stood on end. Why was she saying these things to him, and what did they mean? Ellayne came up to join them, but Martis waved her to silence.

"I don't know what you're talking about," Jack said.

"Prepare the kingdom for Ozias," Jandra said. And then her eyes rolled, and shut, and she would have collapsed if Ellayne hadn't caught her.

"She's fallen asleep," Ellayne said. "She fell asleep standing up! What all did she say to you, Jack?"

"I don't know! It made no sense!"

"But it does make sense, though," Martis said. "The desolation of Obann—that's the old city, the ruins on the south bank of the river. And everyone knows there are pieces of the Scripture missing."

"Oh, that's stupid!" Ellayne said. She couldn't hold Jandra up anymore, so she lowered her gently to the ground. The child slept on. "How would she know anything about it? She's just a little kid."

"Yes, but that's in Scripture, too!" said Martis. He smiled thinly. "Have you never heard that verse from Prophet Cadok—'out of the mouths of infants ye shall hear wisdom?' I may not be a scholar, but I know that much.

"It's prophecy, Jack. Out of the mouth of this infant, God has spoken to you. He's told you what He wants you to do. Go to the ruined city and find something that is missing."

"I thought you didn't believe in anything like that!" Jack said. "And what was all of that stuff about Ozias? King Ozias died a thousand years ago."

"Two thousand, in fact."

"But the Old Books don't say how he died, or where—do they?" said Ellayne.

"The last the Scripture tells us of Ozias, he was on his way to Bell Mountain. He was never seen again. So no one knows where he died or how."

"But I'm supposed to prepare a kingdom for him?" Jack said. "That's just crazy talk."

"So might anyone have said of you, when you told of your dreams about Bell Mountain," Martis said. "And yet the bell was there, just as you dreamed it."

"Even I thought it was crazy," Ellayne said. Jack glared at her; this was news to him. "I went along for the adventure and because I didn't want to be sent away to school. But then I had the dream, too, and it didn't turn out to be crazy."

"I don't mind going to Obann," Jack said. "I'm not afraid. I just thought God was done with us. We did our bit. We rang the bell."

"You also thought the world was going to end," Ellayne said, "and it's still here. Maybe King Ozias didn't die. Maybe he's going to come back."

"He'd be two thousand years old," Jack said. For a fleeting moment, he felt like giving Ellayne a good hard shove.

"I think we'd better leave such matters to the theologians," Martis said. "And I think I'd better put this little girl to bed." He got up and carried Jandra into the cave.

"We shouldn't worry about it," Ellayne said. "If we could get to the top of Bell Mountain, we ought to be able to get to Obann."

"I like it here," Jack said.

But of course, if God really wanted him to go to Obann, he would have to go.

"The closest town to the forest is Caristun. I've been there," Helki said.

"I went there with Van once, on his cart," Jack said. "It has a stone wall."

"From there we might be able to get a boat down the river to Obann," Martis said.

"Although once the Heathen are across the mountains, there might not be any boats available to common folk. But there's always the road by the river—if it's not too crowded by then with troops or refugees."

They'd gone off some distance from the cave so they could talk privately. It was almost sundown, but Jandra was still asleep.

"Getting through the forest shouldn't be too hard for you—not with Wytt and some of the Forest Omah to scout the way," Helki said. Ellayne held Wytt cuddled in her arms. He chirped once, when Helki mentioned his name. "Getting across the plain to Caristun—well, if the Heathen haven't got that far yet, you'll be all right. But I kind of wish you'd stay, if you can make sense out of some of the things Jandra says. If God is using her to talk to me, I'd like to understand Him. Wish old Obst were here. Maybe he'd know what she meant by calling me 'the flail of the Lord.'"

"But that's easy," Martis said. "In the Book of Disorder, that was the nickname given to Vannon."

"Vannon the farmer?" Ellayne said. She remembered her lessons. "The one who killed a hundred Burners with only a cow-prod?"

"Burners?" Jack said. His own lessons hadn't taken him that far.

"They were terrible people who used to throw children into the fire as a sacrifice to some devil they worshipped," Ellayne said, showing off her knowledge. "But Vannon and the Tribes of the Law wiped them out and destroyed their city."

"Sounds like a man I could admire," Helki said. "Too bad Latt Squint-eye doesn't live in a city."

Martis sighed. "We have entered a very strange time," he said. "God has been silent for so long, no one believes in Him anymore—even if they think they do. I didn't believe, until I reached the summit of Bell Mountain."

"Folks hereabouts believe in God," said Helki. "You must've spent too much time in the Temple."

Ellayne couldn't sleep that night. Like everyone else, she had a bed of ferns inside the cave. The cave had gotten crowded, and a couple of the sleepers around her snored.

She envied Jack. He was the one who'd first had the dream that sent them to Bell Mountain, and now he had another mission, to Obann. Who was he, that God should speak to him? He didn't even know the story of Vannon and the Burners.

Just getting to Obann, if the war started soon, would be an achievement. And then they'd have to find a great cellar underneath another cellar, somewhere in the sprawling ruins of Old Obann. If God was so powerful, why didn't He do some of these things Himself?

Outside, choruses of peeper-frogs sang around the little ponds and puddles that dotted the woods. Inside the cave, men and women snored. Tomorrow Helki would take the refugees to a safe place in the middle of the forest, but Ellayne and Jack and Martis would be on their own again.

Beside her, Jack rolled onto his back and groaned. He mumbled something that sounded like "Ozias." Was it another of his dreams? She would have liked to wake him up and ask him, but she didn't. Let him lie there rustling his ferns, she thought: served him right.

Helki was going to be a hero, like Vannon, and Jack was going to find some great secret that had been lost for a thousand years. But I do just as much as he does, Ellayne thought: why doesn't God speak to me, too?

She felt very much put-upon, and it kept her up all night.

CHAPTER 17

The Wise Man in the Tent

Getting a large army over a range of high mountains is by no means easy. The army would have to be split into groups. If the groups were too large, they might not be able to feed themselves. If they were too small, they would be a tempting target for an enemy.

But there were passes in the mountains, and these had been scouted out carefully. The widest of them opened just above Silvertown, a place fortified with a wall of fitted stone. The strongest division would have to take that route and either capture the city or else pass it by. Obst saw no siege equipment in the army: the Heathen could only take a walled city by surprise or treachery.

He traveled with the big division that was aimed at Silvertown. The Abnaks, in whose custody he was, provided him with a conical deer-hide tent that did not leak, all the food and drink he wanted, and even some new clothes for Ryons, decent clothes that would keep him warm at night. They offered Obst a donkey to ride, but he had no need of it.

"For an old fellow, you've got strong legs," Uduqu said, after two days' uphill marching. "Some of the young bucks from the flat lands are already half done-in."

"God has been good to me," Obst said. "He gives me strength."

The old subchief had a sharp mind, and on the second night out, with Obst as a guest for supper in his tent, he asked a sharp question. That there were several other subchiefs present, all smoking beans and keenly interested in the answer, made the question seem even sharper.

"One thing puzzles me," Uduqu said. "You serve the westman's god; he isn't known on our side of the mountains. And you've said he will protect us. But here we are, marching into his country to make war on his people. You'd think he'd protect them, not us."

There was always the chance that these people might kill him if they didn't like the answer to a question, and Obst knew it.

"It's hard to explain, brave one," he said, feeling gingerly for words. "My people worship Him in the Temple and in a thousand chamber houses; but God created the Abnaks, too, and all the nations of the earth. Your people don't know Him, but nevertheless He gives you what you need to live. Food and water, the land you live on, the air you breathe—"

"But we give him nothing in return," said a one-eyed chief with a dreadful white scar across his scalp. "What kind of a god is that? Even the littlest of our gods, in the littlest tree, likes a wee bowl of beer now and then."

"You have asked a question that God answered thousands of years ago, and men wrote it down in a book to remember it," Obst said. "What does the newborn babe give his father and his mother? What repayment can he make to them? And yet they will starve so he can eat: behold, a mother will lay down her life for her child. The Lord loves you as a father loves his firstborn son, and as a mother loves her suckling babe."

Those men, who would just as soon take a man's scalp as get up in the morning, puffed on their beans and pondered the verse. They all had mothers and fathers, and most had children of their own. And they were a long way from their children, their families, their homes.

"The westmen should not have kept this god to themselves," said one.

"But they are his people," said another. "No wonder they're so rich. This god gives them walled cities and all the good land between the mountains and the sea."

"Why does he love them so much better than he loves us?" Uduqu asked. "Why hasn't he given us cities and wide lands and gold?"

Obst faltered, but Ryons took up the question:

"Mighty warriors—what a simple thing to say! Could you live in those cities and still be Abnaks?

"I journeyed with my former master to a city once, when we were in a caravan. The people there, those who weren't slaves, shut themselves up in smelly houses and lived in fear of thieves. Too cowardly to fight for themselves, they had to hire warriors to protect them. If a god ever put the Abnaks in such cities, they wouldn't thank him for it. Has he not put you where you're free and proud, and given you the things you like best—game to hunt, fish to catch, other tribes to fight with? Who would you rather be than yourselves?"

Obst held his breath: the boy had gone too far. But then the chief with the great scar on his scalp laughed so hard he coughed.

"Ho, ho! Who's the wise man in this tent?" he gasped. "The westman's god must love us dearly—otherwise, he never would have made us Abnaks!"

The chiefs all laughed and praised Ryons for his answer. Obst could breathe again.

Much later, when they were back in their own tent and bundling up for the night, Obst admonished the boy.

"You mustn't be so bold with the chiefs, Ryons! They're dangerous men, and if you anger them, how could I protect you?"

"Pooh, my master—pooh! I know them better than you do. Abnaks like a little sass. Besides, they're all afraid of you."

"Afraid of me? I doubt it!"

"For one so old, you don't know much," Ryons said. "All the nations have gods, but there are only two kinds of gods—the kind men are afraid of, and hate, and the kind they only laugh at. They're afraid of your god, so they're afraid of you."

"I don't see how they can be afraid of God, when they don't know Him—although to know Him and not fear Him would be not to know Him at all."

"They know he killed the mardar; they saw it with their own eyes. They were very afraid of the mardar because he served a terrible god. But your god killed the mardar, so he must be a very terrible god, too. Besides, they're still terrified of the Great Man: so they need your god to protect them from him."

Obst sighed. Being a hermit was much more to his taste than being a missionary.

"In ancient days," he said, "God spoke to the people all the time through oracles and prophets. He gave them laws, and when their enemies oppressed them, He raised them up deliverers. He blessed their crops and their herds, and chastised them when they were wicked. People lived every day with God in their midst, as if He were a father to them.

"But things are different nowadays. That's why I became a hermit: so I could live alone in the woods and seek my God.

"We have our great Temple in Obann, and it rules a thousand chamber houses strewn all over the country. It collects fees, trains presters and reciters, buys and sells land: the name of the Lord is on everybody's lips. But it's only a name. As the prophet said, 'These people swear by My name, but know Me not.' For all the little regard they have for Him, for all they leave Him out of their reckonings, He might as well be one of the Abnaks' tree-spirits, content with a little pot of beer—if He even gets that much."

"His people must be great fools, then," Ryons said.

"They are indeed," said Obst. "That's why, at long last, God required the bell on Bell Mountain to be rung, ringing in the last days of the world. I suspect that's why He has moved the nations of the East to come together and invade the West. The day of God's wrath is at hand."

"What do you mean, 'the last days of the world'?"

"Why, just what I say—the end of it all."

"I think that's very silly," Ryons said. "If God went to all the trouble of making the whole world, as you say He did, and it turned out so badly that He got sick of it, that'd mean He didn't know what He was doing in the first place. I wouldn't bother with a God like that. Good night!" And he rolled over in his blanket, without giving Obst a chance to rebuke him.

CHAPTER 18

A Wild Story from the North

While Jack, Ellayne, and Martis made their way to the northwest corner of the forest so they could cross the plain to Caristun, and while Obst toiled up the mountain pass with the Heathen host, Helki got his refugees to safety and prepared to make war.

"How does one man make a war?" Sairy demanded. "You'd better stay here with us."

In the heart of Lintum Forest, at a place known only to Helki and the woodland Omah, stood the remains of a castle. No one knew how old it was, and much of it was ruined; but there was enough left of it to testify that it had been a very grand building in its time. The settlers had never seen anything like it. The roofs had fallen in, one or two towers lay in jumbles of mossy stones, and nature had long since filled in the moat. But it had been built to defy the worst that man could do to it, the walls were thick and strong, and much of it—with a little work—could still be used as shelter. A nearby spring provided drinking water; and although city people would have starved here, the settlers knew how to wrest a living from the forest.

"There's enough room in this place for a hundred of us," Sairy said. "Hadn't you better stay? Someday the war will be over, and Latt Squint-eye will get his comeuppance."

"He'll get his because I aim to give it to him," Helki said. "I'll come back here whenever I can, with tools, weapons, and like as not more people. But someday soon Latt's going to get careless; and when he does—" He spun his rod in his hands and made it whistle.

The seventeen-year-old boy, Andrus, said, "Take me with you! I'm good in the woods, and you'll need help."

"I reckon not," said Helki. He looked to the boy's father, Ival, but Ival only shrugged. "The lad's heart is set on it," he said. "But I'll stay here to help the lasses with the heavy work."

Sairy's husband, Davy, spoke from his litter. "It's time the honest men of this country stood up to Squint-eye and his kind! There must be hundreds of young, able-bodied men in these parts who are ready to do it."

"I'll do everything you tell me to, and I won't be a bother," Andrus said. "But Goodman Davy's right. This fight belongs to all of us, not just you."

Helki thought it over. The forest was full of settlers; no one knew how many. The outlaws bullied them. Maybe it was time for a change. But he was used to doing things alone, without help. Was he ready for a change?

"All right, boy, you can come along," he said. "If we could get the honest men together into war-bands, it might be something for the robbers to fret about at night. Are you any good with a bow and arrows?"

The boy grinned. He was tall, broad-shouldered, and had, Helki thought, the makings of a mighty man. He had fair hair, blue eyes, and strong white teeth. Helki liked him.

"I'm good enough, I guess!" he said. "I'd show you, if I had my longbow with me."

"We'll find you one soon enough."

The last thing Helki did before setting out was to say good-bye to Jandra. "Daddy Helki's got to go and do some work, peeper," he said. "You stay here with Mama Sairy, and she'll take good care of you. And you've got your bird and plenty of the little hairy men to play with." Omah liked ruins, and there were many of them living in and around the castle. Helki had gotten these Omah to agree to protect and help the humans. He was surprised at how easily they'd agreed.

"Daddy go?" Jandra said. She didn't quite understand.

"Yes—but I'll be back again. So you be a good girl!"

She gave him a hard little hug around the neck and a loud kiss on the cheek. He was glad she made no prophetic utterances.

He soon found that young Andrus really was a good woodsman. The boy moved quietly through the underbrush, knew the meaning of most of the bird calls, and skillfully read the stories told by scuffed leaf-litter, bruised earth, and broken twigs. He quickly learned how to summon the Omah and make friends with them.

"A lot of folks live here all their lives," Helki said, "and still don't know the woods are full of little people. Or else they think it's fairies."

"I never knew there were so many," Andrus said.

"Well, there are—only they know how to stay out of

sight. And that's what we're going to do. Find out where Latt makes his camps, how many men he has, what paths he likes to use. He's not to know we're within a hundred miles of him. No fighting, no killing, if we can help it. That comes later."

"Just like hunting a panther, eh?"

"Latt's more dangerous," Helki said.

Lintum Forest wasn't the only place where there were refugees. There were plenty of them in Obann, too, and the rulers of the city had their hands full with them.

People in the east fled before the approach of the Heathen, but there were refugees coming from the north, all the way down from the River Winter. Nor was it any Heathen army that had chased them from their homes.

They brought wild stories with them—so wild, indeed, that Judge Tombo's city patrol arrested a few of the loudest of them, and Tombo had one, as a spokesman, haled before a session of the High Council of the Oligarchy. This convened in the judge's private meeting room inside the Justice Building, away from the public eye. Most people preferred to avoid going anywhere near the Justice Building.

The prisoner, if prisoner he truly was, was a trapper, grey-haired, grey-bearded, born and bred in the Northern Wilds. This was his first-ever visit to Obann. Dressed in worn, stained buckskins, he stared nervously at the six lords in their velvet robes and golden chains of office. A guard made him sit on a stool and stood behind him. Not really necessary, Tombo would have admitted: but useful in impressing upon the man the gravity of his situation.

Lord Reesh sat beside the judge, feigning a detached serenity, but keenly listening.

Tombo spoke first. "Your name, sir? Speak up, don't be afraid. We aren't going to hurt you."

The trapper tried to bow while seated on the stool. "Guddorm, m'lord, son of Gan," he muttered.

"Guddorm, son of Gan, do you know who we are?"

"No, m'lord. I don't rightly know."

Tombo gestured to his colleagues. "We are the men responsible for the peace and good order not only of this great city, but of all the land of Obann," he said. "I don't know if you've heard, but there's a war about to start—a mass invasion of Heathen from the East. People here are fearful. And then you come scurrying down from the northlands with a lot of alarming stories, and we have disorder in our city."

Guddorm looked back at him like a bear cub in a trap.

"But be at ease," Judge Tombo said. "We wish to know what frightened you out of your country. After all, we may have to send an army north. So all we want from you is the truth. We need to know the state of things up north. You're here to tell us, and that's all we ask of you. Do you understand?"

Guddorm nodded. Tombo told the guard to go out and find him a cup of watered wine. "It'll calm you down," he explained. "In the meantime, let's hear your tale. Take your time, and tell the truth."

Guddorm stammered a bit, but when he finally got going, this is the tale he told.

"The river froze this year, m'lord, froze real hard. But you never saw such furs as we were getting on the north bank. Otters as big as sheepdogs, with fur as soft as down.

Tremendous beavers. A trapper could get rich. So we paid no mind to the cold, nor the deep snow, and a lot of us went up there.

"It's all deep woods, m'lord. No one's ever seen the other side of it. And there've always been stories about this or that. You know: funny creatures that lived in the wild lands. You'd meet a man who said he saw something, but couldn't prove it. Once or twice I thought I saw something, too. But I couldn't tell what it was.

"Come midwinter, we had a very nasty cold snap, and snow like you've never seen before. Some men packed up and went home. When the weather didn't let up, after a week we all decided to call it quits. And that's when we saw them."

The guard returned with the wine, and Guddorm was allowed a drink. The cup shook in his hands, Reesh noticed. It took some prodding to get him to continue.

"Trappers like to tell stories, m'lord: the taller, the better. Only this ain't no story. God never love me more if I'm not telling the truth.

"They came out of the woods to cross the river on the ice. The weather must've been too much for them. I can't tell you what they are, because no man ever saw the like before. There's not even a story about animals like these—if they are animals, and not some kind of devil.

"Just imagine a black bear, or a wild boar, as big as one of the big houses in this city, and all covered with black hair. Just imagine a thing like that *moving*, coming at you on four legs, and now and then letting out a scream that'd freeze the blood in your veins. That's what they were like.

"Only they weren't giant bears. Wild boars have tusks, but not like these: a pair of great white tusks, curvy-like, each of 'em bigger than a grown man. And boars have snouts, but not like these things have. Like a giant hairy snake, squirmin' and a-coilin' and lookin' for a man to choke.

"That's what came out of the woods, m'lord. I swear I'm telling the truth. And I don't know how many of 'em there were, because nobody stayed to count. But there were sure a lot of 'em. They crossed the river and just kept heading south, like they wanted to get clear of the woods.

"There's a town up there, what has a trading post where we can sell our furs and ship them to the southlands. Market City, it was called. Only it ain't there anymore.

"Those things passed through Market City, and they wrecked it. There's nothing left of it. I was there, though I got away as fast as I could. But I saw a couple of those monsters flatten the emporium.

"After that, I just snatched up whatever I could carry and took off. There were a lot of us together. People along the way said, 'Go to Obann, you've got to go to Obann,' so that's what we did. That's why we're here. We just wanted to get away from those things. We didn't mean no harm."

Lord Reesh sensed the man was telling the truth, was too scared to do otherwise. He spoke then, along the line he and Tombo had worked out beforehand.

"My lords," he said, "the Temple recommends clemency. Judge Tombo's men have detained a number of these people, and I think we should let them go. They're honest pioneers who've lost their homes: the Temple will provide relief for them until they can either return to their own country or find another place to live. I'm sure they will understand that they mustn't spread panic throughout the city. What say you, Lord Governor-general?"

"I'm sure you're right, my lord First Prester," Lord Ruffin said. "After all, these are our own people. We want to protect them. But I think the time has come to appoint a special commissioner for the northlands and give him a seat among the oligarchs—especially since it may become necessary to build forts, organize a militia, etc., up there. Someone will have to be in charge."

"I'm not sure we have the funds in the treasury for that," said Lord Chutt, Taxes and Revenue.

"My lord Chutt now agrees that strange creatures have appeared among us?" Reesh said. Chutt sighed, and conceded that, on the face of it, it now appeared to be so.

"I haven't got an army to spare for the north," Lord Gwyll rumbled through his beard. "All the troops have been sent east to hold cities against the Heathen."

"Even so, we can't just write off the northern provinces. It would cripple the economy," said Lord Davensay, Commerce. "But by all means let's appoint a commissioner, send him up to investigate, and see what he recommends. A chain of stone forts might do the trick."

"In the meantime," Lord Ruffin said, "Judge Tombo, you may release the refugees into the care of the Temple." He looked down his long, sharp nose at Guddorm. "You may go, my good man. Only have a care not to stir up the people of this city with your stories. You're perfectly safe here. There are no beasts that can break through Obann's city wall."

There were such beasts in Scripture, Reesh thought; but those were only stories.

CHAPTER 19

Bron the Blessed

There was no hiding such a big army, not even in the mountains; so when the Heathen host reached Silvertown, they found the gates shut and armed men on the walls. The defenders shook spears at them and dared them to try it.

"Well, that's that," said Uduqu; for the Heathen had no equipment for breaking down the city walls, and no time for a siege. They would have starved before the city did. What they all wanted to do was to get down to the plain and look for easier prey; and that was what the chiefs decided.

By now it was well into spring and everything was green, but Obst hardly noticed. Ryons kept him busy all day with questions as the army marched. He wanted to know all about the Western lands and peoples, and all about God. And at night the Abnak chiefs and warriors demanded that Obst tell them stories from the Scriptures. Coming from a people who liked to collect the heads of enemies, couldn't read or write, and never built houses that lasted more than a year or two, their interest in the Scripture surprised Obst. Men from other nations represented in the host sometimes came to listen, but the fierce Abnaks had a passion for it.

"The others have bigger gods than ours, and they're afraid to offend them," Uduqu explained. "Our gods are all back home on the other side of the mountains, and they don't care what we do out here."

Obst had spent most of his long life reading the Old Books over and over again, never dreaming he'd someday be called on to be a living book for savages who couldn't read at all. They were especially fond of stories that featured giants, wars, and miracles. Among their favorites was the tale of Bron, grandson of Geb, who was as tall as a tree and twice as strong.

"He is known as Bron the Blessed," Obst would say, "because God was pleased with him, and he lived five hundred years and kept his strength right up to the end. People did live longer in those days, but very few lived as long as Bron.

"In Bron's time, people had spread out all over the earth, and many of them had grown very wicked. Bron and his people, who still proudly bore the name of Geb, lived simply; but some of the wicked people had by then built mighty cities and cared for nothing but power over others. They carved idols out of wood and stone and called them gods; but they were really only worshipping themselves. But Bron's people still worshipped the true God who is the only God. So there was constant war between his people and the people of the cities.

"Now in one of those cities there lived a witch, full of evil wisdom taught to her by devils. Maysah, her name was. Instructed by these devils, she wove a giant robe that the rulers of her city would offer to Bron as a gift, along with false promises of peace. It was a beautiful robe of softest wool, dyed with many colors and woven in cunning patterns to delight the eye. But it was made in such a way so that whoever put it on would be instantly poisoned through his skin; and so they thought to murder Bron.

"Maysah's servants built a great hall just outside the city, big enough to hold Bron. They built a giant chair for him, whom no ordinary chair would fit. They lured him in with vows of friendship and the offer of a feast; but secretly they planned, after they'd poisoned him, to burn down the hall with all his chieftains in it. With their best men slain, Bron's people would be easy to destroy.

"Suspecting nothing, Bron and his warriors came to the feast. The witch had carved a huge cup from a tree trunk, big enough for an ordinary man to bathe in, and filled it with wine for Bron; and there was wine for all Bron's men, and whole bulls roasted over fire, and fresh fruit from the city's fields. And music.

"Now the witch was proud because the rulers of the city had promised to pay her all the gold they had, once Bron was dead. Before she presented him with the poisoned robe, Maysah performed a dance for him.

"Bron drank from his gigantic cup and watched the dance. Some of his men were ravished by the witch's beauty, but Bron only pretended to be. For God sent a snake into the hall, a little brown serpent that only Bron noticed because everyone else was watching Maysah's dance. But Bron watched the snake, and saw it slither up to the gorgeous robe that lay spread out on a giant table, on display. And he saw the serpent brush up against the hem of it that hung down to the floor: and the serpent writhed and spat blood, and died.

"When the dance was over, the witch said, 'Now, Bron, claim your gift!' But Bron said, 'Such a pretty robe becomes you more than me,' and before the witch could escape, he seized her and dropped her onto the middle of the table. The poison in the robe killed her at once; and while the city men outside the hall awaited her signal to set fire to it, Bron rose up, stretched out his arms, and with a great cry, pushed the roof clean off the building. And his men snatched up their weapons and ran outside, and Bron broke off a leg of the great chair for a club, and they slew all the men of that treacherous city and burned it to the ground. Then Bron and all his people thanked God for protecting them."

The Heathen host, finding none to give it battle, marched downhill toward the plains, carrying Obst along as prisoner and prophet. He answered their questions and told them stories from the Scriptures every night.

There was really nothing else he could do.

By the time Jack and his companions reached the northwest fringe of Lintum Forest, Martis' beard had grown over his cheeks. He'd stopped shaving and trimming it. Having no mirror, he had to ask the children how it looked.

"It's white through and through," Ellayne said. "It's like an old man's beard."

"Your hair's still brown, though," Jack said.

"I can fix that."

They made a campfire, and while it burned, Martis cut Ellayne's hair to make her look like a boy, doing a much better job of it than Jack had ever done. Wytt eagerly collected the hair that fell to the ground.

"Why do you like my hair so much?" Ellayne asked him.

Wytt tried to answer in his limited Omah way, which was not quite speech—tried, but didn't entirely succeed.

"What's he saying?" Martis wondered.

"Something about my hair being like sunbeams." You could see Ellayne found that flattering, and liked it.

"And something more," Jack said. "It's hard to make sense of it: something about a Promise that somebody gave them long ago, that they've always waited for. What kind of promise, or by who, I can't make out."

Of course they all knew the Scriptures said "the hairy ones" would inherit the great cities of Obann and possess the ruins. But that was all they knew about it, and Wytt couldn't explain it any further.

Martis kept feeding the fire until he had a goodly pile of ash. He took this up in his hands and rubbed it into his hair. "I want it to look naturally grey, and not just full of ashes," he said. "Tell me when I've done enough."

"It looks pretty good already," Ellayne said; so he didn't add any more.

"We'll wait until we get to Caristun to decide whether to go on to Obann by land or water," he said. "We'll tell people you're my grandsons and we're refugees fleeing from the Heathen, that we came down from the hills. There'll be plenty of refugees. Jack's a common enough name, so you won't need a new one. But Ellayne from now on will just be 'Layne,' a boy's name.

"The closer we come to Obann, the safer we should be. I know the First Prester: he'll have his men searching for you far afield. In the Old City we should be very safe indeed. The patrols never go there if they can help it. And then we can search for your cellar beneath a cellar."

"Whatever that means," Jack muttered.

CHAPTER 20

A New Scripture

The Heathen army came down the hills from Silvertown while Jack and his companions crossed the plain to Caristun. In the forest, Helki and Andrus spied on Squint-eye.

The divisions of the army reunited in a narrow land between the wooded foothills and the northeast spur of Lintum Forest. From there they could either swing around the forest to the south or march alongside it to the north and west. The southern route would be the easy way; if they went north and west, there would soon be fighting. Normally the mardar would have made the decision, instructed by the Great Man's will. Now the chieftains would decide. They brought in Obst to consult with them in the big black tent.

"Is it your god's will that we march north, or would he rather we marched south?" asked Shaffur, the Wallekki. All twelve of the chiefs sat on their stools, and Obst stood before them. Later Ryons chided him for not demanding a stool for himself. "The mardar would have sat, and made them stand," he said.

Obst thought God would best be pleased if the Heathen all went home, but he didn't say so.

"My chieftains," he said, "God will not advise you on the best means of making war on people who never did you any wrong. Nor, it seems, will He restrain you: for the people have wronged Him. He will protect you from the false god in the East if you put your trust in Him. God wills that all men live in peace with one another, but He does not force them to."

"So either way we go is just as well with him: suits me!" said Spider, the Abnak. "North's the best way, toward all those towns along the river."

"And at the end of it, the great city of Obann," said Szugetai, the horse-lord. His eyes glistened. "That's the prize we came for."

"Our friends in the forest tell us the westmen have not yet sent an army to Lintum Forest," Shaffur said; and Obst wondered who those friends were. "Instead, they are strengthening their cities up and down the river. The more of them we kill out there, the fewer to defend Obann. And it may be we'll be able to pen them up in their cities like camels, while we pass by and make straight for Obann. Once we're on the open plain, we can strike in any direction we please." All of the chiefs nodded: this was good generalship.

"So, old man," he said to Obst, "your god will neither help nor hinder us. That's good news."

"He has not told me that He has marked this host for destruction, warlord," Obst said. "Even so, He will be watching you."

"Then we shall give him a good show," said Spider.

Crossing the plain at its narrowest point was only a three days' journey for Jack, Ellayne, and Martis. Once they saw a giant bird in the distance, but it went on its way without attacking them.

"I'd feel better if I had a crossbow," Martis said. He was leading Dulayl, with Jack and Ellayne riding the horse, and Ham the donkey carrying their gear.

Having had his first horse killed and eaten by a bird, and himself with two narrow escapes already to his credit, Martis had a dread of the flightless monsters. But he'd lost the mindless panic they once inspired in him. Now he saw the birds as just another one of many ways to die. But he didn't speak of it.

They found Caristun a beehive of activity—militia drilling on the fields beside the river, crews laboring feverishly to strengthen the walls; boats swarming around the docks, laden with supplies and passengers; crowds milling this way and that; and guards at the gates to bar any more refugees from entering the town.

"We're only taking able-bodied men—no women, no children," an armed sentry told them. "If you want to stay, pop, and lend a hand in the defense, we'll find a place for you. You can send the kiddies on to Obann. But the three of you together can't come in."

"Can we get passage on a boat?" Martis asked.

"Sure—if you've got a wheelbarrow full of gold."

A tent city had sprung up below the walls, the only shelter to a host of people fleeing from the east. Some slept under their carts. Jack, Ellayne, and Martis had only their blankets, and there was no firewood to be had at any price.

"It'll be a long walk to Obann," Martis said, "but at least we have a horse and a donkey. And maybe we'll have better luck at Cardigal, where the Chariot River flows into the Imperial."

"We went to Cardigal once," Ellayne said. "It's a real city, bigger than Caristun." Jack had never been west of Caristun. "My father was a guest at the oligarch's annual dinner for the councilors."

That, of course, reminded her that now her father and her mother and her brothers were all stuck in Ninneburky—which had no stone walls, but only a wooden palisade—waiting for the Heathen. She might never see them again. But she didn't want to cry in front of Martis.

Jack surprised her by saying, "They'll be all right, Ellayne. We'll pray for them. If God's going to send us on these endless errands, the least He can do is keep your folks safe while you're gone."

Ellayne nodded. If worst came to worst, the people in Ninneburky could always flee across the river and take refuge in Oziah's Wood. And the walls of Ninneburky, although not of stone, would be made as strong as possible. Chief Councilor Roshay Bault was not a man to be conquered easily.

In Obann, Lord Reesh sat presiding over a special meeting of the Synod of Presters—all of them, at least, who were able to attend. Many of those in the east had chosen to stay where they were, rather than risk capture by a Heathen scouting party. There were at least two Heathen hosts across the mountains now, with more expected. Wallekki horsemen had been sighted on both sides of the river.

The purpose of the meeting was to announce the discovery of a long-lost fascicle of the Book of Batha the Seer, one of the earliest of the prophets. Batha lived in the days before there was a kingdom of Obann, and little was known of him.

An obscure scholar, a reciter of no prominence, discovered the fascicle in the Temple archives where, for all Reesh knew, many such discoveries remained to be made. It was written on a parchment wrapped around an ancient ledger devoted to Temple finances. Prester Orth, who had composed the verses himself and treated the parchment to make it look old, arranged for the scholar to discover it. As far as the scholar knew, the relic was genuine. He was a little bald fellow named Occus, who'd served the Temple all his life and never came close to being ordained a prester. Today he addressed the leading presters in Obann, under the blue dome of the Oligarchs' Chapel.

He was reading from a copy of the counterfeit scripture, and just coming to the important part of it.

"Hear me, my people," he read, "because you have not destroyed the Heathen, nor cast them out, they shall destroy you, and cast you out. Because you have given them your daughters in marriage, they shall take your daughters without your consent. Because your sons have taken their daughters in marriage, they shall take your sons into captivity. Because you have not destroyed their idols, as I have commanded you, you shall be made to serve their idols.

"Nevertheless, says the Lord, you shall one day obey Me and destroy them; for I shall stir them up against you, and they will be to you as hornets, and a plague of locusts. And you shall know that in those days you must surely destroy them utterly, from one sea to the other sea, lest they expunge you from the face of the earth. For on that day you shall know—"

Occus stopped reading and laid the paper aside. "Here the page is torn away," he said. "It may be that I'll find the rest of it somewhere in the archives. But I think you'll agree, gentlemen, that finding this much of it, at this point in our nation's history, is providential."

A murmur of assent rose from the presters in the pews. Reesh stole a look at Orth's face and liked what he saw—no hint of satisfaction in a job well done.

"Too providential, if you ask me!"

That was Prester Jod speaking up: he came from the city of Durmurot by the mouths of the great river. He was a big handsome man noted for his piety, but not one of Reesh's favorites.

"Prester? I don't understand—"

Jod ignored Occus and stood up, addressing the whole congregation.

"Brothers, there is a curse on any man who adds to or subtracts from Holy Scripture." His voice rang in the hall, and there was some muttering from certain parties who agreed with him. Reesh took careful note of who they were. "We must bear that curse in mind before we accept these verses as authentic."

Reesh had anticipated something like this, and prepared for it. But he would leave the debate to others. He never spoke at synods, except to open and close them. So Orth stood up.

"Our learned brother is quite right to be cautious," Orth said. "However, the fascicle fragment has been closely studied by scholars of no small reputation—including myself—and pronounced authentic. The language, the formation of the letters, the punctuation: all belong to an archaic period, the time of Batha the Seer. Although I grant you it is almost certainly a later copy. We have no evidence that sheepskin parchment was used in Batha's day."

"There is no mention of these verses in even the oldest commentaries on Batha," Jod answered, "nor by any of the prophets that followed him. Nor does Batha himself make mention of the Heathen in any other sayings. At a time when our country is in mortal peril, we should be offering up prayers, not pranks."

This set the whole hall buzzing. Angry voices clashed. Reesh pounded his gavel until the noise subsided.

"Thank you, my lord First Prester!" Orth said. "The authentication committee having approved these verses, I don't know what Prester Jod would have of us. Is it so strange that in these days, when our towns and cities are overrun with false prophets, God would send us a message by a true prophet? But I have heard that Prester Jod, in his own city of Durmurot, has been not unsympathetic to the false prophets in the streets."

Again Reesh had to pound the gavel. Orth was getting carried away with his own eloquence, he thought. He would speak to him about it later.

"My learned brother knows the Scriptures," Jod said. "'Out of the mouths of infants ye shall know wisdom.' And out of the mouths of old women, slaves, and madmen, too! These poor creatures are not out on the streets for their own amusement, presters. I've taken the trouble to question some of them myself. It may be that there are lunatics among them and mere imitators. But there are others who quote Scripture who cannot read it, nor have ever had it read to them. The spirit of prophecy is in them. They haven't the cunning, or the learning, to pretend. And they were all perfectly ordinary, normal people—until they heard the bell."

The hall fell dead silent, and now Reesh had to speak. All eyes were raised to him where he sat on his throne on the dais. But he didn't stand up. His legs wouldn't bear the effort.

"Learned and beloved brothers," he said, "we have not been able to confirm whether the 'bell' we all heard was indeed King Ozias' bell on Bell Mountain. I have sent an expedition to investigate. Whether they'll be able to get to Bell Mountain, with the whole country overrun by Heathen, is in God's hands, not mine.

"Meanwhile, it remains for this synod to accept or reject the authenticity of this fascicle, as recommended by the authentication committee. Your vote on the matter will be final. As for those who dissent, as Prester Jod appears to do, they must follow the dictates of their own consciences: bearing in mind, of course, that if the synod accepts the verses, they must be preached in all the chamber houses in Obann. But they themselves shall be at liberty to resign their office, if they cannot bring themselves to abide by the decision of the synod."

"That I can and will do, First Prester," Jod said. "I shall resign from the synod and from my see with a good will, but I shall never resign from serving God."

In the end, as expected, the synod accepted the verses, and Reesh accepted Jod's resignation, along with several others. He kept all their names on file.

CHAPTER 21

The Assault on Ninneburky

In spite of himself, Helki now had a following of half a dozen men, young bucks with a burning desire to rid the forest of outlaws. He could have had quite a few more, but he only took the best. The others stayed at the castle. He would have preferred to have no one with him at all, but that wasn't possible. If he didn't lead these young men, they'd only get themselves in trouble.

They knew the location of each of Latt's camps, the number and quality of men under him, and the paths by which they traveled through the forest. They also knew that Latt was receiving messengers from the Heathen army that was moving west. Helki's band wanted to capture one of those messengers.

"Never mind that. It'll only put them on their guard," Helki said. "They think they own this part of the forest now, and I want them to go on thinking it."

"But when are we going to do something?" Andrus cried. "I thought we were going to make war!"

"If you just chase a squirrel, boy, you'll never catch it," Helki said. "I aim to trap Squint-eye, not have a battle with him. Get rid of him, and his gang will fall apart."

"Well, then, what are you going to do?" demanded one of the boys. "Walk into his camp one night and just bash in his head?"

Helki grinned. "Something like that!"

There was another Heathen army in Obann, besides the one Obst traveled with. This one came over the mountains in the north and swarmed down the north bank of the Imperial River. That area was poorly defended. Villages and logging camps went up in flames as the Heathen advanced.

These invaders were a people unfamiliar to the folk of Obann, a northern nation called the Zeph, who came from a country beside some great impenetrable swamps that was said to be somewhere "Out East." No one from Obann had ever been there, in living memory.

The Zephites were fierce warriors who wore shaggy helmets with horns, which made them look like bulls on two legs. They went on foot almost as fast as other men could go on horseback. Those few refugees who had escaped them brought tales of terror: the Zeph were cruel, and gave no quarter.

This concerned the town of Ninneburky, which would surely be attacked, and soon. The Zeph were already on the north bank of the river, so evacuation to Oziah's Wood was out of the question.

But the chief councilor, Ellayne's father, was not thinking of evacuation.

Since that day the bell rang on Bell Mountain, Roshay Bault had ceased to fear for his daughter. "I can't tell you how I know," he would say, "but I know she's alive and safe." He knew it surely as he knew his own name; and Ellayne's mother knew it, too.

Roshay bent himself single-mindedly to the task of defending his town. He worked the men as hard as they could bear it, strengthening the walls. He had a deep ditch dug around them, in which he planted upward-pointing wooden spikes to impale any attacker who fell in. He made sure every man in the militia had a bow and arrows, and they practiced archery as if their lives depended on it—which of course they did. Foragers scoured the country for supplies. Everybody knew the Zephites were coming, so they worked at a frantic pace, with Roshay personally inspecting everything.

He also placed the local prester under house arrest and installed Ashrof as acting prester in his place.

"Why did you do that?" asked his wife. "It was the Temple itself that ordered Ashrof expelled from the chamber house. It was his fault Ellayne ran off with the carter's boy after Ashrof filled their heads with foolish stories."

"Peace, Vannett. We heard the bell, so they weren't foolish stories. Besides, the prester is a gloomy character, and I've heard he was planning to desert the town," Roshay said. "But Ashrof is a man of God, and he's the one we need in the chamber house now, praying for us. Would you rather have Ellayne here, with nothing but wooden walls and a few archers between her and the barbarians?"

Vannett nodded. Since the day the bell rang, she and her husband had lost the habit of arguing with each other.

Roshay wished he had the time and manpower to divert the river and make his town an island. But long before that work could have been completed, the Zephites came.

They knew from refugees that the Heathen host was near. Even so, it came as a shock to the man on the watch-tower when he saw the teeming horde gathered on the riverbank. Roshay climbed up to see it for himself, and his heart sank.

"There's an awful lot of them out there, sir," said the watchman. "I think they might have more men than we have arrows."

"I very much doubt we'll have to kill them all," Roshay answered.

There was nothing to do but man the defenses and watch while the Heathen crossed the river. They had no boats, but each man carried an inflated bladder of some kind to keep him afloat. They locked arms until they had human chains stretching from one bank to another, and along those chains crept the rest of the army until they were all on the south bank, facing Ninneburky. The crossing took up most of the day.

"Too bad we didn't have enough men to hit 'em while they were doing it," said a captain of the militia. "Look at 'em down there: they really do look like a herd of wild bulls. Think they'll try a night attack?"

"Not unless they're superhuman," Roshay said. "They must be tired after that crossing. Keep an ordinary watch tonight, but let every man be at his post at first light."

The next day was the worst day anyone in Ninneburky had ever seen.

When the first hint of dawn crept into the sky, masses of barbarians were already drawn up in a dense ring around the walls. Opposite the main gate, looking south, one man stepped out in front of the host and bellowed at the defenders in a language none of them had ever heard before. It was the mardar, but he was dressed as just another Zephite—helmet, horns, and a shaggy cloak. He raised a beribboned rod and shook it at the town, and those countless men behind him roared. And then they rushed forward, all of them at once.

"Hold your fire, boys—wait till you can make every arrow count!" The officers steadied their men as best they could, but many a hand trembled as its owner fitted arrow to the bow. The Zeph war cry sounded like an earthquake.

They had no ladders, no rams, no catapults. They must not have expected the moat. Some actually fell in, to be impaled on stakes. The rest tried to climb down and avoid the stakes, and then climb up again so they could get at the walls. But the air above them hummed with flying arrows, and there was such a crowd of them that an archer couldn't miss.

It was very poor generalship on their part, Roshay thought. Nevertheless, for every Zephite that fell, two or three or four kept coming. They seemed to despise death. Heaps of killed and wounded lay in the ditch, but masses of men crawled out of it and attacked the walls with axes. Those who had no axes hurled short spears; and now men of Ninneburky began to drop off the wall.

The gate was the most vulnerable point. Had the Zeph taken time to shape a great log into a ram, they might have forced the gate in spite of the work done to strengthen it.

Again and again they assaulted the gate, hacking at it, pushing against it fifty at a time with all their strength, while on the other side, crews of women pulled up heavy carts and pushed them onto their sides against the door.

And just when it seemed to everyone inside the walls that they'd done nothing all their lives but fight, and that they could fight no more, deep-voiced horns sounded somewhere and the Zephites abandoned the attack. They crawled over the bodies in the moat, back to their camp on the riverbank; and few were the arrows that pursued them. Only then did the defenders notice that the sun was setting.

"What's our damage?" Roshay asked. It was nighttime now, and he and the captains were meeting at his home. He had never been more weary in his life, and his hands smarted with blisters raised and broken by his own bowstring.

"Half the men either dead or too badly hurt to fight tomorrow," said the senior captain. "The walls are still pretty sound, but the moat's too full of bodies to be a serious obstacle anymore."

"And our arrow supply?"

"Looks like we'll be fighting with spears and clubs tomorrow."

No one said anything. What was there to say? That's that, Roshay thought. Ninneburky had fought valiantly and defended itself with skill; but the defenders were too few, the attackers too many. Tomorrow would see the finish of it. My wife and my sons, Roshay thought—but didn't care to finish that thought.

He heard a knock at his front door, heard Vannett go to answer it. She came into the parlor a moment later, with Ashrof.

"What's the matter, prester?" Roshay had commandeered the chamber house to be used as a hospital: there must be a problem with the wounded, he thought.

"I came to tell you something, gentlemen," Ashrof said. He looked just as exhausted as the younger men who'd fought all day.

"If it's bad news, we don't need any more," said one of the captains. Another rose and offered his chair to the old man, but Ashrof waved it aside.

"Be of good cheer, all of you!" he said. "God will save our city."

"What makes you say that?" Roshay said.

"I don't know! I mean, I think I dozed off for a minute or two, and then suddenly I was wide-awake, and it was in my mind that God was going to save our city. It was as if I'd been praying, and God had answered my prayer. Only I was so busy with all those wounded men, I'm sure I had no time to pray."

As Roshay searched for words with which to dismiss him gently, Vannett came back into the room with a mystified look on her face.

"It's snowing," she said.

It was not unheard-of for it to snow in Ninneburky, even this late in the spring; but it had never yet happened in Roshay's lifetime. At Vannett's urging, he and his captains trudged out to the back porch.

"Will you look at that!" said the senior captain.

The ground was already white, and the night bitterly cold. It was a hard snow, almost ice-pellets. You could hear it striking the porch roof.

"I can't stay out here without my coat," Vannett said. "Why, my teeth are chattering!"

Roshay looked Ashrof in the eye. "Well?" he said.

"Well what?" the old man answered. "Is this how God will save us? I don't know."

"It'll take more than snow to drive away those fiends out there," grumbled a captain.

And there was more than snow. At first it turned to ice and then, without the air getting the least bit warmer, freezing rain. Just to scramble across the street from one house to another, in that rain, was more than most could stand. It was the kind of rain that was colder than snow or ice, that froze you right down to the marrow in your bones. And the longer it went on, the harder it came down. Roshay and his captains could hardly hear each other speak, for the rattle of the rain on the roof.

Harder and harder, all night long, it rained, not so much water as liquid ice. Those who had fireplaces, and wood to burn, used them. The sentries on the walls had to be muffled up in coats and served hot drinks. They steadfastly stood their watch, but they couldn't see anything. The enemy camp was hardly two bowshots from the town, but no one could see that far.

So it was that when the darkness of that long night had passed, and the new day dawned grey and miserable, and the surviving defenders of Ninneburky climbed wearily back to their posts on the walls, and finally it stopped raining, having filled the moat with water and enisled the town—only then could it be discovered that the Zeph had struck their camp and gone away.

Men stared until their eyes ached, but there was no enemy to be seen. Roshay sent out some scouts, who needed no skill to read the trodden, churned-up earth: the Heathen host had marched away to the south, leaving behind the corpses of wounded men who'd frozen to death in the night. In the little time it took the scouts to learn this, the sun came out, the air grew warm again, and vapor began to float up from the chilled and sodden earth, now rapidly thawing.

"Let the people gather in the chamber house," Roshay told his captains, "and let songs of thanksgiving be sung: for God has saved us." And to Ashrof, "Be prepared to lead the town in prayer."

CHAPTER 22

Good News at Cardigal

From Caristun to Cardigal they made good time, Jack, Ellayne, and Martis, on the road that marched along the south bank of the river. But those who went down the Imperial on boats and barges made better, and they brought news—news that they shouted to anyone ashore who was close enough to hear them.

At first it was all bad news. A Heathen host had crossed the mountains north of the river and was driving west, destroying all in its path. "Men with bulls' heads and horns!" was the wildest rumor.

Ellayne could hardly go on: she knew her hometown lay in the path of this army. While she was safe and free, her father and mother and brothers were likely to be killed by savages, and the whole town burned to the ground. It made her sick, and the sickness wouldn't go away. She couldn't help wondering, Is this how God repays me, after I've climbed the mountain and rung His cusset bell for Him?

But then, just before they reached Cardigal, the tenor of the news changed. Some men on a clumsy log raft were the first to tell the tale.

"The bulls'-heads have been beaten!" they cried. "They went up to Ninneburky and got their horns cut off!"

They didn't get the full story until they stopped for the

night, just outside of Cardigal, and a family in a boat came ashore to rest. They weren't from Ninneburky, and Ellayne didn't know them; but they'd stopped there briefly and had the tale from people in the town. Half a hundred refugees gathered around them to hear it.

"They couldn't get over the wooden wall," the man of the family said, "though quite a few of them died trying. And that night, out of nowhere, came an icy rain. It was too much for them! They struck camp and headed south to the plain, getting away from the weather."

"And where are they now?" someone asked.

"Beats me—out on the plain somewhere," the man said.

Ellayne couldn't stand; she had to sit down. Martis carried her back to their own campfire. The night wasn't especially cold, but she was shivering. Wytt crept inside her coat and cuddled up to her.

"Men with bulls' heads," Martis mused. "That'd be the Zeph, a northern people. It's been hundreds of years since any of them came over the mountains. The whole East must be stirred up."

"Maybe that's how God's going to end the world," said Jack. But he was glad Ninneburky was saved, so far. "Maybe He means to set the whole world fighting."

"Don't be silly!" Ellayne said, through chattering teeth. "War can't end the world."

"Your father must have done a good job, though," Jack said.

"He's good at everything he does. That's why he's chief councilor. But it was snow and rain that drove off the Heathen, and God did that. I didn't think He would, and now

He has." Ellayne was ashamed of herself for having thought God was ungrateful. A good theologian might have told her it was wrong to think of God as being in any way obligated to any mortal creature, but there was no theologian handy. All Ellayne could think was that God did care about her and her family, after all, and she'd been wrong to think He didn't.

"There's a bridge at Cardigal where we can cross to the north bank," Martis said, "and it's a good road from Cardigal to Obann, the best in the west. But I think we'd better stay on this south side of the river and enter the Old City without passing through the new. That road won't be crowded, and we'll make good time."

"Is there a bridge between the old and new cities?" Jack asked.

"Only the ruins of a great bridge from ancient times—quite a sight to see. But there are no bridges, no ferries. No one crosses over to the ruins, except now and then a felon running from the hangman. Ordinary people wouldn't go; they think the site is cursed. But it's only ruins. I've been there myself, a few times."

"Why did you go there?"

"Not for any purpose that'd give you a high opinion of me, Jack. The Old City is a good place for meetings and transactions that are best kept secret. I went over on my master's business, which honest people might call crime."

"Hard to think of the First Prester dirtying his hands with crime!" Ellayne said. "What kind of crime?"

"The worst kind—crime in the service of a good cause. I'd be ashamed to tell you about it," Martis said.

"Never mind, then," Jack said. "Will we be able to find

this cellar that's underneath a cellar?"

"We should be able to worm our way into any number of old cellars. I wonder if there are any Omah who might help us. I never saw or heard of any there."

Wytt chattered. "He says all those places belong to the little hairy ones," Ellayne said. He chattered some more. "He says they'll help, all right—once they've been given some of my hair."

Helki knew there was a Heathen army moving across the plain. He would have been amazed to learn that Obst was marching with it.

What perplexed him was that Latt and much of his band was moving through the forest as if in conjunction with the Heathen host, along a parallel course. A military man might have wondered, Was Squint-eye protecting the invaders' flank, or looking for a chance to attack them himself? But to Helki it looked like a fox trailing a bear, hoping to get a few scraps of the bear's next kill.

Helki and his lads, an even dozen of them now, followed Latt, unseen, unheard, and unsuspected. "I reckon it's just about time we took care of him, boys," he said. "I don't know what he's up to, but it doesn't look good. Best we stop him before he does whatever he plans to do."

The weeks of scouting out Latt's paths and camps now showed their worth. Anticipating where the outlaw chief would encamp the next night, Helki and his little band got there first. By now all of the young men were armed with bows and arrows, and they were all dead shots. Helki took only the best of them.

"He has sixty of his men with him," he said. "Once they're settled down for the night and most of them asleep, we'll pick off the sentries—if they bother to post any—and I'll walk straight into their camp to kill Latt. You'll probably have to shoot a few of them. Don't miss! They won't know how many of you there are, so if I tell 'em there are fifty expert bowmen drawing a bead on them, I reckon they'll believe me. Then Latt and I will have it out, while you cover me."

"And what if Latt wins?" Andrus said. Helki guffawed, and all the young men laughed with him.

"But what if he won't fight?" Andrus asked.

"He'll have to, if I call him out in front of all his men. How do you think he got to be their chief? Think his daddy left it to him?"

Andrus wasn't done. "Why don't we just shoot as many of them as we can, and then just melt into the woods? If they all go after you at once, that'll be the end of it."

"Already thought of that," Helki said, "but decided this way's better. Once I kill Squint-eye, and anyone else who asks for it, I'm chief. Then I'll have a hundred men to put to work hunting down other outlaw bosses.

"They're predators, you see, and honest people are their prey. But I'll use 'em to prey on other outlaws. It'll be better pickings for them, anyhow, plundering the plunderers. They won't mind."

So it was that when Latt and his sixty men went into camp for the night—they neglected to post sentries—Helki's dozen bowmen were ready for them. The camp was in a sizeable clearing, and there was a full moon up above, with a dozen campfires still burning on the ground. Hiding in the trees around the clearing, the bowmen had the best conditions they could have hoped for.

"Good luck!" Andrus whispered.

"Just don't miss your targets," Helki said. "Burn it, I'd have done this a lot different, on my own."

Twirling his rod, he strode into the camp.

"Wake up, Latt, you squint-eyed son of maggots!" he bellowed. "Helki the Rod has come for you! Stand up and meet me face to face, if you've got any man's blood in your veins!"

Men sprang up all over. Those who rose up with weapons in their hands went down with arrows in their breasts.

"I've got fifty expert archers covering you fellows, so don't move, if you want to live," Helki said. "My business is with Latt, man to man—if he is a man, and not a cringing coward. Where are you, Latt? Don't tell me you're hiding under a blanket!"

He wasn't. Latt stood up while all of his men sat down—ugly, squat, his hands balled into huge fists, quivering all over, too angry to be frightened, or just too foolish. Helki towered over him; but if you could have seen them both, you might have been the more afraid of Latt. Helki was a hunter, but this man was a murderer.

"I'm calling you out, Squint-eye," Helki said. "The rest of you men, you all know the rules. I've called him out, and no one else can interfere. Somebody toss your chief a sword or spear, so he can die fighting."

A man offered Latt a sword, but that only enraged him further. "A spear, you idiot!" he snarled. "I'll stick him like a pig!" But Latt knew a man with a sword stood no chance against Helki and his rod.

He soon had a spear in his hand, a long spear used for hunting wild boars, and his men hurried to crawl out of the way.

Latt knew what he was doing with a spear, and his rage gave him courage. He would have quickly slain an ordinary man, but Helki was no ordinary man. The rod swept the spear aside, whooshed loudly in a wicked arc, and brought to a swift and sudden end Latt's long career of lawlessness and murder. The fight didn't last a minute.

"Anyone else care to try his luck tonight?" Helki waited for a challenge, but no one offered one. He raised his voice louder. "Who's chief of this outfit now?"

A moment of hesitation; and then, from one man, then another, "You are!" And at last from them all, and not without enthusiasm:

"You are! You are!"

"Burned right I am," said Helki.

CHAPTER 23

How Ryons Earned a Reward

As the army marched, Obst fell into a deep meditation. He could do that and still keep walking. This amazed Ryons, who waited anxiously to catch him if he stumbled.

"What's he doing?" asked an Abnak warrior who marched along with them, guarding against their escape.

"Shh! He's walking with God."

The warrior's eyebrows went up. "Oh! Shaman stuff."

"Shows how much you know!" Ryons said. "He's no shaman. He hasn't got time for the puny gods that shamans know. His god would just laugh at all that dancing around and screaming that shamans do."

The plain upon which they marched wasn't much different from the plains on the east side of the mountains, except for one thing. Not far ahead, and a little to the north, there rose a brown, flat-topped hill. Ryons knew from Obst that it wasn't a hill at all, but the remains of an ancient city. The plain was dotted with them. God destroyed those cities long ago, Obst said. The men who'd built them and lived in them were wiser and mightier than men today, Obst said: "Wise enough to become fools."

Before the discussion of shamans could get very far, there was a distraction. A few men were running back and forth, spreading news throughout the army.

"What's up?" the guard called to the nearest runner, a half-naked Fazzan in a wolf's-head cap.

"Don't know—but be ready to make camp. Some of our horsemen just came in, and they were in a big hurry. We might have fighting soon!" And he ran on to spread the word to others.

The chieftains very soon called a halt to the march, and up went the big black tent, a sure sign that they were going to hold a council. Ryons shook Obst out of his reverie.

"We've stopped," Obst said, looking all around and blinking.

"Some scouts came in," Ryons told him. "I wonder when we'll find out what it's all about."

They didn't have to wait long. A warrior came to fetch Obst; the chiefs wanted to see him. Ryons went with him.

"This time make them give you a stool so you can sit down," the boy said. "Don't act like a slave. They'll have more respect for you if you don't."

"I don't think about things like that," Obst said.

"Well, you should. You want them to listen to you, don't you?"

They found the chieftains with some of the Wallekki scouts standing before them, men drenched with sweat, who'd ridden hard to get there. Ryons found Uduqu and tugged on his arm. "Make them give my master a seat," he said. "He's old, and he's been marching all day." Uduqu ducked into the crowd and returned with a stool. He planted it before the chieftains, and none of them objected when he maneuvered Obst into it.

"We need the help of your god, old man," Chief Shaffur said. "Two of these men before us are scouts attached to another army. They scouted for Zephites from the north, who have no horsemen of their own. They've deserted the Zeph and come to us with tidings."

"The Thunder King is angry with us," Szugetai said. He looked angry himself.

"The mardar who commands the Zeph has commanded them to attack us," Shaffur said. "He pulled them out of a fight against a city on the river. It seems the Great Man knows what happened to our own mardar. Now he means to punish us. The Zeph move fast. They'll be here by this time tomorrow."

"A lot of them will stay here, too—forever," Chief Spider said.

"What must we do, to be sure of your god's protection?" Shaffur demanded.

What a time for a theology lesson, Obst thought. How was he to answer? He rose from his stool and held up his palms. "My chieftains," he said, "there is nothing for you to do but join with me in prayer, here and now. We must submit ourselves to God and ask for His protection."

"Is that all?"

"Yes."

"Who ever heard of a god who doesn't demand sacrifices!" snapped Szugetai.

"My God doesn't, warlord," Obst answered. "There's nothing you can give Him that He doesn't already own. What He desires is for you, of your own free will, to confess that you belong to Him.

"So let us pray. I'll lead you. All you have to do is close your eyes and raise your hands to heaven. Open your hearts to the true God. When I've finished saying the prayer, just say, 'Amen.'"

And so, for the first time ever, the men of a dozen Heathen nations prayed to the true God. Ryons closed his eyes and reached for heaven; and a very strange thing happened to him.

Immediately after all the chieftains said "Amen," the boy cried out, "My lords! My masters! God has shown me something—I know what He wants us to do!" And Obst's heart sank; but the chieftains waited on Ryons' words.

"My masters," he said, "I've heard of these Zephites, and it's true they have no horsemen. That's why the Wallekki have to lend them scouts.

"There is a hill up ahead of us, a big one with a flat top. We should go there right away! Let the Abnaks, and all the others who like to fight on foot, line up along the top of the hill where the Zeph can see them. Let a few men with firepots hide in places where the grass is long, down below.

"When the Zephites see you waiting for them on the hilltop, they'll attack. Set fire to the grass, then. It's not dry enough to burn well, but the fires will make it look like you're desperate.

"But let the Wallekki, and Szugetai and his men, and everybody else who fights on horseback, gather on the far side of the hill, where the Zeph won't see them. Once the battle has started on the slopes, let the horsemen charge out from behind the hill, half of them from the east, half from the west. The Zephites won't expect it, and you'll have them—like that!" He clapped his hands together, making Obst flinch.

For a long moment no one said anything. Then Shaffur, with an angry glare, looked to all the other chieftains. "Are we to be schooled in warfare by a child, and a slave?" he said.

But Szugetai barked out a laugh, and smacked his own knees. "It's a good plan—I like it!" he said. "We'll catch them going up and coming down."

"It'll serve them right for attacking us," Spider said. "I won't mind fighting on a hilltop, but just make sure you horsemen come along before we kill them all."

Shaffur frowned at Ryons. "You say the westmen's god showed you this, boy—while we were praying?"

"It's true, warlord. Would I dare to speak, otherwise? You'd kill me if I lied."

"But why did the god show this to you, and not to him?" Shaffur pointed at Obst.

"Well, He's my god, too!" Ryons said. And the Abnak chieftains laughed so loud no one else could say anything.

"Did God really show you all those things?" Obst asked, as the army marched toward the hill. "I must warn you, it's a grave sin to tell lies in His name. He is a God of truth."

"I wasn't lying," Ryons said. "I was praying, like everybody else, and all of a sudden I saw the hill, with men on it waiting to fight; and I saw the horsemen waiting on the other side."

"What do you mean, you *saw*?"

"What's the matter? You're angry."

"I can't help it," Obst said. "You're too free with your mouth. Bad enough to speak like that to men who might decide to kill us because you've annoyed them. But God is greater than man! How can I make you understand?"

"I wasn't making it up. And it wasn't a daydream, either. Why don't you believe me? Why wouldn't God show me what He wants us to do? And if He didn't show me those things, who did?"

There was no way to answer that. Obst patted the boy's shoulder.

"I suppose stranger things than that have happened lately," he said. "You've always believed in me. I'll try to believe in you."

Ryons had never seen a battle, only a few duels between young Wallekki men touchy about their honor. The Wallekki liked to recite long poems and sing long songs about great battles, but they seldom managed to arrange one.

So he was excited the next morning, as he waited on the flat hilltop beside Obst among the Abnaks, in the place assigned to Uduqu and his clan. As the sun rose, they could all see the cloud of dust in the north that betokened the coming of the Zeph. On the south side of the hill, men waved banners to signal to the riders that the enemy had been sighted.

When the men of the advancing army could actually be seen, the Abnaks launched into a frightful racket, like a pit-full of wild dogs fighting with demons. It was their way of preparing for a hard fight, Uduqu explained. "We sing out the names of all our ancestors and the names of enemies they killed, so that they'll know that many of us will soon be joining them."

He had a stone axe and a javelin, and all the Abnaks had long knives. The Fazzan would fight with spears and leather shields. They howled like wolves—"for religious reasons of their own," Uduqu said. "The Fazzan are very funny people."

Obst stood as straight as a spear, praying; his lips moved, but Ryons couldn't hear the words. The Zeph came on fast, and now Ryons could see they really did look like shaggy bulls on two legs. And then the men in hiding down below set fire to the grass, and the smoke blew into the enemy's faces, and the battle was joined.

It all turned out just as Ryons had seen it in his mind's eye, yesterday. Infuriated by the smoke and by the taunts of the men atop the hill, the Zeph swarmed across the plain and up the slope. There were more men there than Ryons had ever seen in his life, more than he thought existed. Old Uduqu shrieked in triumph when he hurled his javelin and hit his mark. He waved his axe over his head and dared the Zephites to come up and get it.

At just the right time, the horsemen charged from around both sides of the hill and took the Zeph in the rear and on the flanks. For them there was no way up the hill, and no way down. By the end of the day, Szugetai had taken the head of the Zephites' mardar with his own hands, and the few survivors of the great northern host had fled in all directions, leaving the slopes and the flat ground blanketed with dead and wounded. For the Abnaks and the Fazzan had charged down the hill and crushed their enemies.

Going into the dusk, exultation kept the victors on their feet. The Wallekki heaped a vast number of Zeph helmets into a trophy. The chieftains came for Obst and Ryons and set them on litters made of spears and shields, and had men parade them all around the hilltop while the entire army cheered in a dozen different languages.

Their chieftains held council under the evening stars, everyone being too exhausted to raise the big black tent, planting their tribal standards on the middle of the hilltop. That was where the parade ended for Obst and Ryons, and they were allowed to come down from their litters.

"For a thousand years our poets will sing of this day!" Shaffur said. "You, boy, are a slave no longer, but a chieftain with a seat in the council of chiefs. You shall have a chieftain's share of all the spoils, a fine tent of your own, and a horse of your own choosing."

"Take one of mine," Szugetai said, grinning. "Mine are the best!"

"As for you, old man," Shaffur said to Obst, "your god has delivered us from the Thunder King, just as you said he would. So you must tell him that all of us, by the vote of all the chieftains in this council, have decided to become his people. We will not worship any other gods, except to pay honor to our ancestors, as is only right and proper. You shall teach us how to serve this god, and we'll be faithful to him. We don't think those Zeph will be the last army that the Great Man sends against us."

They all cheered, but Obst pitied their ignorance. How could he begin to make them understand?

"My chieftains," he said, "God has indeed protected you this day. But you're like babes and children in your understanding."

"That's why we need you to teach us!" Spider said. "We're going to need your god: we've just wiped out an army of our allies. Everyone in this country will be against us now, westmen and Easterners alike. We came here to sack great cities; now it'll be a good job just to stay alive."

"We can't turn around and go home," Szugetai said. "There's a bigger army coming in behind us, say our scouts. Besides, I'm angry with myself that I ever agreed to serve the Thunder King and for groveling before his mardar! It wasn't our fault that your god struck down the mardar, but King Thunder tried to destroy us—and he'll try again."

He was still spattered all over with dried blood, with dust plastered to his face. He looked ready to collapse on the spot. But now he raised his voice.

"Tell your mighty god that we'll go wherever he sends us and do whatever he commands. We are his people now! If he didn't want us, he wouldn't have sent you to us. He wouldn't have shown the boy how we ought to fight our battle. If we are only children, then let this god be our father!"

"So be it," Obst agreed; and how he ought to carry on from there, he couldn't imagine.

CHAPTER 24

What the Blind Man Saw

The road from Cardigal that ran along the south bank of the river carried very little traffic. When Jack looked across the river, he saw masses of carts and people slogging along the road. But that road linked Cardigal to the New City; the south road led only to the ruins of the old.

Spring was here, at least: a little cooler than normal, but a lot greener. Wildflowers bloomed everywhere—purple kiss-me-not, crocuses in white and yellow, duchess' doilies in pale blue, and little red babies' buttons, bright red, peeking out from the grass. Birds sang from every tree, and here and there smoke curled from the chimneys of widely scattered farmhouses. And yet the travelers had the road to themselves.

"You'd never guess there was a war on, or anything wrong at all," Ellayne said.

"All you have to do is look across the river," Martis said.

"Is it true that if you keep going west, you'll reach the sea?" Jack asked. Martis nodded. "How far is it, and how long would it take to get there? I'd like to see it."

"From Obann to the coast is about half-again as far as from Cardigal to Obann, so it wouldn't take us all that long. But I doubt you'll find your cellar anywhere along the seashore."

"In King Ozias' time, people used to sail the sea in ships," Ellayne said. "How come there are no more ships?"

"No one knows," Martis said.

"Abombalbap met a magician who came from an island in the sea, in a ship," Ellayne said; she was young enough to believe in most of Abombalbap's adventures. "Do you have to be a magician to be able to sail the sea?"

"No—of course not. But some scholars believe that when the Empire was destroyed, there was some great horror that came from the sea: something so terrible, no one recorded what it was. But certainly the coast is richly endowed with ruins. Today there's no city nearer to the sea than Durmurot, and even they don't have any business with the ocean."

They were still talking about the sea when they saw three men coming from the west, an old man supported on each arm by two younger ones. All three were on their way to growing beards, and their clothes were dirty. When they saw Martis and the children coming, they stopped to wait for them. Jack thought they looked like beggars, and in this he was at least partly right.

"God's blessing on you, travelers," one of the young men greeted them. "Do you have any food to spare—not for us but for our master, who is old?"

"We haven't much to spare," said Martis. "Why don't you ask at one of those farmhouses?"

"Tell them, Odys," said the old man. "Let us not beg the bread of deception."

"That's from one of King Ozias' Sacred Songs," Ellayne said, recognizing the phrase.

"And if I'm not mistaken," Martis said, "you're of the

Temple, you three."

"Not anymore!" said Odys. "We've been put out of the Temple—I mean, our master was, and my brother and I couldn't let him go alone. He's blind."

"He was prester in the town of Wusk, a long way's walk from here," said Odys' brother. "I was sexton in our chamber house, and my brother was reciter. We can't ask for food at any farmhouse because we're banned."

Jack didn't know what that meant, but Ellayne gave a little gasp.

"May I ask why you were banned?" Martis said.

"For disobedience," the blind man said.

"Cuss that!" growled Odys, the reciter. "Prester Konn is too forbearing. They banned us because he wouldn't let their damnable false Scripture be preached in our chamber house. The Temple made him resign, and then they banned him."

"I want to hear about this," Martis said. "Why don't we sit down under that oak tree over there? We'll give you the food you need. We're not banned, so we can get more from a farmer."

He never told them that he was a servant of the Temple, too. Once they had some bread to chew on and water to drink, they told their story freely.

"The Temple came out with a long-lost fragment of the Prophecy of Batha the Seer," Odys said. "The synod approved it and required it to be preached in every chamber house; and further, they required us to preach against the so-called false prophets of these days."

"What false prophets?" Martis asked.

"Oh, the poor devils you find in the streets of every

city, every town—old slaves, children of paupers, broken-down old tosspots. All spouting Scripture and speech that sounds like Scripture even if you can't make any sense of it. The Temple hates them like poison. And so someone in Obann cooked up this fragment that miraculously turned up in the archives—all this pap about how God commands us to destroy the Heathen from sea to sea."

"Prester Konn may be blind, but he saw through this," said Odys' brother, the reciter. His name was Pagget. "He's seen for years the growing corruption of the Temple—"

"Enough, enough!" The old man silenced him. "We have nothing to boast of. The temple is ordained of God. Don't try to tear it down."

"Too bad we can't!" Odys said. "Well, we knew there'd be trouble when Prester Jod stepped down. But they wouldn't dare ban him. He's too big for them, and everyone in Durmurot loves and honors him. There'd be riots if they banned him. But Prester Konn, in a little nowhere town like Wusk—him they banned."

"They're the ones who are blind," Pagget said. "They don't see how many chamber houses—little ones like ours, all throughout the country—will serve God before they serve the Temple."

The banned prester quieted them with a loud sigh.

"Brothers, you'll weary these travelers with your complaints," he said. "Besides, we've hindered them. They have a journey to perform, do they not?"

He turned to Jack, with sightless eyes; but Jack had a powerful feeling that they weren't sightless, but saw things no one else could see. It made him shiver.

"We're going to Obann, sir," he said.

"Yes," said Konn, "for God has sent you. I rejoice and give thanks that I have met you, all three—for God has chosen you. Go on your way valiantly and full of confidence: for God is with you." And he made the sign of blessing over them.

When they parted, Ellayne opened the lining of her coat and gave the men some of her money. It was the first money she'd parted with since she'd left Ninneburky.

"Be careful with that money," Martis said, when they were on their way again. "We may have great need of it someday."

"We haven't been anyplace where I could spend it," Ellayne said. "It's funny, carrying money all over the world and never spending it. But I wanted to help that poor blind man. How did the Temple ever get to be so wicked? It's supposed to be good!"

"I'm living proof it isn't," Martis said.

"And old men like Obst and Prester Konn are proof it is!" Jack said. "He said God chose all three of us—even you, Martis!"

"Two children and an assassin." God's ways were truly unfathomable, Martis thought.

Wytt crawled out from his hiding place among the baggage on Ham's back and hopped onto Ellayne's shoulder: he didn't let strangers see him, if he could help it. She reached up and petted him, glad he was there. It was a daunting thing to be chosen by God. She'd supposed they were finished with their work, once they'd climbed the mountain. Now she wondered if it would ever be finished.

CHAPTER 25

How God Spoke to the Heathen

It wasn't long before the people in Lintum Forest got to know of the great battle on the plain. Some of the Zephites reached the forest and got lost in it. Most of them were killed by outlaws. With Latt gone, the country at first grew more lawless and more dangerous, not less. Helki's men captured one of the fugitives, but no one could make head nor tail of his language. Someone killed the captive when Helki wasn't looking.

After that, he had to fell two more men with his staff before all of Latt's followers would accept him as their chief. To find work for them, he sent scouts out onto the plain, with orders to find out who the Zeph were and what had happened to them. One of these parties returned with a tattooed Abnak, who greeted two or three of Latt's former lieutenants by name when he arrived at their camp. He spoke a passable Obannese.

"Where's Latt Squint-eye?" he asked, when he was brought before Helki. "I have a message for him."

"There have been some changes here," Helki said. "Latt's dead and gone; I've taken his place."

"Then my message is for you. I am Hlah, son of Spider, chief of the Abnaks in the host of many nations."

"I'm Helki, son of a man who never told my mother his name." He already knew from Latt's men that this was the Heathen army that had come down from the mountains. Latt had agreed to alert them to the approach of any force from Obann, and they had acknowledged him King of Lintum Forest. "What's your business here?"

"Only this: we ask your leave to take refuge in the forest, should we ever need to. We promise to harm none of the people who are under your protection; and if you should ever have need of us, send word, and we will come."

Before he agreed, Helki made Hlah tell him about the battle. It was Heathen against Heathen, which surprised all the outlaws who heard it.

"Every hand is raised against us now," Hlah said. "Another army is crossing the mountains after us, by way of Silvertown, so we can't go back the way we came. We have not yet met any of the westmen's armies, but they'll fight us when we do.

"The East is being emptied of fighting men, all coming over the mountains, host after host. This is the doing of the Great Man, who says he is a god who takes other gods captive. But our teacher says he is a false god. The real God has allowed him to be a scourge and a destroyer; but he, too, will be destroyed when God has had enough of him.

"Our teacher told me to tell you that our host now serves the true God, who made the heavens and the earth, and to offer you friendship in His name. I have spoken."

Andrus, standing close beside Helki, said, "It's a trick—they're Heathen."

Helki ignored him. "Who is this teacher of yours?" he asked.

"An old man from the West who speaks and understands all tongues. When he prayed, God struck down the mardar, the servant of the Great Man, who commanded our chieftains. No one could save him. Our teacher is a man of miracles. He says God sent him to us, and we believe him."

Helki's thoughts raced. He'd been worrying about how to control the outlaws and stop them from preying on the settlers. Maybe he could do it with a Heathen army. The outlandishness of the idea appealed to him.

"How am I to believe you now serve God?" he asked. "I never heard the like of it before."

"We'll give you hostages—the sons of chiefs," said Hlah. "Besides, we have sworn to obey the westmen's God. I can't speak for others, but we Abnaks don't lie. Everybody knows that."

Helki nodded. The Abnaks had a bad name for cruelty, but no one ever said they were liars.

"I reckon we'll talk some more, after I've had some time to think it over," he said. "But don't be deceived: there is no King of Lintum Forest. There's only a lot of people who want to survive the war and be left alone."

Hlah grinned at him. "Anyone who survives this war will have done well!" he said.

Helki couldn't sleep that night. What was he to do? He liked to live alone and go his own way. All he'd ever meant to do was kill Latt so the forest could have peace. He would find people to take care of Jandra and then go back to wandering. Spring was his favorite season in the woods, and he was missing it. How had all this happened to him?

He woke Andrus. "I want you to do something for me," he said; and it galled him to say it. "I want you to hurry back to the castle and fetch me Jandra, as quick as you can. One of the women ought to come back with you to take care of her."

"What do you want Jandra for?" the young man wondered. "This is no place for a little girl."

"She'll be all right. Just go get her."

It was too dark to see the look on Andrus' face, but Helki could imagine it.

"All right—I promised to obey you, so I'll go. But I hope you know what you're doing."

So do I, thought Helki.

He made Hlah stay until Andrus could return. "I think I'd like to go back with you and talk with your chieftains face to face," he said. "I'd like to meet your teacher, too."

"No one would object to that," the Abnak said.

The whole camp was astounded the next day when a worn-out Andrus arrived with Jandra and a fair-haired young woman named Abgayle. Not the least of their astonishment was due to the hideous toothed bird that Jandra carried in her arms, and its penchant for hissing at anyone who got too close. The outlaws kept their distance and indulged in a lot of superstitious muttering.

"Daddy!" Jandra put her bird down and ran to Helki for a hug and a kiss.

"Your daughter?" Hlah asked.

"She thinks so." Helki picked her up, and the bird stalked jealously around his ankles. "But sometimes she's also my teacher, although usually I can't understand what she's trying to teach me."

Hlah pointed to the bird. "I saw one of those, once, just before we all went off to war. The shaman said it was an omen, but he couldn't say what it was an omen of. How is a child your teacher?"

"God sometimes speaks through her. If He does it again, I want to hear it. I was thinking maybe your teacher might be able to explain some of these things to me."

"These are interesting times we live in," Hlah said.

Helki decided to take the whole band with him to meet the Heathen chiefs. A following of sixty men might make him look like someone to be taken seriously: he could always say he had many, many more. Besides, he didn't trust them so far as to leave them to their own devices in the forest.

"You're not afraid to come with us?" he asked Abgayle.

"My own baby was born dead. She'd be just about Jandra's age, if she'd lived. I'll stay with Jandra."

"What about your husband?"

"He died, too. Chopping down a tree, and it fell on him."

She'd been lucky not to have been carried off by outlaws, Helki thought. He told Andrus to stay close to her at all times: "And don't be slow to use your knife on any man who troubles her."

"As long as that thing is with her, I don't think anybody will," Andrus said, meaning Jandra's bird.

It was a long day's march to the Heathen camp, which had been moved closer to the forest and fortified with a ditch. They might have camped atop the hill where they'd won their battle, but no one wanted the labor of burying the enemy dead.

Helki had never seen so many men in one place before. But this was very far from being the biggest army to come out of the East, Hlah told him. "All the armies coming after us are bigger," he said.

Jandra had not yet spoken any words of prophecy, intelligible or otherwise. She prattled with Abgayle, talked baby-talk to her bird, and was delighted whenever Helki carried her. He wondered if she'd just gone back to being an ordinary little girl. If so, he envied her. He wished he and everybody else could go back to being what they were.

Riders came out to escort them into the camp, over a bridge of split logs laid side by side. These were lean, brown-skinned men with long spears and tall headdresses. Helki recognized them as Wallekki. The last time he'd seen Wallekki horsemen in Obann, they were heading home with slaves.

"Horses!" Jandra cried, pointing at them. Helki was carrying her. The bird hopped along beside him; it always stayed close to her.

"It might not be easy, getting out of here alive," one of the outlaws said.

"Pretend you're not afraid," Helki told him.

The camp was a confusion of tents and lean-tos of all shapes and sizes. A military man wouldn't have seen much hope of defending it in any organized way. But to Helki it looked like the army didn't mean to stay there very long. He wondered how they got themselves organized at all.

"We have twelve chieftains who decide everything—thirteen, if you count Chief Ryons," Hlah said. "But we're never sure of what to do from day to day. We don't have a mardar to command us anymore. Not that anybody wants one."

He led them to a big black tent in the middle of the camp, where the chieftains were assembled in their council. Helki's men grew more uneasy with every step they took. Helki put Jandra down, and Abgayle took her hand.

"Whatever happens, stay close to me," he said.

"I don't feel any temptation to go exploring on my own," she said. "Jandra, sweeting, why don't you carry your bird?" It fluffed and rattled its dirty purple feathers as Jandra picked it up.

There wasn't room in the tent for all of Helki's men. As much as he would have preferred to have Andrus with him, Helki left him outside to be in charge of the others. "See that they stick together and behave themselves," he said. He picked a dozen to go in with him as his bodyguard.

He was unused to being in enclosed places. He didn't like the uncertain light inside the tent and the way the smell of unwashed bodies blended with the smell of burning lamps. Warriors of a dozen nations stepped aside, making a lane for him and Abgayle, Jandra and her bird, with the bodyguard following close behind.

Twelve chieftains sat on stools—or rather, twelve chieftains and a small boy dressed up as a chieftain with a gold chain around his neck and feathers in his hair. But Helki ignored them all, the moment he clapped eyes on someone else.

"Obst!" he cried, so surprised, he almost dropped his staff. "Well, I'll be burned!" And he let loose a great bellow of a laugh. "Whoever would have thought you were a man of miracles!"

Obst rose up from his stool among the chieftains. He'd been expecting Latt Squint-eye. To see Helki in Latt's place left the old man speechless.

"Aren't you going to say you're glad to see me?" Helki said. "By thunder, I'm glad to see you!"

"Teacher, do you know this man?" demanded a Wallekki chief.

"Know him? My chieftains, God is good to us beyond my hopes!" The old man's eyes filled with tears. He crossed over to Helki and threw his arms around his neck, weeping for joy. Helki patted his back and said, "There, there." The chieftains waited patiently until Obst collected himself. At last he released Helki and turned back to them.

"Yes, warlords, I know this man," he said. "This is Helki the Rod—my friend, and the strongest and most valiant man in all of Lintum Forest."

"This is our teacher," Hlah said; but Helki had already guessed that.

"What are you doing here, Obst? What happened to those two kids who were with you? I've never been so surprised to see anybody, not in all my life."

"It's a long, long story," Obst said.

"I like a good story," said the Abnak chieftain. That was Spider, Hlah's father.

But he would have to wait for the story. They all would, because of a distraction.

Jandra slipped loose from Abgayle, and, with her bird

cradled in her arms and glaring red-eyed at everyone else in the tent, she was suddenly walking among the Heathen chiefs. Helki couldn't see her face, but he could see the chieftains' faces. They were amazed.

The whole crowd in the tent fell silent. Abgayle would have rushed after Jandra, but Helki caught her arm. She must have had some experience of Jandra's spells; she stayed where Helki held her.

Jandra walked straight up to the boy chieftain and stood before him. Obst cast a wild glance at Helki, but Helki kept him quiet with a look.

The bird hopped out of Jandra's arms, spread its clawed wings, and uttered a series of sharp, ringing barks. Its feathers rattled like mail. Then Jandra spoke:

"I shall give you the throne of Ozias, which I have promised to Ozias, my servant. He shall tread down all his enemies. Have I not held him by the hand, for all his days? Shall I not punish them that persecute him?

"Their houses shall be made desolate, but Ozias' house shall I exalt. I shake the earth, but Ozias' throne shall be established forever."

Jandra kissed the boy softly on the lips while he sat frozen in astonishment. Without another word, she turned from him and walked back to Helki. Her face was the face of a child who sleeps with her eyes open, seeing nothing. But then her eyelids fell shut, and Abgayle just caught her before she could fall. Helki helped her.

"She's asleep!" Abgayle said.

"Yes. That's what usually happens."

But the chieftains all stared at the boy. He looked back at them helplessly.

"What was all that?" demanded the Wallekki chief.

"Something that needs to be considered very deeply, my lords," said Obst. "Very deeply indeed—for God is speaking to us, here and now." And those fierce and warlike men were all afraid.

CHAPTER 26

The Old City

Long before they got there, Jack and Ellayne could see the ruins of the Old City. It was a much bigger place than the present city of Obann, Martis said.

"It's hard to believe ordinary people ever lived there," he said. "I was never in it but I wanted to be out of it as soon as possible."

"If it scared you, what'll it do to us?" Ellayne said.

They had the road practically to themselves. No one went to the Old City, and the road was in very poor repair. They would have been bumped sick if they'd been riding in a cart. There weren't any more farms or villages to be seen, although the gently rolling countryside seemed fertile enough.

Wherever the road climbed to the top of a rise, they could see the dark brown mass of ruins hunkered below the silver band of the river. It wasn't like the ruined cities of the plains, which anyone would take for hills. Here you could still see the outlines and remnants of colossal buildings.

"What happened to it?" Jack wondered.

"Who knows?" Martis said. "God destroyed it, say the Commentaries; but they don't say how. It was built on the site of the first city, which the Heathen sacked and burned. Many of its buildings were of stone with steel skeletons. No one knows how to build things like that anymore. It's all we can do to turn out enough steel blades and spearheads for the army. Lord Reesh would dearly love to know the secrets of the Empire; but they've eluded him."

"We were in an ancient tunnel in one of the mounds," Ellayne said. "It was all full of dead people's bones!" she shuddered.

"There's nothing down there that will hurt us," Martis said. It wasn't altogether true.

The site wasn't as close as it looked. For two more days they traveled toward it. Soon they could see the New City on the north bank of the river and the hulking obstacles in the water that were all that remained of a gigantic bridge. The whole place might have been built and inhabited by giants, Ellayne thought. There were a few giants in the stories of Abombalbap.

"Look how beautiful it is—the New City," she said. It had domes and towers, many of which glinted in the sun, and mighty walls. "I wish we were going there instead."

"It is a lot littler, though," Jack said. It was the greatest of all cities between the mountains and the sea, but four or five of them would have fit comfortably inside the ruins. It was distressing to think of that, somehow.

One more stretch of decayed road, just a few miles downhill, and they'd be among the ruins.

"It's so big!" Jack said. "How are we ever going to find the right cellar? There must be a thousand places to look."

"To say nothing of our 'finding what is lost,' when we don't even know what it is," Ellayne said.

"It's a missing book of Scripture: that's what I think," Martis said. "And the best place to start would be the ruins of the Temple."

"Do you know where, in all that jumble, the ancient Temple was?" Jack asked.

"Yes—that I do know," Martis said. "Come on, let's go. We can be there before the sun sets."

Thanks to teams of swift relay riders, the High Council got war news promptly. But the news was not good. Lord Gwyll summoned his colleagues to come secretly, one at a time, to his own townhouse. He didn't want anyone to know they were meeting.

"It's very bad news," he said, when they were all assembled in his parlor. "Silvertown has been taken, and burned to the ground."

"I thought the Heathen withdrew from Silvertown!" cried Lord Davensay, Commerce.

"This was another army, a bigger one. They had good equipment: armored rams to break the gates, plenty of ladders to keep the defenders busy on the walls—even some primitive engines to hurl stones. Not as good as our own catapults, but good enough. Most of the people are either dead or carried off to slavery."

Gwyll paused. He'd been chewing on his beard, and it stood out at odd angles. The other councilors waited for him to continue.

"We have been invaded by four main armies. South of Lintum Forest—we didn't expect anything from that direction—there is a Heathen host marching toward Caryllick.

We have five thousand men on the way to give battle, in addition to four or five hundred already there.

"Then there's this big army coming down from Silvertown. We have no single force strong enough to meet it head-on.

"There was a third army that came down from the north—the one that attacked the town of Ninneburky, but marched away after one unsuccessful and poorly coordinated assault. This army has been destroyed—but not by us.

"For reasons we've been unable to discover, the northern army attacked the first Heathen army—the one that bypassed Silvertown—on the plain, north of Lintum Forest. Those Heathen annihilated that northern army."

"If they're destroying one another, that's good news," said Lord Chutt, Taxes and Revenue.

"Yes, of course it is. But not knowing why they fought among themselves, we can't count on them doing it again," Gwyll said.

"Meanwhile, where are the rest of our armies?" asked the governor-general.

"In addition to the five thousand on their way to Caryllick, I've positioned another five thousand at Cardigal and five thousand more in newly constructed forts along the river."

"Do we want them spread out like that?"

"It's a defensive strategy, Lord Ruffin—the forts are close enough to reinforce one another," Gwyll said. "What else would you have me do? If the opportunity presents itself, these forces will attack. Otherwise, the orders are to defend the fortified places and let the Heathen bleed away their strength trying to take them."

Judge Tombo sighed. "We're going to have our hands full here in Obann, once the news of Silvertown gets out. How many men have you held back to defend our city, Lord Gwyll?"

"Enough, my lord—seven thousand, fully trained and equipped. And we can get more if we need them. But Obann's walls are not to be taken by any power the Heathen can command, and the city is extremely well provisioned. If it ever comes to a siege, they'll starve before we do."

Throughout the discussion Lord Reesh said nothing. Eventually the governor-general noticed it and bade him speak.

"We've all heard rumors that the Heathen have raised up to themselves some new false god, in whose service they invade us. How does the Temple plan to heighten the valor of our people, my lord First Prester? Have you and Judge Tombo found a means to silence the false prophets in our streets—the ones who proclaim the end of the world?"

Reesh shrugged slightly. "We preach this war as God's war, and a holy war. It will take some time before we can see the effects of this."

"I congratulate you on your discovery of long-lost Scripture so apt to that purpose!"

So Ruffin saw through that, Reesh thought. It was to be expected. But he doubted Lord Gwyll had seen so deeply. Gwyll believed in God. The governor-general ought to be careful not to disillusion him.

"We must all keep our tempers, sir," Reesh said. "Our city is impregnable; so should our hearts be, too.

"Give the presters time to preach, and the people time to hear them. Meanwhile, my agents are learning all they can about the state of affairs beyond the mountains.

"We have heard the Heathen's new false god is a man, who lives somewhere out beyond the lakes. He must be an extraordinary man. Give us time to find out more about him. It may be he has a weakness."

Late in the afternoon, Jack, Ellayne, and Martis entered the Old City, first built a thousand years or more before Ozias' time. A heathen people lived there first, the Kassites. The tribes that would someday become the nation of Obann captured it and made it their city and the seat of their kings. The mightiest of them, Ezkasaiah the Wise, first built the Temple there. And on the ruins of his city an even greater city grew, the greatest city that had ever been.

The road, the little bit of it that still peeked out from tufts of hard grey grass, led right into it. Even broken by the wrath of God, and battered by a thousand years of weather, pieces of great buildings soared high over the travelers' heads like cliffs. Broken stone lay everywhere in heaps and hills, enough to make a good-sized mountain. Leathery vines ran down like waterfalls from the tops of roofless structures, and here and there, unseen doves cooed mournfully.

"It's bigger than anything else in the world!" Jack cried—and then lowered his voice because he did not like the echoes. "It must be bigger than all the other cities put together."

"It very likely was," said Martis. "This was the heart of the Empire. When it beat, they felt it all the way out to the Great Lakes and beyond. There's enough stone piled here to build several dozen cities, and very strong walls to protect them."

"I don't like it!" Ellayne said. "There's bad magic in it." She was thinking of the stories of Abombalbap, replete with sorcerers and shape-shifters, witches, elves, and goblins.

"There's no such thing as magic," Jack said, and he hoped he was right.

"It won't be long before sundown," Martis said. "We'd better find a comfortable place to camp. Tomorrow I'll take you to the Temple."

"Do you believe in magic, Martis?" Ellayne asked.

"I never gave much thought to it. Lord Reesh said the men of the Empire could do things that people nowadays would call magic; but he also says that we could do them, too, if only we knew how. It wasn't magic, he said. Only knowledge—and from knowledge, power."

"It doesn't look like it did them much good," Jack said.

From his perch on Ellayne's shoulder, Wytt launched into a muted string of yips and chitterings.

"There are Omah here—I guess he can smell them," Jack said. "But he doesn't like this place. He's warning us to be careful."

"He does well to warn us," Martis said. "I've heard of pits suddenly opening in the streets and belching out clouds of poison air. And I saw an ancient structure collapse, once, for no apparent reason but extreme old age. We will indeed be careful."

They found a spot sheltered by a bit of broken wall that was crowned by a twisted tree, dead and lifeless, but still rooted in the weathered stone. Plentiful vines, which Martis cut with difficulty, provided inexhaustible fuel for their fire. When the sun went down and darkness fell, owls called to one another and bats fluttered overhead, chirping. Ellayne kept her hat on.

"What if someone sees our fire?" Jack asked.

"No one would be fool enough to try to move around in this place by night," Martis said. "We're perfectly safe. For us, this may be the safest place in all Obann."

CHAPTER 27

How the Heathen Got a King

Ryons used to be afraid, most of the time: afraid his master would beat him, or that the other slave-children would gang up on him, or that he would be sold into some barbarous country where even worse would happen to him. He learned to keep to himself and do as he was told, and he became the kind of boy to whom people paid no attention. His fears subsided.

But then he met Obst, and he began to speak up whenever the spirit moved him, and these past few days had been by far the best days of his life. When he was seated among the chieftains, with feathers in his hair and a golden chain around his neck, he would not have believed life could get any better. Only a very great God could have done such things for him; and so he believed in Obst's God, who'd saved him from the mardar.

But now he was afraid again.

The chieftains sent all of the warriors and subchiefs out of the tent so they could closely question Obst and the big westman with the staff. The woman stayed, too, holding the sleeping girl in her arms; and some kind of monster with both teeth and feathers stood guard over her.

They all had their eyes on Ryons because it was he to whom the little girl had spoken. He didn't think it would take much for Shaffur to order him burned: the Wallekki lived in mortal fear of witches. It didn't seem to matter that there weren't any.

Obst tried to explain.

"King Ozias was the last anointed king of Obann. He lived two thousand years ago. After usurpers drove him from the throne, your ancestors, warlords, burned his city to the ground. Ozias himself fled into exile, no one knows where. But on his way, he climbed Mount Yul and erected a bell on its summit. That's how it came to be called Bell Mountain. I was with the two children who climbed the mountain and rang the bell—the bell that Ozias believed God would hear, if someone rang it.

"But Ozias was more than just a king. God loved him and blessed him. Ozias wrote most of the Sacred Songs that are included in our holy books. We believe God inspired him to write them; that's why they're sacred to us. We also believe, because various prophets said so, that God promised Ozias that his kingdom would endure forever: that if it ever departed, it would be restored again. That it might sleep, but would never die."

"But this Ozias," Szugetai said, "did he not die? Or did he become a god and live forever?"

"Certainly he died! No man can become a god," Obst said.

"And you say God used this girl to speak to us—like the Great Man spoke to us through the mardar?"

Obst shuddered. "No, no—please! The Great Man is only a man, and a very wicked one. But if we could actually hear the voice of God, it would be too much for us. No one has ever seen God; only a chosen few have heard Him. God would choose a little child like this so that we would know that it was really Him speaking to us, and not some clever trickery. This girl is much too young to make up the kind of things she said, or even to learn them by heart. I knew it was prophecy as soon as I heard her."

"But she spoke to this boy!" Shaffur said. "Why? Who is he, that God should speak to him?"

I'm nobody at all, Ryons thought. Besides, he hadn't understood a word the girl said.

"Who was your father, Ryons?" Obst asked, gently.

"I don't know. I hardly knew my mother. My master sold her away when I was little."

"How old are you?"

"I don't know that, either. I don't know anything."

Obst turned to Helki. "What can you tell us about this girl?"

"Not much," the big man said. "I found her wandering the plain, all alone, and I had to take care of her. I reckon her ma and pa were settlers in the hills, and something happened to them. So I took her with me, back to the forest.

"She gets these spells, like you saw. She says things no one understands, like you heard. That was not her normal way of speaking."

"She can't be more than three years old," the woman put in.

"How can we know it's not witchcraft?" Shaffur asked.

"Chieftain—would a witch speak of God?" Obst said. "It's out of the question! You can be absolutely sure she spoke prophetically. Alas, that's all we can be sure of."

"God speaking to us does not seem to have done us much good," said Szugetai. "What does it matter what God says, if we can't understand Him?"

"I don't think it's so hard to understand," said the woman. "God says He will give this boy the throne of Ozias. We all heard it, as clear as a bell. This boy will be King of the West someday, a king like Ozias. What else could it possibly mean? It means what it says."

At the moment, Ryons would have almost preferred to be a slave again. Him a king! What could it mean? He knew perfectly well that slave boys do not become kings. And king of what? He wasn't even sure he knew what "two thousand years ago" meant. Beyond thirty or forty, he didn't know much about numbers.

Old Chief Spider chuckled. "None of our Abnak gods would ever think of anything like this!" he said.

A Fazzan chieftain spoke up, too excited to use the common language. The Fazzan were a river valley people who seldom ventured out of their own territory, and were almost never seen west of the mountains. But Obst understood every word he said, and translated for the others.

"Chief Zekelesh is sorry to change the subject," Obst said, "but he would like to know how many hostages you would require before you let this army into Lintum Forest. He and his people know nothing of kings; but since the way back to their own country is blocked, they would rather be in the forest than out here on the plain."

Helki didn't take long to answer. "Tell him I'd be ashamed to take hostages from people who serve God and have you for their teacher, Obst. As far as I'm concerned, they can enter the forest as friends, and I'll help them all I can. Maybe they can help me with a thing or two."

The chiefs were all agreeable to that, although Shaffur the Wallekki had his doubts.

"Why should you trust us?" he asked. "My people have sold some of your people as slaves. Why would you not take vengeance on us?"

"I don't reckon God would like it if we did," said Helki.

"My horsemen aren't used to forests," Szugetai said. "We came here to win fame and to get rich by sacking cities. Now what shall we do?"

Ryons startled when the monster bird, which had been quiet for some time, suddenly squawked and shook his feathers. It was a loud and piercing cry, but the little girl slept on.

"Warlord Szugetai," said Obst, "we are all in God's hands now. We'll have to wait and see what He calls us to do. As for becoming rich and famous, we shall all do well just to stay alive."

The horse-chief nodded.

"Well, that's settled, then," said Spider. "Meanwhile, as long as everyone else is against us, East and West alike, I would like for us to take this boy to be our king."

The other chieftains stared at him.

"Have you gone mad?" Shaffur sputtered. "Are we to be commanded by a child?" And Helki laughed out loud.

"Not that kind of king!" Spider said. "But he could be something to hold this army together through the hard times that are bound to come. And you heard what the little girl said. If God is going to make him a real king someday, we'd be wise to be his men."

Shaffur couldn't answer that, but the Fazzan chieftain broke into a broad grin.

"I am Zekelesh: I speak for the Fazzan people from the Green Snake River," he said. "I accept this child as my king! As long as we've broken with the Thunder King and thrown in with the westmen's God, let's hold nothing back."

Another chieftain spoke, the captain of a little band of copper-colored, black-haired people called the Dahai, who came from a faraway country Ryons never heard of.

"I, Tughrul Lomak, chief of the Dahai—who will never see their homes again—also accept this child as my king. As long as the Great Man means to destroy us, let's see how angry we can make him first."

One by one, eleven chiefs swore loyalty to Ryons as their king. Ryons, knowing how changeable they were, could only shudder. Their making him a chief had something of a joke in it; but they weren't joking now.

The big man from the forest swore, leaving only Shaffur. The tall Wallekki glared at all his fellow chiefs.

"Very well!" he said. "Since you've all sworn this oath, then in the name of the Wallekki in this army, so do I! We're flaming fools for doing it, too." He fixed his angry stare on Obst. "Well, old man? Have we succeeded in pleasing God? Was this what He wanted us to do?"

Ryons felt sorry for Obst, having to answer such a question. But this time Ryons held his tongue.

"May He have mercy on my soul for saying so," Obst answered, "but yes—I think it was."

CHAPTER 28

The Way Down

That first night in the Old City was not one that Ellayne would have liked to repeat.

Jack and Martis fell asleep right away, but she couldn't. She was used to sleeping outdoors; she could hardly imagine, anymore, what a real bed felt like. She'd heard owls before, too; they didn't scare her anymore.

Wytt squirmed out of her arms once, snatched up his little sharp stick, and stood there sniffing the air and trembling all over. When Ellayne asked him what was wrong, he didn't answer. Two or three minutes passed before he relaxed.

"What was it?" Ellayne whispered. "Did you hear something? Should I wake the others?" But she hoped she wouldn't have to do that. She wouldn't want them thinking she was imagining things and scaring herself.

Wytt made chirps and chock-chock noises that, ever since she and Jack heard King Ozias' bell, Ellayne understood as if they were words.

"Something bad here—don't know what," he answered. "Should be many Omah here, but only a few. They won't come close to us. Very quiet Omah."

"Are there bad men around?"

"No men nearby. Maybe much farther off."

"Is it animals, then? Dangerous animals?"

He chattered in a low tone, frustrated because he couldn't make himself understood. The little hairy men, Ellayne and Jack had come to know, had no words for many things that mattered to human beings. They could only speak of things that they could see and hear and smell and touch. They didn't imagine things. Their senses were so much keener than humans' that an imagination might have been a burden to them.

"Are you afraid, Wytt?"

"Yes. A little."

"Well, so am I," Ellayne said. "People lived here, long ago—more people than you could imagine. But they were wicked people, and they just kept getting worse and worse until God destroyed them, and all their cities. And this city, where we are now, was the heart of all that wickedness. I wouldn't be surprised if there were ghosts."

But Wytt knew nothing of such things; and by mentioning them, Ellayne succeeded only in keeping herself awake an hour longer.

After breakfast, Martis led them to the ruins of the Temple.

"Not the Old Temple, that the Heathen burned—this would be the Temple that was built in its place, the Temple of the Empire," he said, as they set out.

There was a fog coming off the river, and everything was grey and still. Martis picked out a careful route amid the rubble. Pieces of colossal stone walls towered over their heads.

"Do any of these ever fall down?" Jack asked.

"Sometimes. It's very old."

With many a detour, they followed what had once been broad, straight streets. "Lord Reesh says the people of those days used to travel in carts and carriages that propelled themselves without horses," Martis said. "He's made a deep study of those times."

"What did the people do that was so wicked?" Ellayne asked.

"No one knows for sure. Long before that time, the prophets said the people would turn away from God and worship themselves and the works of their own hands. But we know more about Ozias' time, and more ancient times still, than we do about the Empire. At least some people do. I was never a scholar," Martis said.

Except for vines and weeds, flying and crawling insects, and a few birds, they saw no other living thing.

"Where are the Omah, Wytt?" Jack asked.

"They watch us," Wytt answered, from his perch on Ham's back.

"I don't see them," Ellayne said.

"They watch."

"Will they be friendly?" Jack said.

"Maybe."

Having made an early start, they arrived a little after noon.

"Oh, no," Jack said. "Is this it?"

Never having seen the Temple in the New City, nor even a picture of it, he'd been expecting to see a building much like the chamber house in Ninneburky—only bigger and grander, of course, and in poor repair. He'd thought it would be an empty old place you could just walk into and start looking for the way to the cellar.

But this, the ruins of the old Temple of the Empire, was like nothing he'd imagined. It was a heap: it was a wilderness of tumbled stone. Where parts of walls still stood, rubble choked the space between them. The whole ruin towered higher than any building Jack had ever seen. It was too big to permit a guess as to how much ground it covered. It was too big to be seen all at once.

"We're standing in front of what was once the main entrance to the Temple complex," Martis said. "Do you see those pieces shaped like giant stone barrels? They were once great pillars that must've stood as high as heaven. Beyond them was an open courtyard for assemblies, and then the Temple itself, under an enormous dome."

"How could anything so big be turned into ... this?" Jack wondered.

"No one knows. Lord Reesh says the men of those days had the power to destroy a whole city in the blink of an eye. But there are no writings to tell us of that time. It was all destroyed, even their books. Only the Holy Scriptures themselves survived."

"Maybe it was an earthquake," Ellayne said. Her father had told her about earthquakes.

"Some scholars think so," Martis said, "but they can only guess."

Somewhere under that mountain of ruin, under those mighty walls and broken stones, there ought to be a cellar, Jack thought. And then another cellar under that. Where else would God have meant them to look, if not here? But the idea of being under all that mass, which might fall down on them at any moment, was not a pleasant one.

"Do you know the way to the cellar?" he asked Martis.

"No. We'll have to find it."

"The Omah will know," Ellayne said. "We could never find it on our own, that's for sure. We could spend years looking for it. Wytt, see if you can call them. See if they'll help us. We have to get under *that*."

Wytt hopped down from the donkey. He raised his head and voiced some piercing, peeping cries. They echoed endlessly, all around. Listening to the echoes die away among the stones, Jack would have found it easy to believe that he and his companions were the only living things left in all the world. The thought that the biggest and most populous city in Obann lay just across the river seemed fantastic.

The echoes died away at last, and silence fell. No one dared to break it. Ham snorted, just once, then looked around nervously, his long ears twitching. Dulayl, born and bred to open spaces, pawed the stony earth, but only once.

They aren't coming, Ellayne thought. But she was wrong.

One by one, without a sound, they came. They appeared out of the mist, out from behind great stones, up out of the earth. They looked like Wytt. As well as she knew him, Ellayne was hard put to tell him from the others.

Two dozen of the little hairy men looked up at them with bright eyes. Wytt began to chatter at them.

"These are my friends," he let them know. "We come from far away. They ask you to show them the way to a place under the big stones." He looked up at Ellayne. "Show them your hair. Let them see."

Ellayne took off her hat. The little men stared at her, and pointed, and began to chatter and cheep excitedly among themselves.

"What are they saying?" Martis asked in a whisper.

"They're making a fuss about my hair!"

"'Hair like sun, hair like sun!' Something like that," Jack said.

The Omah began to chirp and squeal, they were unnervingly loud; and more and more of them came out of hiding. Dulayl whinnied and tossed his head. Jack didn't blame him. Martis was afraid; you could see it in his face.

"It's all right," Jack said. "They're happy. But don't ask me why."

"I wish we could understand them better!" said Ellayne.

Had Obst been with them, he might have warned them not to be too sure that God only spoke to human beings: that the Omah, too, belonged to Him, and there was no way of knowing how He spoke to them, or what He said. But Obst was not there, and Jack and Ellayne were only children, and Martis an assassin. They knew little of such things.

It took the Omah quite some time to rein in their excitement and produce a spokesman. This was an old male with patchy fur, who stood shivering as he spoke to Wytt.

What he said, in substance, was this:

"Yes—there is a cave-place under the big stones here. We go there when it's very cold. Big people can go there, if we show them the way. Four-legs can't go.

"Yes—there are many cave-places like that, under many places of stones. Some go deep, deep into the earth, farther than any Omah knows. Some go so deep, Omah never use them. Bad air! When bad air gets loose, Omah who breathe it die. And some places have good water, but some bad.

"Big people come sometimes. Not many. Sometimes the big stones fall on them and eat them. We know how to stay away from those places. Big people never see us. Sometimes they come here to kill each other.

"Yes—we will help you go down below. She with sunshine hair, we know to be good to her. Omah from far away, we make you welcome. We never before see any Omah from far away. But we know there are Omah everywhere. One day, all Omah everywhere shall dance at the same time."

And Wytt said, "Yes—my Omah think so, too."

Martis had not told the children all he knew about the ruined Temple. In fact, he was afraid.

Children who grew up on the streets of Obann heard all sorts of stories about the ruins across the river. There was treasure buried in the ruins, but it all had curses on it, people said. There were entities called gawnks that prowled the ruins, and if they caught you, they would suck out all your blood and you would become one of them—lifeless, grey, and silent, always hungry, never satisfied. The Old City was full of ghosts. And somewhere in a secret chamber under the ruins, King Ozias himself lay sleeping, with all his mighty men around him, to wake again when Obann was no more. Anyone who disturbed them would be turned into dust.

It was all nonsense, of course: but if you'd grown up hearing it, you could never quite dismiss it from your mind.

Bits of it clung to dark corners where the broom of reason couldn't reach.

But even without gawnks or curses, the Old City could be dangerous. Some of the worst criminals in Obann escaped into the ruins, and the patrols never hunted for them there, for none of them ever returned. Martis had visited the Old City often enough to know that the stones shifted, walls fell down, and ancient floors gave way. Freezing and thawing, burrowing animals, and the roots of living trees undermined the stones, wormed their way into cracks and pried them farther apart. Someday there would be nothing left of it but gravel.

So crawling down some passage to the cellar of the Temple was not something that appealed to him. The passage might collapse behind them, burying them alive.

For the sake of the children's morale, Martis kept all these things to himself. They'd already climbed Bell Mountain, so who was he to hold them back from this?

Martis had learned to be afraid of God—more afraid of God than he was of collapsing passageways. Reesh would despise him for it; but Reesh hadn't been to the summit of Bell Mountain.

A party of Omah led them into the ruins of the Temple. Dulayl and Ham remained behind, hobbled, munching on tough grass. The Omah scampered up and down the rocks like squirrels, but there was some tricky climbing for the humans.

"I was thinking we'd be going down a flight of stairs," Jack said.

"We might," said Martis. "There are still some stairways left, here and there. But most of them are broken."

"Does the new Temple have a cellar?" Ellayne asked.

"The new Temple extends deep into the earth; it has enormous cellars. We keep some of the archives down there, plus storerooms for all kinds of things—including the First Prester's wine." He didn't mention two or three little rooms where the First Prester kept people who'd displeased him, but for one reason or another were not to be killed.

"Do they keep any treasure?" Ellayne asked.

Martis laughed. "The Temple's expenses don't allow much treasure to be accumulated," he said.

The day was overcast, with a threat of drizzle in the air. Up and down they climbed over heaps of shattered stone. Some of the stones were seared pale grey, and bits of it flaked off under their shoes. Whatever had destroyed the Empire Temple, Martis thought, fire had been a part of it.

The Omah brought them to an expanse of flat pavement strewn with small stones, under the shelter of a piece of standing wall. It didn't stand quite straight. Below it gaped a square black hole.

"This is the way down," the Omah told Wytt. "Omah know many ways, but only this way for big people."

Jack, Ellayne, and Martis stood over the hole in the pavement, looking down. They saw stone steps, cracked and broken in the middle.

Ellayne hugged herself against the damp. "That could lead anywhere!" she said.

"We can't try it without torches," Martis said. "And lamps would be better."

"I wonder how far down it goes," said Jack.

"We'd better not attempt it today," Martis said. He would have been glad not to attempt it at all. "We ought to set up camp here, and spend the rest of the day making torches. Who knows how many we'll need? And maybe we can find some vines strong enough to serve as ropes. I might have to cross into the New City to buy some lamps."

Jack would have preferred to descend those stairs right away. He should have been afraid, and he was; but he felt an even more powerful urge to see the cellars. They'd come a long way for this.

"This is where we're supposed to be," he said. "This is where we'll find the missing book, if that's what we're supposed to find. Where else could it be, but in the Temple? And this is where King Ozias' Temple was—under all this."

"From King Ozias' bell to King Ozias' Temple—it must be right," Ellayne said. "It's like an old story, in which all these things fit together in the end. A story about Ozias that began two thousand years ago and isn't finished yet."

"Story" was hardly the word for it, Martis thought: God's hand is in this. After all these centuries of lords and presters and merchants and peasants going about their business as if there were no God, suddenly we feel His hand on us. Or has it been there all along, and we knew it not?

Martis shivered, too; but he wasn't cold.

CHAPTER 29

A Prophet on a Scaffold

Once they were decided on it, the Heathen lost no time in moving into the forest.

Ryons had not yet learned how to ride a horse without falling off, so he marched on foot, sticking close to Obst and the big man with the staff. The man's clothes, a patchwork of every crazy color you could think of, fascinated him.

The little girl went back to being an ordinary little girl—which was a relief, because she took a liking to Ryons and always wanted to be near him. He hadn't much experience with small children, but he liked it when she took his hand and swung it and sang silly little songs that made no sense. Even her strange bird seemed to like him; at least it didn't hiss or snap at him when he came near it. But it still struck him as a thing more like a snake than a bird, and he never ventured to touch it.

Being a king with no power to command was easy. The chieftains still decided everything. Still, it made him uneasy that the Abnaks insisted on calling him King Ryons and touching their foreheads before they spoke to him.

"It's a grand thing for us to have a king," Uduqu told him. "We Abnaks never had a king before. You must always remember, O King, that it was our own Chief Spider who first said it would be a good thing to make you a king."

"It wasn't my idea," Ryons said.

"Cheer up, Your Majesty!" Helki said. "I knew a low-down bandit chief who called himself the King of Lintum Forest, and he's king of nothing now. But as it's someone else's doing that you were called a king, I reckon that's a different story.

"Look at me. I never wanted anything but to be left alone, and here I am, marching with an army. There's several dozen people in the forest who look at me like I was their father, and sixty outlaws who have me for their chief—and none of that was my idea.

"Look at Obst. He's like me, just wants to be left alone. And what happens to him? He has to be a father to all this host of Heathen. Be thankful you're only a king!"

The woman who took care of Jandra spoke up. "At least be thankful you're not Helki," she said. "He'll have to get all these Heathen settled in the forest. They'll need houses, and food, and water. Some of them have probably never even seen a forest before. They'll need taking care of."

Uduqu grunted. "Not Abnaks," he said. "We know how to hunt. We come from the forests on the hills."

"Then you can help us keep some of these plainsmen alive," Helki said.

"We'll help. It shouldn't be too hard, as long as there's fighting sometimes. Men with no one else to fight will fight each other."

"That's one of the things that worries me," said Helki.

Even as they spoke, there was a battle south of Lintum Forest. The legion sent out by Lord Gwyll lost the battle, and many were the survivors who fled into the forest to save their lives.

Relay riders brought the bad news to Obann, and it was all over the streets before the oligarchs could muffle it. Rumor made out the defeat to be worse than it was, and in spite of Obann's mighty walls and thousands of defenders, the mood of the city verged on panic.

"You must do something about those crazy prophets in the streets!" the governor-general told Lord Reesh.

"I'm afraid there's nothing for it but to hang one of them," Judge Tombo said. "We can't have them going all around the city preaching the end of the world. But a public hanging might steady the people's temper."

"Or shatter it," Reesh said. "Lord Ruffin, you must give my ministers more time to preach the holy war."

"It's not a good idea to kill a prophet," Lord Gwyll grumbled; but his was the only dissenting voice.

This was the last thing Reesh wanted to do. Not that he had any objections to hanging anyone; but he thought that would make the situation worse, not better.

"I will not have the Temple's name attached to this, my lords," he said. In the end, he and Gwyll were the only councilors who voted against it. But in spite of their disagreement, he still rode home in his friend Judge Tombo's carriage.

"Don't worry," Tombo said. "The charge will be creating a public disturbance in time of war, and sedition. I'll make sure it doesn't reflect on the Temple."

"It can't help but reflect on the Temple," Reesh said. "There are too many instances in Scripture of prophets being put to death by ungodly rulers. This will only make people take those fools more seriously."

"I know what I'm doing," the judge said.

Overnight a gallows was erected in High Market Square, near the public stables and quite far from the Temple. In plain clothes and in a covered litter, Lord Reesh came to see the hanging; and he made sure nobody saw him. Their attention focused on the event itself, the gathering crowd paid no attention to him.

In due time the prisoner arrived in a cart. It was a nondescript old man who had once been someone's doorkeeper. Guards led him up the scaffold, where a herald read out the charges against him:

"For disturbing the morale of the city in a time of war, for alarming the public with false rumors and seditious fabrications, and for treason, the prisoner having been duly convicted by a court of law, sentence is hereby executed upon him. Prisoner, have you anything to say?"

This was what Reesh was afraid of, and there was no avoiding it. Not even Tombo could change the custom, hallowed as it was by centuries of use.

"Only this," the old man said, in a cracked voice that somehow managed to carry to the limits of the square. "Woe to you, you false and hard-hearted nation! The Lord has looked for righteousness, and not found it in this city, nor in all the land. The sword, the pestilence, the famine, and the end of days—woe to you, for the terrible day of the Lord is at hand! He has numbered your sins, and they are like the multitude of ants in the earth, which cannot be counted for their multitude. The bell has been rung, you wicked nation, and the Lord has heard it—woe, woe, woe to you!"

He might have said much more, but as soon as he paused to catch his breath, the guards clapped a hood over his head, put the rope around his neck, and hanged him. And the crowd made a noise like thunder rumbling on distant hills.

Tombo, you fool! Reesh thought. The people might have ignored this wretched lunatic, but now they won't.

CHAPTER 30

Under the Temple

While the crowd was dispersing from High Market Square, Martis prepared to lead the children into the depths of the ruined Temple. They had vines coiled around their shoulders for use as ropes, and bunches of chopped vine for torches. Jack used the last of his matches to light them.

"Ready?" Martis asked.

"Not exactly," Ellayne said; but Jack said, "Let's go. I want to see the cellar."

Wytt and a few of the Omah went down first, springing lightly from ruined step to step. They could see in the dark. Martis went next, carrying in his heart a sense of dread, then Jack and Ellayne. The stairs sagged in the middle, but seemed solid enough. But it was best to climb them using hands and feet.

"It'd be really something if we found a treasure," Ellayne started to say; but she didn't like the way the sound bounced off the walls, so she said no more.

"I wonder if anyone else has been down here, besides the Omah," Jack whispered.

"Over the course of a thousand years, it's possible," Martis said. "But there can't have been many here before us. The Old City has been mostly left alone." Because the shadow of God's wrath still hangs over it, he thought, even after all these years.

They descended slowly, carefully. Little by little, the square patch of sky above them grew smaller. It was another grey, overcast day; but now that little patch of sky seemed most enticing, Ellayne thought. It would've been nice to stay up there. The air down here was close and clammy. The torches gave light enough, but the darkness seemed to press on them, like an animal waiting for the moment to pounce on its prey.

How far down they went, or how long it took, there was no way to tell. They just kept going until their feet rested on a level floor and they could stand again. Overhead, the entrance looked as small as a lady's dainty handkerchief.

The Omah chattered among themselves. "They're saying this whole space used to be filled with bones," Jack told Martis, "but the Omah took them out so they could use it."

"Dead men's bones," Ellayne said. She didn't like to think of it.

There was more darkness and more space than their torches could light. Jack turned slowly, holding his torch above his head, to see all he could.

Except where it was piled with rubble, the floor was flat and seamless, as if it were all one impossibly great stone. Stout pillars held up a high, flat ceiling, although a few of them had fallen. Everything looked stained and splotched, old and dirty. Here and there, Jack saw empty doorways piercing the wall, pits of sheer blackness in the murk. They must lead to other rooms, or corridors that hadn't seen light for a thousand years.

"We should've brought lamps," he said.

"Paint would be useful, too, to mark our trail and keep from getting lost," Martis said. "But I can cross over into the New City and get anything we need."

"I got lost in a place like this, once," Ellayne said. "Good thing it wasn't underground! Wytt found me, and Jack and Obst pulled me out. It must've been a cellar like this, once, and it somehow got unburied. There was a great big room in it, bigger than this one; and on the floor was a map, that Obst said was a map of the whole world, with lands beyond the sea."

Nobody said anything. It had been a thousand years since anyone in Obann had sailed across the sea. Whatever lands and peoples might be found there had no names that anyone remembered.

"Well," Martis said, "there's been a lot of water down here, and fire, too, from the looks of it. Any decoration has been worn away."

Jack addressed the Omah. "Wytt, there should be another cellar like this one, underneath all this. Ask the Omah if they can show us how to get down there."

The Omah chattered for several minutes before Wytt gave an answer.

"He says there is another place below," Jack said, "but the Omah never go down there. It's hard to understand just what he means: something like, 'All these places belong to Omah, but not this place.'"

"Bad air, maybe," Martis said.

"No, that's not it. They can't go there because it's not allowed."

Wytt added something: "Girl with sunshine hair can go there. Omah say this place is for her, always."

"I don't like the sound of that!" Ellayne said.

"What do you mean, Wytt?" Jack asked.

"Omah always know that someday the girl will come and see the place that belongs to her. Now she is here." That was the best he could do by way of explanation.

"They might as well show us where it is," Jack said.

The Omah led them into one of the black corridors, and then another, and another. Martis left unused torches on the floor so they could find their way back. They passed by many rooms, some large and some small, some choked with rubble and some empty. Floor, walls, ceiling—it was all flat, smooth, stained, undecorated stone. Here and there, bands of rust ran along the ceiling.

Martis would have given all he had to return to the surface. One chance shifting of the stones, and there would be no return. He thought of the immense weight of the ruined Temple piled over their heads. These cellars had supported it for a thousand years: for how many more days, or hours, would they continue to support it?

At any hour of any day, a thousand men might be found in the new Temple, going about their business. On holy days it might hold ten thousand. But this ruined place was bigger, and once upon a time it had been full of people. They were all dead now, Martis thought. The Omah had carried out their bones. But some vestige of those people's doom still brooded over the place.

The Omah led them into another big, bare room; but this one had a great crack in the floor, running diagonally from one corner to another. That was the way into the deeper cellar, Wytt said.

"I'm not going down there—not down into any crack in the floor," Ellayne said.

"Ask them if it's safe," Martis said.

"Yes, very safe," was Wytt's answer.

"How do they know, if they've never been down there themselves?" Ellayne was thinking of rats. There could be a thousand rats down there.

"Oh, I'll go first, then!" Jack said. But as he prepared to lower himself feetfirst into the crack, the Omah crowded around him and made a noisy fuss. He got back up. "They won't let me go first. It has to be you." He didn't see why. Wasn't he God's servant, and Ellayne just his helper?

"It'll be all right, Ellayne," Martis said. "The Omah won't let you come to any harm; and we'll tie one of these long vines under your arms so we can pull you out again."

"Wytt, it's all right if Jack goes first," she said; but the Omah insisted it had to be her, although they couldn't explain why. There were so many things they knew, but didn't know how to say.

If she didn't give in, their quest could not continue. The books she'd read had made her understand that much. So she had to agree, and Martis tied a vine around her, under her arms. "I'd better tie two together," he said. That proved difficult, but he finally managed it. "Ready?"

"I suppose I am. As ready as I'll ever be."

"Then start climbing—and take it slow."

Martis held on to the vines while Jack held both their torches over the crack. Ellayne went down feetfirst, feeling for holds. The floor was an immensely thick slab of that seamless stone the builders of the Empire used, but the edges of the crack were rough. Proceeding slowly, she had no trouble finding footholds. And it was a wide fissure: a grown man would easily fit, with room to spare.

She inched along, downward into the dark, careful not to drop her torch. Looking up, she saw Jack's and Martis' faces and the glittering eyes of the Omah. They weren't really far away. She kept going, an inch at a time, until her feet encountered empty space.

"Hold it!" she cried. "There's nothing underneath me now."

"Can you see anything?" Martis said.

"Wait a minute."

She didn't like to, but now for the first time she looked down. She clung to the vine with one hand, dipped her torch with the other. She wouldn't have been surprised to see a bottomless chasm, or a pool of black water with dragons in it.

"There's a floor," she reported, "about ten feet under me. It's hard to tell because it's so dark. That's all I can see."

"I'm going to lower you the rest of the way, so you can look around. When you're ready ..."

"Go ahead." Ellayne was too excited now to be afraid. After all, this was a place mentioned in the Scriptures. Kings and prophets had been here, men whose names were in the holy books. "Just take it slow!"

"Slow and steady," Martis answered.

Jack held the torches steady, but his feet felt like jumping up and down. Martis let the vine-rope out so slowly that he felt like screaming at him. The man's face shown with sweat.

"All right so far?" Martis called.

"Slower, slower! I'm starting to swing around."

"Slower it is."

Jack wondered how it could take so long to lower someone ten feet. And like as not, it'd only turn out to be another empty cave, like the room they were standing in now. He was surprised the Omah could have superstitions.

"I'm at the bottom!" Ellayne sounded like she was at the bottom of a well.

"Can you see anything?" Martis said.

It took her a moment to reply.

"A lot of things," she said. "I think—I mean—well, it looks like maybe people live here."

CHAPTER 31

What They Found in a Jar

Obst sat alone in a tiny clearing in the woods, thinking.

Ozias as a child fled to Lintum Forest with his mother. He stayed there, hunted constantly but never caught, until he was old enough to lead men, conquer his enemies, and claim his throne. But the wickedness that was Obann in those days raised up new enemies against him; and he was the people's last anointed king.

Now the boy Ryons was a king, and hiding in Lintum Forest like Ozias. But king of what? A ragtag host of Heathen with nowhere else to go and only lately come to God. And yet the girl, Jandra, speaking with the authentic voice of prophecy, said the Lord would give this boy Ozias' throne.

But there was no throne to give him! The Obann that came after Ozias never had a king. No one knew, exactly, how the Empire rose, nor how it fell; but in the intervening thousand years, Obann never had a king. It had tyrants, warlords, a multitude of petty princelings, and now the oligarchs.

What could the prophecy mean?

Just that day the army had crowned Ryons King of Lintum Forest—crowned him with a circlet of oak leaves. Against Obst's advice, Helki added his assent to theirs.

"The oligarchs won't like it," Obst said. "They'll have you up for treason."

"Oligarchs—hah! They never gave a snap for anyone in Lintum Forest. They let the woods fill up with outlaws. And the same goes for the Temple.

"Well, I'm going to use this army to scour the place clean of outlaws. And if there still is an oligarchy when this war is over, we'll see what they have to say about it. Just be thankful they didn't crown you Prester of the Forest."

And so there was the wretched boy with a crown of oak leaves on his head, hailed as king by outlaws and barbarians—what was this world coming to? He thought of a verse from Scripture: "Your wisdom is foolishness with me, says the Lord."

Helki said he knew a castle in the middle of the forest where the king could hold his court and no enemy could get at him. From there, he said, detachments of the army could strike out in any direction, putting down the outlaw bands, dealing with any force from the outside that invaded Lintum. How so many men were to live in the forest, Obst could hardly imagine; but Helki said it could be done. "Some will have to hunt, and some will have to farm, and the settlers will have to feed the rest. They won't mind: they'll like having a king and an army to protect them. And once it's all been sorted out—" Helki grinned—"I can go back to living on my own."

Obst doubted that would ever come to pass.

Martis couldn't go down the crack; he'd have to stay behind to pull the children up again.

He tied the vine around Jack's body, made sure of the knots, and then Jack began his descent. He had to force himself not to hurry. In a few minutes he was standing beside Ellayne, holding up his torch and looking all around.

"What do you think?" she said.

He didn't answer. He was looking at tables, their tops littered with cups and other objects, stools, and shelves stacked along the walls with earthen jars lined up on them. The floor was clear of rubble: it had all been piled up in several columns to support the roof. Someone had come down here and done that; and yet there was dust all over the floor, undisturbed.

"Well?" Martis called.

"Just a minute! There's a lot of stuff down here," Jack said.

He handed Ellayne his torch and undid the vine, then helped her out of hers. He wanted a closer look at one of those columns of broken stone between the ceiling and the floor.

"This must've been a lot of work," he said. "It's all jammed tight. They must have pounded it tight with mallets, to keep the roof from coming down. I guess all this stone came from the ceiling when it cracked open."

"But who could've done the work?" Ellayne said.

"Maybe the Omah know. See if they'll come down."

She called Wytt. Soon he and several others clambered down the vines. "It's all right for them to be here now," she said, "as long as I was the first one in. Wytt, ask your friends if any other big people have ever been here."

They chattered among themselves until Wytt had the answer.

"No—all the time Omah have been here, no one ever comes into this place. No one can come until you come in."

"But all this furniture," Ellayne said, "these are all things that big people use. Someone must have brought it down here. And someone must have piled up these stones."

"Omah never see this place before," Wytt said.

So the little men, who had lived here since the city became a desolation, knew nothing about this cellar. That meant the work had all been done before there were any Omah living in the ruins.

"A thousand years ago!" Ellayne said.

Jack wasn't even sure of what a thousand was. He supposed it had all happened so long ago, it might as well have been at the beginning of time.

"Whoever they were," he said, "I'll bet they didn't come down here through that crack. There must be another way in." He asked the Omah if it were so.

"Other ways all blocked, all filled with stones," Wytt said. "This is the only way."

There were hallways leading out of this room, but it didn't take long to discover that all of them were filled with rubble. "A mouse couldn't get through," Jack said.

He tried to sit on a stool, but it snapped to pieces when he put his weight on it. After that they were careful about touching anything.

"What do you see down there?" Martis called. Because of the irregularities of the crack, they couldn't see him when they looked up; but a little bit of light from his torch reddened the stone, so he wasn't all that far away. It just seemed so.

"There's a lot of furniture and things," Jack said.

"Please tell me exactly what you see!"

So they did, and he thought it over for a minute, then

said, "See what's inside the jars—but be careful."

"It's probably just food that's all turned into dust," Jack muttered, as they crossed to the nearest set of shelves. These were made of wood, and they were careful not to break them as Jack removed a jar. "It's heavy," he said. "But not heavy enough to be full of money."

"Don't drop it," Ellayne said.

He set it on the floor. They were all big jars, tall, narrow at the top, with closely fitted stoppers. Something had been poured over this jar's stopper to seal it, some substance now black with age. Jack had to use his penknife to scrape it off, but even then the stopper was fitted so tightly that he couldn't pull it out. He told Martis.

"Listen, Jack—I've seen jars like that before, in the First Prester's collection of antiquities. The ancients used earthenware jars to store their writings. You have to break off the top of the jar to see what's inside. Do you think you can do that without shattering it?"

Ellayne said, "Why don't you pull us up again, and we'll bring the jar with us? We can open it when we're outside in the sunshine."

"I could break off the top right now," Jack said. "You just don't like it down here, do you?"

"No, I don't! Do you? There's something about this place that feels like no one ought to be here. Can't you feel it?"

Had Obst been there, he would have said the place was holy, set aside by God for some very special purpose. But Ellayne knew little of such things.

Jack passed up a chance to quarrel with her and just stood still, listening: not that there was anything to hear.

"You're right," he said. "But I don't think it's wrong for you and me to be here. We only came because God sent us."

"Are you coming up?" Martis asked.

Jack went up first, leaving his torch with Ellayne so he could carry the jar. He bumped his head once or twice as Martis pulled him back up through the crack, but he didn't drop the jar.

Once he was on his feet again, in the cellar of the Empire Temple, he understood more clearly what Ellayne meant. There was something special about that older place below. He could feel the difference, even if he couldn't say what it was.

Ellayne came next, and after her the Omah, swarming up the vines like squirrels. Martis had to light new torches.

"That does look just like one of Lord Reesh's jars," he said.

"But let's get a better look at it outside."

Their first exploration of the Temple cellars had taken longer than Jack thought. It was early morning when they went down the cracked stairs, and just after noon when they came up. The sun had driven away the morning mists, and birds were singing somewhere: it was a relief to hear them. By the light of day, and by comparison with the dark places down below, the ruins of the Temple seemed a safe and cheery place.

Martis sat on a stone, cradling the jar on his knees, studying it. But there was nothing to see: no decoration, no inscriptions.

"Whatever was put inside should still be here: you found the seal intact," he said. "Like as not it'll be some kind of tithing record, or an inventory."

"Stop talking and open it!" Jack said.

Martis couldn't budge the stopper with his fingers, nor could he insert his knife between it and the rim of the jar. "It's sealed, all right," he said. "They must have coated the stopper with wax or tree-sap before fitting it in, and when that hardened, it made a perfect seal. Whoever did it must have wanted it to remain sealed for a very long time. We'll have to break it open."

He tapped and tapped with his knife, harder and harder, until finally he cracked the jar around its rim. Prying with the point, he soon broke off the whole neck. He reached in with his fingers and slowly drew out something rolled into a cylinder and tied with a black cord. The knot fell apart with his first tug on it.

"That's a scroll, isn't it—what they had before books were invented?" Ellayne said.

"A sheepskin scroll, I think," Martis said.

The children leaned over his shoulders. Writing covered the scroll, in brown ink that had once been black.

"I was afraid this would crumble to dust if I unrolled it," he said, "but I suppose the seal was perfect. The skin's in very good condition. Lord Reesh would pay a fortune for it."

"Never mind him," Jack said. "What does it say? I can't quite make it out."

"I can't read it, either," Ellayne said.

"Nor can I."

"Well, what good is it if nobody can read it?" Jack said.

"We can't read it," Martis said, "but there are men who can. There are many of them in the Temple, just across the river."

Ellayne clenched her fists. What if Martis just took this scroll to Lord Reesh—and took her and Jack with it? What was to stop him? He was Lord Reesh's servant once; he could be again. She backed away from him.

"What's the matter?" Jack said.

"She's afraid," said Martis. "Afraid of me. And who can blame her?

"You're wise not to trust me, Ellayne. I'm no good. I've done too much evil ever to be good."

"I was only thinking—" she started to say; but he held up a finger to stop her.

"I know what you were thinking," he said. "But if you can't trust me, then trust the white hairs of my beard. God put them here: He could just as easily have struck me dead. He still could, at any moment He pleased. That's what I'm afraid of. Every breath I draw is on trial, so to speak. I stand on God's scaffold with His rope around my neck. I wouldn't dare betray you."

She believed him. She let out a sigh.

"Even so," Jack said, "we can't just walk into the Temple and ask someone to read this for us."

Martis smiled sadly at him. "No—we can't," he said. "So the scholar will have to come here. You can leave that to me."

CHAPTER 32

King Ryons and His Chieftains

Among the nations represented in King Ryons' army was a little band of men from the flatlands north of the Green Snake River; and these spent only one day in the forest before deciding they wanted no more to do with the enterprise. Attakotts, they were called: small, wiry men with curly hair, swift and tireless runners, experts with the sling, and a bad reputation for being quarrelsome. A man named Looth spoke for them in the council of the chieftains, but he was not really a chief. On the morning of the army's second day in the forest, he brought his people's complaint to the council.

"We don't like being under all these trees," he said, speaking the Tribe-talk with a singsong accent. "It isn't natural. We don't like being under a king, either. We're going to go back across the mountains to our home."

"You swore an oath to follow our king," Chief Shaffur said; but the Wallekki took oaths very seriously.

"I did," Looth said, "and I'll stay here if I must. But none of the rest of the Attakotts swore."

"You'll never get across the mountains," Szugetai said. "The whole country is full of the Great Man's armies."

"Why did you take the oath," Shaffur said, "if your people never meant to honor it? What kind of chieftain are you?"

"Foo! What do the Attakotts know of oaths or chieftains? Back home, we have neither. Once a man is a man, he does as he thinks best. We only joined this army because our people feared the Thunder King. His mardar came among us and spoke the secret names of our ancestors, a thing which no man knows. But he knew, so we were afraid.

"We are the best fighters among the Attakotts. Our place is with our own women and children. Our place is out in the sun, not under a lot of trees."

The chiefs could not convince the stubborn little man to keep his people with the army. He couldn't, he said; he had no authority over them, but only spoke for them among the chieftains. Old Chief Spider nodded.

"We Abnaks have always known the Attakotts," he said. "There's no other people we'd rather fight with. They take our scalps, we take theirs: it's always been so. No one understands better than the Attakotts the joy of fighting for its own sake. We take home no horses, no furs, no gold from them—because they have none. The only thing they have that's worth having is the bravery of their warriors. I would be very sorry to think that someday they would be no more. But King Thunder will exterminate your people, Looth. There will be no place in his kingdom for a people who don't have chiefs. And after you, it'll be the Abnaks' turn."

The chiefs fell silent, pondering his words. Better than Obst or Helki, Ryons understood what Spider meant. He'd seen the Wallekki, his masters, swallow their pride to serve the Thunder King. Every nation did what the Great Man demanded of them, because they were afraid. There was not a chief in this council who wouldn't have cut off his own fingers, one by one, or put out his own eyes, if the Great Man's mardar commanded it. Was not the Great Man greater than their gods?

Had he taken a moment to think about it, Ryons would not have spoken a word. But the words came out before he had a chance to think.

"Chief Looth! Why don't you give God a chance to protect you? The God who struck the mardar dead before your eyes, who gave you victory over the army of the Zeph—why not put your trust in Him?

"Chief Spider's right. The Thunder King will swallow up a people like yours and never spit them out again. But I think the real God will swallow him before he gets a chance to do it!

"Besides, you won't have to stay in the forest all the time. You'll be out scouting on the plains, along with the Wallekki and Chief Szugetai's horsemen. We can't just sit here in the woods and not know what's happening anywhere else. And I don't think we'll be staying in the woods forever. There's a throne waiting for me in Obann—but I'll never get there without you and all the other people in the army.

"I know you'd all go home, if only you could. But you can't! The only way you'll ever have a chance to go back is if you trust God and try to do what He wants. Tell them, Obst. You can tell it better than I can."

Ryons suddenly felt dizzy, and he almost fell off the tree-stump that served him as a throne. What was he doing, speaking like that to chieftains?

"He's right, my lords," said Obst. "The enemy will empty the Eastern lands. Army after army will come, rolling in along the same route we followed over the mountains. You can't possibly get back. Your only hope is in God and in the courage that He gives you."

Looth looked all around, catching the eyes of all the chieftains. Spider grinned at him.

"It'd be a great shame to us Attakotts," Looth said, "if we ran away while a lot of tattooed Abnaks stayed. They would tell their women and children, who would make up shameful songs about us. Their men would not want our scalps anymore."

He turned to Ryons and clapped, a gesture of respect among the Attakotts.

"Very well, Boy King!" he said. "I think I can keep my people here a little longer. I'll tell them what you've said, and give you their answer."

And he was back by noon, with his men's decision: the Attakotts would stay, as long as they were sent out onto the plains on scouting missions. Ryons thanked him. There weren't many Attakotts in the army, but he was glad not to lose them.

"You did mighty well, young king," Helki told him afterward. "It's a hard thing, when a man's home calls to him and he can't come."

"I don't know," Ryons said. "I was a slave. I don't think I know what a home is. I can't imagine wanting to go back to the Wallekki country. I'd much rather be here."

"You could do a lot worse for a home," said Helki, "than this forest."

CHAPTER 33

Martis in Obann

Martis crossed over to the New City by night, in an old boat that he'd left in a safe hiding place a few years ago. He'd been careful about hiding it, and it didn't leak.

The children didn't like being left behind at the ruined Temple.

"What are we supposed to do if you don't come back?" Jack said.

"You're much safer here than you'd be in Obann," Martis said. "Besides, I'll be back before sunup. It'll take me a few days to find a scholar and work out how to bring him here without a fuss. Judge Tombo's men will be patrolling the streets, on the lookout for trouble. Much better for you to stay here, where the Omah can watch over you."

So Jack and Ellayne remained in camp, huddled over their campfire—which they each wished, silently, they hadn't built so close to the hole leading down into the ancient cellar. Ham and Dulayl were still outside the Temple, but Wytt saw to it that they had water, and his friends protected them.

"Abombalbap stayed in a ruined castle overnight," Ellayne said, recalling a story from her book of adventures. "In the middle of the night, a beautiful lady came up out of the floor and made love to him; but the next morning, when he came out of the castle, he found out that a whole year had passed in a single night. The lady was an evil spirit, and a holy hermit had to come and drive her away. When he did, the whole castle crumbled into dust. My father read me that story when I was sick in bed."

"When I got sick, Van made me keep on working," Jack said, not missing his stepfather even a little bit. "Nobody ever told me a story."

"I just told you one."

"I'm not a little kid. I don't need stories."

"Everybody likes stories," Ellayne said. "Your mother would have told you stories, if she hadn't died."

In truth, Jack liked Ellayne's stories and liked having her tell them to him; but he wouldn't admit it.

"I wonder if there are any stories on that sheepskin in the jar," he said. "I wish we could read it. But Ashrof never taught me how to read that kind of writing."

"Do you trust Martis, Jack?"

"That's a silly question. Of course I trust him, after all this time. Don't you?"

"I suppose I do. But he says such terrible things about the Temple! If the First Prester was really as bad as all that—"

She never finished her sentence. Somewhere in the sprawling ruins, some creature howled. It wasn't quite like the howling of a stray dog on the streets of Ninneburky, or the howling of a wolf on the plain. This was a howl that belonged to some kind of animal that didn't have a name. Both of the children startled badly when Wytt and a couple of the City Omah burst unexpectedly into the circle of their firelight.

"Burn it, Wytt—don't do that!" Jack said.

"What was that howling, Wytt?" Ellayne asked. "Do you know?"

The Omah chattered together, then tried to answer.

"Big animal lives in a hole, comes out at night sometimes. We think it cries for a she-animal, but gets no answer."

"What kind of animal is it?" Jack asked.

"New kind, never seen before. Comes from outside. Big, with big teeth. Hunts rats. Black hair, but smells like snake. Omah stay away from it."

"So it's not a wolf?" Ellayne said.

"Not wolf. More like lizard. We have no name for it: new animal, no one ever see it before."

Jack added more vine-chunks to the fire.

Martis came back just before sunup, bringing some oil lamps, a bag of apples, a small jug of wine, and a couple of loaves of bread.

"I think I've picked out a scholar for us," he said. "I'll watch him for a few nights, find out all I can about the route he travels to and from the Temple, and where the patrols are in his neighborhood. When I can do it safely, I'll bring him here. But I'll have to be careful: the city's in a very uneasy mood."

"Why's that?" Ellayne asked.

"Everybody's worried about the war, and they hanged a prophet the other day. There are still a lot of prophets preaching in the streets, and the oligarchs don't like it."

"You can't hang a prophet!" Ellayne cried.

"That's what most people seem to be saying. The hanging was supposed to settle the people's minds, but it's done more harm than good."

They built up their fire, and as the night faded into dawn, made an early breakfast. One of the City Omah had his first taste of bread, and loudly chirped his approval. It wasn't such a bad place to camp, Ellayne thought, now that Martis was back. So it must be I do trust him, after all, she thought.

"I don't think there's much point in opening any more of the jars until we have our scholar present," Martis said. "Tonight I'll pick up some good, strong rope for us. We may as well make ourselves comfortable; we'll probably be here for a while."

"But not forever," Jack said. Ellayne and Martis didn't understand. "What I mean is, what do we do if it's true that these are the missing books, under the Old Temple, and we've found them? What do we do after we read them? Do we just let the scholar go? He'll tell everybody about us."

Martis answered with a sickly smile. "He will certainly tell Lord Reesh," he said, "and the patrols will come for us. When I kidnapped someone for my master, that was usually the last anybody ever saw of him."

"But we can't do that!" Ellayne said. "We can't murder anyone. We shouldn't even kidnap anyone!"

Jack had thought of that, too. But how could they just let a kidnapped scholar go, once they didn't need him anymore?

"She's right," he said. "We need an honest man, who'll help us because he wants to. We need someone like that old blind prester we met—except he couldn't see to read."

"You want me to just *ask* someone to come across the

river with me?" Martis said. The idea had never entered his head. "It seems I picked up some bad habits in Lord Reesh's service. I never thought of trying to find an honest man in Obann—certainly not anywhere near the Temple."

"There must be someone we shouldn't have to kidnap!" Jack said.

"God never sent us here to commit crimes," Ellayne said.

"No—I don't suppose He did," Martis agreed.

He caught a few hours' sleep, then returned to Obann late in the afternoon. "Skulking around in the dark, and acting like a man who doesn't want to be noticed, is the best way to get noticed by the patrols," he said.

Martis knew the city better than anyone. He grew up on its streets, fatherless. He'd been a thief and a cutpurse. As long as he could get a good start, he could escape any pursuit: he knew all the hiding places, and how to navigate the maze of streets and alleys.

He browsed the shops, keeping his ears open. Outside a fishmonger's, he found a little group of citizens huddled around a prophet. They had to huddle because this prophet was whispering, almost. She had no desire to be hanged. Martis edged closer so he could hear her.

"They can say what they please in the chamber house," the old woman was saying, "but this is what the Lord God says—He has forsaken them! Behold, their hearts are closed to me, says the Lord; but I shall open the gates of their city and give entry to the sword and pestilence. They shall all die in their sins."

A young man interrupted. "But the prester says we're going to win the war! God wants us to conquer the Heathen all the way out to the edge of the earth and do away with all their idols."

"Woe to them that preach a lie," said the old woman, "and to lying prophets who fill the people's ears with vanities! Cursed is that prophet who says, 'The Lord has said,' when I have not said, nor spoken to him."

"Keep your voice down!" said a younger woman. "Do you want to be hanged?"

Martis moved on. The city's mood was full of doom, and as yet the Heathen hosts were far away. The mood the people were in now, they'd never stand a siege.

He came within sight of the Temple. The rays of the setting sun turned into blood against the golden dome. People trudged slowly up and down its great stone steps, as he himself had done so often. But how many of them knew the secrets of the Temple as he did?

And then he froze, because a man who knew many of those secrets, and knew him, came walking down the steps straight toward him. It was Dicken, one of Lord Reesh's secretaries, a man who'd sometimes given him Lord Reesh's orders. If Reesh were to learn that his assassin lived and was in the city—well, that would be the end.

Martis relaxed, made way for Dicken to pass, and even caught his eye. And Dicken, seeing him but not recognizing him, nodded politely and walked right past him, intent on whatever errand sent him forth.

Martis wondered: have I changed so much that old friends don't know me—or had God dulled Dicken's sight? He sighed. There was no answering that question. But one way or another, he supposed, it was safe for him to talk to people, even to servants of the Temple.

The next day, with the aid of some of Ellayne's money and the clean, respectable clothes it bought, Martis had his supper at a public house in the shadow of the Temple in the company of reciters, archivists, and students of theology. He'd eaten there many times before, with Temple servants who knew him only as a lowly clerk of inventory. A few of those old acquaintances were there now, but no one recognized him. He introduced himself as a clerk for the prester's office in Durmurot, come to Obann to tie up a few loose ends left by the resignation of Prester Jod.

"Prester Jod, yes—he'll be missed," said a man at the other end of the table. "Pity about him."

"I confess I never understood why he had to resign so suddenly," Martis said. "But I was visiting one of the outlying chamber houses when it happened, and by the time I returned to Durmurot, he was out of office."

"It's no secret," a reciter said. "He didn't like the new Scripture Dr. Occus found tucked away in the archives."

"Don't let your prester hear you saying that," a student said.

Another student butted in. "Burn all that! Anyone can see it's just a forgery. Occus is the laughingstock of the seminary."

Martis generously bought a round of ale to keep them talking. They didn't need much encouragement. Without asking too many questions, he heard the tale of a scholar named Occus who'd discovered a hitherto unknown fragment of the Book of Batha the Seer—a few fascicles exhorting the people of Obann to destroy the Heathen and prophesying, so it seemed, the current war. A special committee under Prester Orth—Martis knew him as a sly one—authenticated the fragment; it was added to the Scripture and now being preached in every chamber house in the land. But Prester Jod and a few others had resigned rather than accept it. At least among his fellow scholars, Occus' reputation lay in ruins. This could be the man we need, Martis thought.

"But why?" he asked. "Was he not an able scholar? But perhaps he's in this room somewhere ..."

"He doesn't show his face here anymore," said a student. With subtlety, so that they hardly noticed he was asking, Martis learned where the disgraced scholar lived.

He's the one, Martis thought, and discarded all the other names he'd considered. No one will think it strange if he leaves the city for a while. And maybe he now has a grudge against the Temple hierarchy: something I can play on.

He decided to pay the man a visit.

CHAPTER 34

The Scholar and the Scrolls

The following evening found Martis loitering on a street under the north wall of the city, where Dr. Occus rented rooms in a respectable but inexpensive rooming house. He got a description of the scholar from a neighborhood shopkeeper, and so he knew him when he saw him come walking slowly up the street, home from his duties in the Temple archives. Martis scanned up and down the street with a trained eye, pleased to discover that Occus wasn't being followed. He walked alone with his thoughts, a little, bald fellow with little, bald thoughts—or so Martis imagined him to be.

As the man was about to walk past him, he spoke.

"Dr. Occus!"

The scholar stopped, looked him up and down.

"Yes—but do I know you, sir? I don't think I do."

"I know you by reputation, doctor. May I speak with you?"

"My reputation is not what it was, and I'm late for my supper."

"Forgive me for intruding," Martis said. "My matter is

of some importance, and must be discussed in privacy. You won't be sorry you listened, I can promise you that. Permit me to buy you something to drink."

It was the pot of ale that got him a hearing. Martis bought it at an alehouse across the street, then accompanied the scholar to his rooms. Occus had a sitting room and a bedroom on the second floor of the rooming house, with a flight of rickety wooden stairs in the back leading to his own private entrance. He had bread and smoked fish waiting for him. For all he hungered for knowledge and prized scholarship, Martis reflected, Lord Reesh was miserly about remunerating scholars. Occus sat down to his meal and didn't offer Martis anything to eat. He had none to spare.

"Suppose you start by telling me who you are and what you want with me," he said.

"My name's of no importance," Martis said. "What is important is that I need the help of a scholar, a man skilled in reading ancient documents—and who will think twice about running to the presters with any new discovery he might make."

Occus glared at him. "What makes you think I'm interested in making any new discoveries at all?"

"You've devoted your life to the pursuit of learning. I doubt you're ready to give it up. But you're probably disillusioned with the way the Temple handles new discoveries, and inclined to be cautious in your dealings with the presters. I'm looking for a man who can keep a secret, if necessary."

"What kind of secret?"

Martis leaned over the table and lowered his voice. "What would you say if I offered to show you some scrolls from the First Temple, still sealed in their original storage jars? What if you could be the first to read them?"

"I'd say it was poppycock," Occus answered. "I'd say anything like that was bound to be a forgery."

"I think, when you see them for yourself, you'll conclude that they are genuine."

"Let's see them, then."

"I didn't bring them with me," Martis said. "I've left them where I found them, jars unopened, except for two. If you come with me, I'll show them to you. But I'll ask you to swear an oath not to mention them to anyone else until I say you can."

"And why should such a find be kept secret?"

"Because I can't read the scrolls, and I have no idea what they'll say. It may be something that the Temple would pay a great deal of money for. It may even be something they would choose to suppress—something embarrassing to the powers that be."

Occus chewed his fish and sipped his ale, thinking. He would very much enjoy embarrassing those who had embarrassed him, Martis thought.

"May I be candid, doctor?"

"I think you'd better be."

"I came to you because you're the one who discovered, in the archives, a long-lost fragment of the writings of Batha the Seer," Martis said. "As was your duty, you passed it on to a higher authority. The presters authenticated it, proclaimed it Scripture. But among your colleagues there are serious doubts about it.

"Through no fault of your own, those doubts have come to rest on you. Those who believe the fragment is a forgery suspect you lent yourself to a dishonest purpose. Your good name has suffered. Not daring to criticize the Temple, the doubters criticize you. They even suggest you forged the document.

"You've suffered from this incident, but the Temple has neither defended nor rewarded you. You have reason to resent it—reason enough, maybe, to permit me to trust you.

"But if you don't want to see the scrolls, just say so, and I'll take my leave of you. I'll find someone else to read them for me. There are many scholars in Obann."

He'd seen a man's eyes light up like this before, for money. Occus had the same reaction to the prospect of obtaining knowledge—knowledge that no other scholar would possess, and that came with a subtle aftertaste of revenge.

"Where are the scrolls?" he asked.

"I'll take you to them."

A worldly man would not have gone along with him; but Occus had spent most of his life holed up in a cubicle with ancient documents or in a classroom, teaching. He was more like a child than any of his students were. Before the night was out, Martis had him in the boat and was rowing across the river. Occus hadn't even asked Martis his name.

"I've always believed there were great finds to be made in the Old City," he said. "I shouldn't be surprised you found something there. One of these days I meant to go over myself, with some of my students, and see what we could dig up. There must be troves of valuable material awaiting discovery."

"Why didn't you go?" Martis asked.

"Oh, there's always something else to do. One gets caught up in one's work. But I remember when we found King Azzam's signet ring—there was quite a bit of excitement over that."

He prattled on as Martis rowed. It was a clear night, with starlight glinting off the black water. Obann displayed clusters of lighted windows; but the ruins of the Old City brooded dark against the starry sky. Occus had had enough ale to fortify him against superstitious musings.

Martis lit a lantern and led him carefully through the rubble. He was sure Omah were watching them, but the little hairy men stayed out of sight. By now Martis knew the way even in the dark, and they reached the Empire Temple before the night was very old.

"Is it safe to go in there at night?" Occus asked.

"We have our camp within the Temple. It's perfectly safe."

Jack and Ellayne were waiting by the campfire. Wytt was nowhere in sight.

"Is this the scholar?" Jack asked.

"These are my grandsons, Jack and Layne," Martis said. "We came from the east, from the mountains. Boys, this is Dr. Occus. He has come to read the scrolls. Sit down by the fire, doctor."

"If I might see a scroll ..."

"Sit, and we'll show you."

When he was comfortable, Martis put the jar in his hands. Jack and Ellayne watched suspiciously as he examined it.

"You had to break the seal?"

"The seal was intact. The scroll is inside, rolled up, in an excellent state of preservation."

"May I take it out?"

"Of course."

With slow and delicate movements, he withdrew the scroll and set the jar aside. He handled the treated sheepskin as if he feared it might crumble to dust in his fingers. He'd probably had that experience, Martis thought.

By light of fire and lantern, he spent some long minutes poring over it.

"The paleography is perfect for the Late Kingdom period," he said, mostly to himself. "Of course, there are dozens of men in Obann who can imitate that kind of writing. But surely a forger would have aged the skin, or used a bit of ancient material that had no writing on it."

"But can you read it?" Jack said. "What does it say?"

"I'll read it better by the light of day," the scholar said. "The ink has faded just a little; and, as is typical of this period, there are no breaks between the words. But it appears to be some kind of itinerary—I think these must be the names of towns along a route traveled by the writer. But I can't do it justice by this light." He sighed and put the roll back into the jar. "You say you have more of these? In sealed jars like this one?"

"Lots of jars—thirty-seven of them, counting this one," Ellayne said.

"Where are they?"

"Under the Temple," Jack said, "in a cellar underneath the cellar."

Occus stared at him. "But that would be part of the original Temple!" he said, as if he thought it impossible that any part of the First Temple could exist.

"We think it is," said Martis.

"But this is incredible! You're not scholars. You're refugees in Obann, a man and his grandsons, chased out of your country by the Heathen. And yet you came here, to the Old City, to the ruined Temple—and found the remains of the First Temple. I think you ought to explain how you came to do that!"

"There's not much to explain," Jack said. "A prophet sent us."

CHAPTER 35

Remnants of the Legion

Helki didn't trust his men, who not so long ago were happy enough to follow Latt Squint-eye. But he trusted the Abnaks and their woodcraft. While the rest of the army followed him to the castle, he sent Abnaks out on scouting and foraging missions. He would much rather have gone foraging himself and let Andrus lead the way to the castle. But it didn't seem wise, just yet, to leave the army to its own devices. Those Heathen who were unused to woodlands grew more and more restive the farther they got from the open plains. Still, they did enjoy the venison that Helki's hunters brought them.

Once they arrived at the castle, the great task would be to get all these people settled down somehow.

"I've got plans for this place," he told Obst. "We may not be able to build it up into a proper castle again, but we can build a town around it with a stockade around the town. You can see the settlers have already gotten busy with their axes.

"Folks will need a safe place, and the king will need a place to hold his court. It might as well be here. There's plenty of water, plenty of game in the woods, and the land, once cleared, ought to be good for raising crops. Otherwise nobody ever would've put a castle here, I reckon."

The same evening Martis met with Dr. Occus, three of the Abnaks brought to the castle a dozen militiamen with a sergeant, survivors of the lost battle in the south. These had been wandering in the forest for days and were in no condition to fight. They might have, had they known the reputation of the Abnaks. But they were farm boys from the land around Trywath, far out to the west, and they'd never heard of Abnaks. They came with the scouts willingly, bringing the news of the destruction of their legion.

"Are there many more of you?" asked Helki.

"I suppose there must be," said the sergeant, a grey-haired man named Vord. "Once our front line broke, everybody started running. It was kind of shameful; but I thought I might as well run, too. The battle was lost, no mending it; and I had to stay with these boys.

"But who are all these people here? They look like the enemy!"

Helki grinned. When Obst translated for the chieftains, they laughed.

"They were the enemy," Helki said, "but now we're all together in the forest, trying to survive. But we're not so badly off. We've got a teacher, a prophet—and a king."

Now everyone knew that Obann had kings in ancient times, as told in Scripture; but to speak of a king today was unheard-of. The sergeant's jaw dropped.

"Don't let the oligarchs hear that you've set up a king for yourselves," he said. "You'll swing for it, that's certain."

"I don't think so," Helki said. "Anyhow, it was God's doing, not ours.

"Look around you, Vord. The whole world's changing. You heard the bell, didn't you? Out on the plains, there are birds as big as horses. Here in the woods, there are animals that have no names. A couple of little kids climbed all the way up Bell Mountain and rang King Ozias' bell—and God heard it.

"When this war's over, if it's ever over, there might not be any oligarchs. There might not even be an Obann City. Might not even be a Temple. But we have a prophet who says God means to give Ozias' throne to this king of ours, and we believe her."

Vord shook his head. "The country's full of prophets, nowadays. They all talk moonshine."

"Ours doesn't," Helki said; and saying it, he finally believed it in his heart: Jandra was indeed a prophet and spoke the words God gave her.

There might be hundreds of militiamen still alive but lost in the forest, and Helki wanted to round up as many as he could and add them to the army. If there ever came a day when the army would have to emerge from the forest and give battle, Helki wanted it to be as strong an army as possible. But first these militiamen would have to be won over to King Ryons.

Before presenting Vord and his men to the king, Helki told them Ryons' story.

"He was the lowest of the low," he said, "a Heathen slave, and only a child. He was about to be sacrificed to one of the Heathen gods when the true God struck the priest dead in front of all the chiefs.

"This was once an enemy army come to Obann as invaders. But the other Heathen hosts turned against them, to wipe them out. So they put their trust in God, and He saved them. Of their own free will they chose this slave boy to be their king. That's when the prophet spoke."

In an open space within the castle's walls, the chieftains pitched their big black tent. Helki brought the militiamen there to meet the king. Abgayle brought Jandra, and Jandra brought her bird with teeth.

Ryons had no throne, just a square-cut building stone to sit on. The chieftains sat around him on their stools, in all their finery.

Making a show of it had been Shaffur's idea. "If we're going to call this boy a king, we ought to treat him like one," the Wallekki chieftain said. He'd once visited a real king, in a city far to the south in a great oasis in the desert, so he knew how a king's court ought to look. The other chieftains agreed with him: no royalty without a show of royalty. For Ryons this meant a thorough scrubbing in cold springwater. "I'd almost rather be sacrificed!" he said; for Helki and Uduqu administered the scrubbing, and their hands were hard. But he looked more like a king now that he was clean, Shaffur said.

He sat on his makeshift throne and received the militiamen. The chieftains had draped him in a scarlet cape, and Shaffur laid a sword across his knees. And Obst taught him that a king, more so than other men, was a servant of the Lord. "Always remember that, my boy," he said. "To whom much is given, from him much will be required."

Ryons understood very little of it; but he did understand that the fierce men who had made him a king could just as easily unmake him, and he had no desire to provoke them.

"Your Majesty," Helki said, "these are men from one of Obann's legions. Their sergeant, Vord, is a veteran man of war. They'd be a very useful addition to your host."

"Here, now!" Vord said. "I never said we wanted to join up."

"Then we'll have to send you away," Helki said. "You're in the forest by the king's leave. There's no oligarchy here."

"But he's just a boy!"

"So were all the kings of Obann, once," said Obst. "But he'll be a man someday. And someday he will have Ozias' throne."

The militiamen looked at one another. Few in Obann had ever read the Scriptures for themselves, but all knew the name of Ozias, the last of the anointed kings.

"The Temple preaches that this war is a holy war, by God's will," one of them said. "If we joined up with you, we'd be going against the Temple. And that'd be going against God, wouldn't it?"

"What do we care for your Temple?" Chief Spider said. "But we do care very much for God, who gives us victory over our enemies and protects us from the Thunder King. I thought He was the westmen's God, your God—but it seems you care more for the Temple than you care for Him."

"You said you had a prophet," Vord said. "Show us this prophet."

"You're looking at her," Helki said. He bent down to touch the top of Jandra's head. She was sitting on the stony ground, intently watching a beetle. "This is our prophet. God speaks to us through her."

Vord's lip curled. "This is foolishness!" he said. He might have said something more cutting, but one look at the chieftains' faces restrained him. "But you can't be serious!" he said. "She's just a little girl. You can't expect us to believe she's a prophet and this boy a king."

Some of the chieftains scowled at that. Ryons quieted them, holding up his hand.

"Let these men go, Helki," he said. "We can't make them believe. I don't think I was made a king just so I could make a slave of someone else. Show them the way out of the forest."

Helki made no answer, but bowed—as Shaffur had taught them all to bow when receiving a command from the king.

"As you wish, Your Majesty," he said. "We'll give them a meal and a night's rest and send them on their way tomorrow morning. Andrus, take them away and give them something to eat."

When the militiamen were gone, Ryons looked uneasily at his chieftains.

"I didn't say the wrong thing, did I?" he asked.

Spider shook his head. "We didn't need them, Majesty. Let them go and lose more battles for their Temple."

Even so, when the militiamen departed the next morning, three stayed behind to serve the King of Lintum Forest.

CHAPTER 36

King Ozias Speaks

As soon as it was light enough for him to read, Occus bent over the scroll and studied it.

There was something about him that made Ellayne uneasy. Maybe it was the gleam that came into his eyes when he touched the scroll: you'd think he was going to eat it. And since his arrival, Wytt hadn't shown himself, nor any of the City Omah. She doubted they were afraid of him; he'd be more likely to be afraid of them. But she was a little bit afraid of him—which was silly, with Martis here to protect them.

The scholar didn't say a word until Martis finally prodded him. "Well, doctor? Can you read it?"

"Of course I can read it!" he snapped. "As I suspected when I glanced at it last night, it's an itinerary. The narrator journeyed up the river, and he lists the cities and towns he visited. Some of the names are familiar to me, and some aren't. He also mentions various persons, local officials and the like. Now do be quiet!"

Jack wandered off a little ways, out of earshot. Ellayne joined him.

"What do you think of him?" she whispered.

"I'm thinking Wytt doesn't like him for some reason—I can't imagine why," Jack said. "And I'm thinking that at the rate he's going, we'll be all grown up by the time he reads all the scrolls."

They went off to tend to Ham and Dulayl, still hobbled outside the ruined Temple. Omah watched over them, although none were anywhere in sight just now—which didn't mean they weren't there. Jack slipped the hobbles, and they led the beasts to a hole in the pavement where Martis had found good water and then took them for a walk to stretch their legs. By the time they returned to camp, Occus had finished reading the scroll.

"You say there are thirty-seven of these?" he said.

"I counted them," Ellayne said.

"I need to see more. I'd especially like to see the place where you found them."

"I'm afraid that's not possible," Martis said. "The way in is safe enough for children, but would be dangerous for a grown man. My grandsons will have to bring the jars up to you."

Jack and Ellayne exchanged a look, both wondering why Martis had said that. He doesn't quite trust Occus, either, Ellayne thought. But Jack thought it would just be too hard for Martis to haul Occus up out of the ancient cellar.

"I must see the site as it is," said the scholar. "There might be suspicions of fraud, otherwise. You do understand that a skillful person, with no more knowledge than I have, might have fabricated these scrolls."

"Of course," Martis said. "But we would need a long and sturdy ladder to get you down into the crypt, and we haven't one."

"Then I suggest you go back across the river and buy one! This is important work, and it must be done properly."

Martis promised to get a ladder the next day. "But in the meantime, I think we ought to open another jar. We don't know that there are scrolls in all of them."

After an inner struggle, Occus agreed to that. *He's greedy*, Ellayne thought. *He can't wait, even if he knows he should.*

"Wait for us here, doctor. We won't be long," Martis said.

"Can't I come with you into the cellars?"

"Not until we get a ladder for you."

"What if he runs back to the city while we're down here," Jack asked, as Martis prepared to lower him into the cellar beneath the cellar, "and comes back with a bunch of people from the Temple?"

"He won't. Believe me, he has no cause to trust the Temple. The last thing he wants is for any other scholar to see these scrolls—not until he's seen them all."

So Jack went down and got another jar. They were all exactly alike, so there was no reason to choose one over another. And Occus was still there when they came up again. Martis handed him the jar, and he examined the seal.

"The ancients made a special glue to seal these jars," he explained. "Very few have been found intact. Jars do get broken, after all. We'll have to break this one open. But wait!"

He'd been turning it over in his hands, and he did something that Martis hadn't thought to do with the first one: he looked on the bottom. What he saw excited him.

"Look!" He jabbed at it with a finger. "This jar is stamped

with the insignia of the royal house of Obann!"

Stamped into the clay was a circle enclosing a figure of a king's crown and a shepherd's crook. It was a small thing, easy to miss. Martis picked up the first jar, looked at the bottom, and found the insignia there, too—only worn away a little.

"Open it!" Jack said.

Occus hemmed and hawed, muttering something about anyone being able to make an earthen jar and stamp a seal on it. "Doesn't mean it's genuine," he said. But when Martis offered to crack it open, the scholar got busy with his knife. Finally he drew out another rolled-up sheepskin.

"It's either a forgery," he said, "or in an excellent state of preservation."

Jack and Ellayne traded a look. They knew it couldn't be a fake. Had anyone been in the ancient cellar, the Omah would have said so.

"Read it," Martis said. "Aloud, if you can."

Occus read slowly, tracing the words with his finger.

"The testament of Ozias, the son of Halgar: So says the Lord, you are old and you shall die here, and be gathered to your fathers—" He looked up from the scroll.

"It can't be!" he said.

"Read," said Martis.

"Nevertheless, you have written down all the deeds you have done under the sun. I have led you by the hand through many countries, and swept away your enemies before you. And I said, Yes, Lord: they have not profited from the evil that they did to me; I have seen the destruction which you visited upon their heads, and there are none of them left upon the earth.

"I have obeyed your commandment and wandered east and west, and sojourned with the heathen; and now I am indeed old, and have returned. Behold, I have planted my seed where none shall find it; and now I plant your Word where none shall read it."

Occus stopped again. His face shone with sweat.

"What's the matter?" Martis said.

"You are asking me to believe that I hold in my hands the last writings of King Ozias—that he came back to this place after the Temple was destroyed. Impossible!"

"Why impossible? Scripture doesn't tell us where Ozias died, or when, or how—only that he fled into the East, across the mountains, and was never seen again. Why couldn't he have returned here, many years later?"

"If I were to present these scrolls to my colleagues," Occus said, "I'd be laughed out of the city! Who knows that better than I?

"There have always been legends about Ozias. God translated him into Heaven, so he never died; God removed him to an island on the far side of the sea, where he enjoys eternal youth. Or this one, that he came back to Obann as an old man and saw the ruins of the city. But those are tales for simpletons and children! Who else would believe them?"

Ellayne thought of her book that chronicled the adventures of Abombalbap, which her father always said were make-believe. "Don't your scholars believe the stories that the Scriptures tell?" she asked.

"You mean the Children of Geb crossing the sea on stepping-stones miraculously raised up for them by God?" he snarled. "Or those tales of Bron the Giant? Or maybe the one about the Imperial River parting so that Arza and his wives and daughters could escape from the chariots of the pagans!

"Those were primitive people who first told such stories and whose descendants wrote them down. They lived in a world that was half their own imaginations. They dreamed up stories to explain things they couldn't understand. A great deal of Scripture consists of such stories. No one takes them literally. If things like that ever really happened, miracles and all, they wouldn't stop happening. They'd still be happening today!"

Jack thought he'd never heard such foolishness. "That shows how much you know!" he said. "Burn it, all you have to do is look around! Well, we've been—"

Martis held up a hand and gave him such a glare that he fell silent. Jack had been about to say, "We've been up Bell Mountain." But Martis was right, he thought: better not let that slip out.

"Never mind, Jack," Martis said. "Occus, read the rest."

It didn't take too long. The letters on the scroll were large, and there wasn't room for much.

But Jack's heart raced. King Ozias, who'd lived so long ago, was speaking to them out of these scrolls: King Ozias, who'd put the bell on Bell Mountain, was speaking to the very persons who'd rung that bell.

Jack had no doubts. It had been Ozias himself who'd been in that cellar beneath the cellar, writing the scrolls and sealing them in jars. He must have had servants to do the heavy work of clearing the rubble and shoring up the ceiling. And whatever he'd written on these scrolls, it must have been important.

"'I shall tell you of the things to come in latter days, and you shall write them down and seal them with a seal: so that when these things come to pass, those generations shall confess, Behold, the Lord has told us! And they shall know that my words which I have caused you to record are true words.'

"It ends there," Occus said.

The sun was by now low in the sky, so they would learn no more until tomorrow.

CHAPTER 37

Ozias' Prophecy

Before the army was settled on the land around the castle, Helki sent scouts to the northern plains to watch for the arrival of the Heathen host that had destroyed Silvertown. It was a good thing he did. The scouts came back in a hurry, reporting that the great host was making straight for the eastern end of Lintum Forest. The chieftains assembled in the tent to interrogate the scouts.

"It's a great army, my lords—much bigger than ours," said the Wallekki horseman in command of his scouting party. "They have thrice our number, at least."

"What kind of men do they have?" Shaffur asked.

"Wallekki cavalry, mostly of the Wal-Kallut clans in the south: at least a thousand. Of footmen, maybe ten thousand, mostly Easterners from around the lakes. Uskut spearmen, Shurun archers, and some black men from much farther south, Hosa with short spears and long shields. They have machines, too, but those are for battering down the gates of cities—not much use in a forest."

"You're sure they're coming here?" Helki said.

"Had they meant to stay on the plains, they would have turned before now. But I left the Attakotts to make sure of them and Abnaks along the fringes of the woods."

"Well, then, it's bad news for us, but good news for the oligarchs in Obann," Helki said.

"There is another army close behind this one, my lords," the scout said.

"It seems we've made the Great Man very angry indeed," said Chief Zekelesh, of the Fazzan.

"These nations that you mentioned: I've never heard of most of them," Helki said. "What kind of countries do they come from?"

"They are all plainsmen, chieftain."

A grin spread itself over Helki's face. "Then they won't know much about fighting in a forest, will they?" he said. "Your Majesty, give me the Abnaks and all my own men who were outlaws, and we'll go to meet these Easterners."

"If there's going to be fighting, we want to come, too," said Szugetai.

"It won't be fighting fit for horsemen," Helki said.

"Then we'll fight on foot! We may not get rich in this war, but we can still try to get famous."

Obst shook his head. "Warlord, we fight to stay alive. We are all servants of the living God. The glory is His, not ours."

"Surely He can understand a warrior's heart," Szugetai said. "We didn't come here to sit on our shields while the Abnaks do the fighting."

"Very well said!" Shaffur cried. "We have scores to settle with the Wal-Kallut. We won't be left behind."

Helki and Obst wrangled with the chieftains, and Ryons sat on his stone throne not daring to say a word. What if they should start fighting among themselves? I'll be the first to have his head lopped off, he thought.

They were still at it when they were interrupted and silenced by an unearthly shriek. Into the tent came strutting the toothed bird that belonged to Jandra, rattling its dirty plumage. Some of the chiefs shrank back from it, thinking it no natural creature. After it came Abgayle, holding Jandra by the hand. The little girl's face was blank; by now they all knew what that meant. They kept silence for her. Still holding Abgayle's hand, she spoke—in that voice that was not her own.

"I have heard my people, and I will surely make them famous. If they keep my commandments, I shall make their names honorable among men.

"Szugetai the son of Ogotai shall go to this battle, but he shall not return. He shall humble himself before me, and I will keep his soul; nor will the generations of my people ever forget his name.

"Let my people go forth against the Heathen, for I have delivered them into your hands. Be bold and of good courage, for the Lord shall fight for you. But take not the whole army out against the Heathen, but only a thousand picked men; and by these I will destroy ten thousand. And I shall give glory to Helki, for I have chosen him."

With that, Jandra fell asleep and Abgayle gathered her up in her arms. But all the chieftains looked at Szugetai.

He shrugged. "If I've offended God, I'm sorry," he said. "But at least He has given me what I asked for."

Eventually they had to let Occus go down into the cellar. They couldn't bring up all the jars. What would happen to the scrolls if it rained? Martis bought a ladder and more lamps, and for the first time, went down with them.

"Now do you believe the find is genuine?" he said.

Occus went all around the room, studying it, even getting down on his hands and knees to examine the floor. Jack and Ellayne wondered what he was looking for. He studied the rocks in the rock-piles, too. Some time went by before he spoke.

"There can be no doubt of it," he said. "This floor is natural stone, small pieces cut to fit. This room is part of the original Temple, not necessarily the cellar. The Empire Temple was built on top of it."

"And King Ozias' scrolls?" Jack asked.

"If they are a fraud, at least they are a very ancient fraud," said the scholar. "It may be some of Ozias' followers, or people who remembered him, hoping to reestablish the monarchy, thought this would be the way to do it: create a message from Ozias. There's no way to know. But what I would like to know is exactly how you found this place!"

"We've told you—a prophet sent us," Martis said.

"A prophet! Did he tell you exactly where to look, in all this vast ruin?"

Wytt had still not shown himself since Occus' arrival, nor had any of the Omah.

"Someone showed us," Jack said, "but we can't tell you who it was."

"What kind of someone?"

"Why don't you just read the rest of the scrolls, doctor?" Martis said.

It took him three more days to read them all. He read them on the spot; he didn't want any more of them taken out of the room.

When he read them exactly as they were written, he was the only one who could understand the language.

"What language is it?" Ellayne asked. "Is it one of the Heathen languages?"

"Oh, no—it's our own, as it was spoken two thousand years ago. It's changed a lot since then."

"But it does sound like I could almost understand it; only I can never quite make it out," Jack said.

"It wouldn't be hard to learn, then?" Martis said.

"Easier than any foreign language."

But of course it was the story, not the language, that mattered; and much else besides a story.

The story was the easy part. Ozias wandered in the East, settled somewhere beyond the Great Lakes, married a Heathen woman, and had children. No more a king, he lived as just a herdsman. But when he was old, and his children were all grown up with children of their own, God called him to return to Obann. The city had not yet been rebuilt. With a few loyal priests—they were like presters, only there were no chamber houses then: just the Temple itself—to minister to him, Ozias settled among the ruins of the Temple and spent a year writing the scrolls. God showed him things in dreams and visions, and he wrote them down; and then he died.

But there were thirty-seven scrolls, and most of what they had to say was obscure even to the scholar. He couldn't explain it to them.

"It's prophetic visions—and who knows what they mean!" Occus said. "Some of it seems to foretell the rise of the Empire, and its fall. Some of it speaks of things that would happen long after the Empire fell. It says the city of the Temple, this city, will be destroyed by fire from the sky. And there seems to be a prophecy concerning still another Temple—that would be three—and its destruction, too.

"But it's all couched in prophetic language: it will not give up its secrets easily! There's enough here to keep a whole college of scholars and theologians busy for a hundred years. So don't ask me what it means!"

"I don't think we need to ask," Martis said; and there was something in his eyes that suddenly made it easy for Jack to believe he used to kill people for a living. "Three temples, three destructions. We're in one; the second lies in ruins, over our heads; and the third still stands, across the river."

"That means Obann's going to lose the war, then—doesn't it?" Ellayne said.

Occus shook his head. "That's just a simpleminded way of looking at it!" he said. "Laymen think they can interpret prophecy, but they deceive themselves. I've studied ancient writings all my life. I don't need children to interpret them for me."

"Nevertheless," Martis said, "what people think the writings mean can be much more important than what they really mean."

"Listen to me—please!" Occus appealed to them with outstretched hands. "It's pointless to argue about these things down here. These scrolls need to be taken to a safe place and studied, for years, by the most learned scholars in the land. It's a wonderful thing you've done, finding them; but now your part in this business is over.

"These scrolls must be copied. They must be compared to other scrolls we have. Savants must be allowed to study and discuss them. You have no idea how much work has to be done before we can even try to interpret them. No idea at all!"

Jack and Ellayne didn't understand, but Martis seemed to.

"I suppose you must be right," he said. "You're the scholar, after all. Certainly we aren't accomplishing anything, arguing about it down here, other than to use up the oil in our lamps. I suggest we go back up to camp and have our supper."

CHAPTER 38

The Flail of the Lord

Helki divided his thousand men into small parties, with his own Lintum Forest men to guide them to their places. It was no pitched battle that he planned to fight; that couldn't be done in dense woods.

"I don't know about battles," he said, "but I do know a thing or two about hunting. We're going to hunt the enemy like you'd hunt a wild boar."

Before he left, Szugetai requested an audience with the king and Obst. They met in a room of the old castle that had no roof, but four solid walls to ensure their privacy.

"I have told my men that I will probably die in this engagement," the horse-lord said. "That will leave them without a master of their own blood. Among our people, only a man who is born to be a chief can be a chief.

"We are farther from home than any of our race has ever been, in lands that have no names among us. There is no way back. So we might as well stay with you! And this is what I have done: hear me.

"When I die, my king, my men will become your men, as if you were their father and they were your sons. They will be faithful to you to the death. They will protect you. When you are older, you will protect them. They have sworn an oath before God—not any of our gods, who are not worth very much, but the Great God who has made you king.

"If He really is God, then He will overthrow the Thunder King no matter how many armies he commands. You, old man, have taught us to believe in this God.

"We were brought up to believe that when a man dies, he joins the spirits of his ancestors in the World of Darkness, and only his fame lives on after him. We now understand that that was a silly thing to believe, when there is a real God, up above, who knows us all by name. We have not yet learned much about Him, but those of us who live will learn more.

"Be good to my men, O King. You may find some of our ways peculiar, but you'll find my men brave and loyal. And I think you'll have need of them."

Szugetai bowed at the waist. He would have turned on his heel and walked off, just like that; but Ryons cried out after him.

"Szugetai! Wait!"

"Yes, my king?"

Ryons held back tears. He'd been afraid of this man: squat, bowlegged, who spoke a language that sounded like dogs barking. He'd seen him in battle: he was terrible. But now, at the thought of seeing him no more, he felt as if his heart would crack. He was sure a real king wouldn't feel like that, but he couldn't help it. Nor did he know what a real king ought to say.

"I'll be as good to your men as if they were my brothers," was all he could think of saying. "I'll try to be as good to them as you've been to me."

Szugetai grinned. "Then that will be good indeed!" he laughed. And that was the last Ryons ever saw of him.

Then the tears came, and he glared at Obst.

"I really hate being a king!" he said.

"I think that's one of the attributes of being a good king," Obst answered.

"But I don't want men going out and dying for me! I'd rather be a slave again!"

Obst put an arm around his shoulders. He had no way of knowing that Ryons had very early in life lost the habit of crying. No one listened when a slave cried, and he might get a beating if he cried too loud.

"They don't die for you, Ryons," he said. "They fight and die because the human heart is dark and sinful, and in these days there is a great evil loose in the world. Men have to fight to save their lives.

"By the mercy of God, these men who are with us fight against that evil. They came west as servants of the Thunder King, but now they are his enemies. They came as Heathen, but now they are God's. Who could have imagined it?

"You're God's, too. You were a slave, but He made you a king. I was a hermit, and He made me His minister to an army of barbarians. We're not to blame for where we are today. All we can do is trust in Him and do the best we can."

A forest is no place for an army of plainsmen. The Easterners felled trees to cut a road for their supply wagons. Their Wal-Kallut cavalry, so useful on the plains, could go no faster than the men on foot. Black flies tormented horses and riders alike.

The army couldn't have ventured into the forest at all if they hadn't hired a score of outlaw woodsmen as guides. Helki let the host advance some distance into the woods before letting his bowmen pick off the guides. The enemy tried to press on without them—a mistake.

Acting under Helki's orders, little bands of Abnaks would burst out of the underbrush along the army's flanks, shriek like devils, cut down a few men, and be gone before the enemy could resist. Szugetai's men, unseen by the enemy, sang unnerving war songs in their own language: they had a way of singing from deep down in the throat, and it sounded hardly human. Helki's bowmen shot riders out of their saddles; and ahead of the army's line of march, his woodsmen chopped down trees to block its path. These could only be removed with hard labor.

Helki changed his plan when he realized the weather was about to change.

"It's going to rain tomorrow," he told Szugetai, "and hard, too. I want everybody brought together tonight so we can hit them on both flanks tomorrow—but only after they've been rained on for a while. If that doesn't chase them out of here, I miss my guess."

"They won't run," said Szugetai. "Have you seen that man in the feathered headdress, the one with half his body painted blue? He's their mardar. While he lives, they will all obey him."

"It won't be easy to get him," Helki said. "He always puts himself in the middle of the crowd."

"Leave him to me," Szugetai said.

True to Helki's prediction, it began to rain the next day, late in the morning, after the army had been marching for an hour. It came down hard and cold, as Helki knew it would: as it always did in this part of the forest in this season of the year. But the strangers from the East could not know that.

Helki let them struggle in it for another hour, then launched his attack. The men made as much noise as they could, and it broke the invaders' spirit. Having grown accustomed to an enemy they could not see, its sudden appearance made Helki's force seem many times its number. For all the ten thousand knew, they were being attacked by twenty thousand.

As he'd promised, Szugetai cut down the mardar; and then the mardar's bodyguard felled him. But with the loss of the Great Man's agent among them, the men of the East panicked. They stampeded into the woods in every direction. Later, most of them rallied behind their surviving chieftains—but only to retrace their path out of Lintum Forest. Helki let them go, forbidding the Abnaks to give chase.

"It's a shame," said Hlah, the son of Spider, "not to harvest so great a crop of scalps. They'll be back someday."

"But not soon," Helki said.

They found Szugetai beside the body of the mardar, dead, but with a smile on his face. No more than a dozen of King Ryons' men had died in the assault, but there were hundreds of dead Easterners—some, oddly, without a mark on their bodies. Hlah thought they must have died of fear.

"What'll we do with them?" asked Andrus. "It'd take a week to bury them all."

But Helki gave that task to the hundreds of prisoners they'd taken. With one of the Wallekki subchiefs to translate for him, he addressed them in a group.

"It would serve you right, all of you, if I sold you for slaves and pocketed the money," he said. "But King Ryons is my chief, and he's merciful. So we'll let you live and provide you with an escort out of our forest—once you've finished burying your friends. If you're wise, you won't come back.

"And one more thing you can do: you can take the head of your mardar with you and tell the world that King Thunder doesn't have a future. Whether he comes over the mountains himself, or stays in his castle out beyond the lakes, the true God will find him out and deal with him."

One of the captured Wal-Kallut was bold enough to ask a question: "Who shall we say has dared to speak thus?"

Helki pondered his answer for a moment.

"It doesn't much matter who I am," he said. "I'm just a man named Helki. It's God your Great Man ought to be afraid of—the true God, who is Lord of all."

The prisoners looked here and there at the shambles all around them, and many of them nodded. But Hlah cried out, "Helki, the flail of the Lord!" And all the men in Helki's following took up the cry, to celebrate their triumph: "The flail of the Lord!" It made Helki uneasy to hear it, but he didn't know how to stop them.

CHAPTER 39

How Occus Escaped

Occus continued to plead for the scrolls to be taken to his seminary, and Martis kept putting him off—never quite saying no, but never saying yes. They wrangled all through supper and into the night.

"If it's money you want—and I agree that you deserve a reward—I'm sure my school will be generous," Occus said.

"How generous?" Martis asked.

"I don't know! Do I strike you as a man who has a lot of experience with money? You can discuss that with the preceptor of the seminary."

Ellayne gave Jack a worried look. He knew what she was thinking: if Martis sold the scrolls, he might as well sell them, too. And the world would never see King Ozias' message, buried in the ruins for ages, now to be buried again in a scholars' library.

At last the two men agreed to sleep on it, and everyone lay down for the night. Jack lay on his back and fell asleep trying to count the stars.

A sharp jab in his arm and a shrill cry in his ear jarred him awake.

Wytt was back, along with several of the City Omah. The fire had just about died, and it was dark. The little hairy men were frantic, jumping up and down. Wytt jabbed Jack again, with his little pointed stick.

"Wake, wake!" he chirped. "City man hurt White-face, and he takes your things!"

Ellayne got up, too. They found Martis sprawled on his back with his forehead bleeding. Around him lay the fragments of an earthen jar.

"He took the scrolls!" Ellayne said.

"Can you stop him, Wytt?" Jack asked.

The Omah showed his teeth in something very like a grin. "Oh, yes! We can stop him."

"Then let's go. You look after Martis," Jack told Ellayne.

The Omah all rushed off, Jack following. Ellayne ran after him, but he didn't know that until she caught up to him.

"Why didn't you stay?"

"Somebody had to bring a torch!" she said. "We can't see in the dark like Wytt."

They couldn't keep up with the Omah, but they could follow them by the high-pitched squeals and squeaks they made. Occus must be hearing it, too, Jack thought. He'd get a nasty surprise when he saw what was making all the noise.

"You shouldn't have left Martis," Jack said.

"Well, what was I going to do for him?" Ellayne answered. "What do you do for someone who's had his head bashed in?"

"You might have looked to see if he was still alive!"

"He is. Didn't you hear him snoring?"

They couldn't stop to argue. By moonlight, starlight, and torchlight, they tried to overtake the Omah. Their cries were always somewhere ahead of them, the criers out of sight. Jack and Ellayne scrambled up and down heaps of rubble. Jack fell once and cracked his elbow.

"I knew there was something wrong about that man," Ellayne panted, as she helped him up.

"Martis wouldn't have expected a little toad like that to clout him one," Jack said. "Dear Lord, I hope he'll be all right! What if he needs a doctor?"

"We'll have to get him one, somehow. But I think—"

She never finished the sentence. Somewhere up ahead, in the dark, a man's hoarse scream drowned out the shrilling of the Omah.

Jack and Ellayne rushed around the corner of a ruined wall. The screams had stopped, but the Omah were louder and shriller than ever.

They were amazed to find themselves only a stone's throw from the water. There they saw two things. The first was a rowboat on the river, with a man in it paddling clumsily away from the bank. It could only be Occus, in Martis' boat.

But the other thing they saw was a crowd of Omah hopping about, scolding, threatening, surrounding a strange beast that hissed and snapped at them. This was the sight that stopped them, skidding, in their tracks.

What was it? It had a long, flat head with long jaws full of pointed teeth, with long, sharp fangs up front. It was big, as big as a grown man, and it pounced and feinted on short, stout limbs. Behind it swung a long, stiff tail. You'd think it was some kind of giant lizard; but its body was covered with stiff, dark hair, and it had a pair of ridiculous little ears behind the corners of its mouth. And it dripped and slavered like a dog.

It kept lunging at the Omah, but they were too agile to be caught. Its eyes gleamed in the moonlight.

When it saw Ellayne's torch, it froze for a moment, glared at her, and hissed like a snake. And then, with a leap, it scattered the Omah out of its way and scuttled off into the ruins. A few of the little men gave chase, chirping and squealing. And Jack and Ellayne could breathe again.

But Occus had the only boat.

"Burn it, he got away!" Jack said. "That's trouble."

"Here, here!" Wytt called. "Come see!"

Ellayne went first, Jack following her to the water's edge where the boat must have been. Wytt was waiting for them, pointing at something with his stick.

Three scrolls lay on the ground. When Ellayne bent to pick one up, she saw something else.

"Look at this, Jack. There's blood on the ground."

"Snake-beast bit him: then he dropped your things," Wytt said. "We came, the beast turned on us, and man went out on the water. Omah can't catch him on water."

"He'll tell people about us," Jack said, "and then the First Prester's men will come looking for us."

"Then we'd better not be here when they do," Ellayne said. "Come on, let's see if we can wake Martis. They'll kill him if they find out who he is."

"At least we've got the scrolls," said Jack.

He was sitting up when they got back to camp, with his head in his hands. Wytt had to lead them back, or they never would have found their way.

"Are you all right?" Ellayne said.

"It's my pride that's hurt," Martis said. "I never dreamed he'd have the nerve to hit me. I was careless."

"He got away, Martis," Jack said. "He tried to take some scrolls, but he dropped them and we got them back. But he got away with your boat."

"An animal bit him," Ellayne said. "Something like a snake, with hair and legs."

Martis sighed, and looked at the blood on his hands. "He was just coming up from the cellar when I woke," he said. "I was a fool to buy him a ladder. I asked him what he was doing, and he picked up a jar and broke it over my head. I never even had a chance to stand up. I never thought he was the type to do it."

"He's going to tell them all about us, isn't he?" Jack said.

"He wants the scrolls. He can't get them without help. I suppose he thinks he can sell them to Lord Reesh, the more fool him."

Jack clenched his fists. It was robbery, and he was furious.

"We can't take them with us in the jars," Martis said, "so I guess we'll have to break the jars. We can wrap the scrolls in a blanket, and Ham can carry them."

"You rest for a little while," Ellayne said. "Jack and I will get the scrolls. It won't take long. But you're hurt. You're going to need a bandage. Your head looks terrible."

"It doesn't feel very good, either," Martis said.

CHAPTER 40

Lord Reesh's Awakening

A chamberlain pulled the bed-curtains aside, and with profuse apologies, awoke Lord Reesh.

"Cusset criminal knave! What's this?" The First Prester growled through his teeth and squinted his eyes against the feeble lamplight.

"Your pardon, Your Holiness! It is a messenger from my lord Judge Tombo, and the judge himself is on his way here to see you. The matter is very urgent."

"What matter, flea-face?"

"My lord, I was not told."

Knowing as he did that nothing short of a disaster would get his friend out of bed in the middle of the night, Reesh submitted to the circumstances. His servants dressed him in his warmest robe, gave him warmed wine to drink. When he asked, they informed him it was still two hours before sunup. His only consolation was that Tombo would be feeling even more miserable than he did.

The judge was waiting for him in his private office, with a heavy cloak thrown over his sleeping clothes. Reesh dismissed the servants and had them shut the door.

"You look wretched," he said.

"That well, eh?" Tombo said. "Better than I feel, no doubt. But I have news that won't wait."

They both sat down.

"One of my patrols picked up a man in a boat that was grounded on the riverbank," the judge said. "They heard him groaning, whimpering. He'd just come over from the Old City, and such were his rantings that my people thought it best to wake me. When I found out who he was, I thought it best to wake you."

"So who was it? I'm not in the mood to guess!"

"Your favorite scholar, Occus of the archives. Remember him?"

"Of course I remember him! What in heaven's name was he doing?"

"Fleeing from the Old City. He's hurt rather badly and fallen into a fever. Some kind of dragon bit him, he says. He's delirious, and they saw he might die suddenly.

"But he says he was in the Old City for several days, in the ruins of the Temple, with some people who'd discovered ancient scrolls. They were in a crypt beneath the Temple, a place that he says was part of the original Temple. These people brought him over because they couldn't read the scrolls. I don't know about such things. But Occus said it was a man and two boys."

Reesh wasn't sleepy anymore. What was a man with two boys doing in the ruins of the Temple?

"Did he describe them?"

Tombo shrugged. "He mostly carried on about the scrolls. Said they were priceless, genuine, they had to be copied and studied—on and on about it. Said they were written by King Ozias himself: the King Ozias in the Scriptures. Can such a thing be possible?"

What a question for such an hour of the morning! Reesh's mind raced. He was glad he wasn't standing.

"I'll tell you what's possible," he said. "A nasty little plot by a nasty little insect of a scholar—that's possible. He must have decided that the fragment of Scripture that I arranged for him to discover really was a fraud. That seems to be the consensus of opinion nowadays, behind closed doors in the scholarly community. I understand his colleagues have decided he's a fraud."

"I got the impression he was telling the truth about this, though," Tombo said.

"About long-lost works by King Ozias? Don't be ridiculous."

Tombo reached under his cloak. "I thought you'd better see this for yourself," he said, and produced a sheepskin, which he gently unrolled on Reesh's desk. "The blood's from Occus," he explained. "He had this tucked into his belt. He said he lost the others when the dragon attacked him."

"Dragons!" snorted Reesh. He bent over the sheepskin. He read the ancient scripts almost as easily as he could read his own writings, and he knew at a glance that this was truly writing that dated from Ozias' time—or at least a flawless imitation. But how could this sheepskin possibly be so old, and be so well preserved? Surely forgers would have thought of that and aged it artificially.

"Can you read it?" Tombo asked.

"Yes, of course I can! Not that this miserable lamp's much help. Do be quiet for a minute, will you?"

"So what does it say?"

Reesh squinted, ran a finger slowly over the printed words, and read aloud, translating as he went along:

"On the tenth day of the tenth month, I was taken up in the spirit and an angel of the Lord showed me a heavenly city that shone in the night like stars. But the angel said, Behold, the light of that city shall be extinguished, for they do wickedness therein. And he showed me the destruction of that city, by fire and great shakings, until I woke on my bed, sick and drenched with cold sweat, and bitter tears.

"Ah, Lord! I prayed. Why should you preserve my seed, but preserve no kingdom for him to inherit? You have showed me nothing but evil. But He said, The evil is in the hearts and minds of all the people, therefore my wrath burns hot against them. Their priests have corrupted themselves—"

Lord Reesh stopped reading. There was too much of Occus' blood on the page. It would have to be cleaned off somehow.

"Send your men across the river—in force, and at once," he said. "I want those scrolls, and I want Occus' confederates. For the time being, I wish to question him."

"My men are already getting set to cross the river," Tombo said. "The ruins are too dangerous by night, which you know. They'll leave at first light. As for Occus, if he's still alive, you can have him. When I left, he was raving about imps of Hell coming up out of the ground and dancing all around him."

"Let's go see him now," said Reesh.

Tombo's carriage was waiting outside to take them to the justice building. This early in the morning, with a sharp chill in the air and only a faint hint of approaching dawn, the city of Obann slept. Reesh was thankful for that. He huddled under a thick blanket and ground his teeth.

Occus lay on a cot, breathing shallowly, attended by a city-paid physician.

"I don't think he'll last much longer. I'm sorry, my lords," the healer said. "He's burning up with fever. There must be some kind of poison in his blood."

"Wake him," Judge Tombo said. "We need to question him."

"My lord, he's much too weak—"

"I said wake him. Try."

The doctor tried, and the patient died.

"Get your men across the river now," Lord Reesh said. "I must have those scrolls."

"But if they're only counterfeit—"

"It doesn't matter if they're counterfeit!" Reesh cried. "Just get them!"

All the jars were broken, all the scrolls wrapped tightly in a blanket. Ham would have no trouble carrying that.

They worked fast, not bothering to load up with firewood or make a meal. Martis was obviously in pain, but he didn't let that slow him.

"Nothing would be worse than to fall into Lord Reesh's hands," he said. "Believe me, I know. Even if somehow he failed to learn who we really are, he'd kill us just the same. He'll kill Occus, too. I could have told him that. The fool betrayed us for nothing. I never thought he would."

"But why should he kill someone who tried to bring him the scrolls?" Ellayne said.

"Because he doesn't want anyone to know about them. Weren't you listening when Occus translated them for us?"

"All that about temples being destroyed—that must be it," Jack said.

"To say nothing of the problems it'd pose for the oligarchs if the people started looking for a king!" Martis added. "But it's all prophecy, and I don't understand a tenth of it."

"Obst would understand it," Ellayne said. "But he's all the way back in Lintum Forest."

"Then that's where we've got to go—isn't it?" Jack said. "King Ozias' mother hid him in the forest when he was a baby. He grew up there. Only thing is, how do we get there before they catch us?"

"I don't know," said Martis.

Ham was all packed up, with Wytt perched atop the load, screeching his farewells to the Omah of the ruins. Hidden in the dark and in the rubble, they answered him. Martis made Jack and Ellayne ride on Dulayl.

"Shouldn't you be riding, not us?" Ellayne said. "How's your head?"

"Better than it'll be if Lord Reesh catches us. And I can still walk faster than the two of you."

Lintum Forest was a long way off, Jack thought, as they began to pick their way amid the heaps of broken stone; and this time they wouldn't dare stop in any of the cities. Once the First Prester's men failed to find them in the ruins, they'd be scouring the countryside on horseback. Dulayl was a fine horse, but he couldn't carry all three of them.

It always comes back to King Ozias, he thought, and to Lintum Forest.

If we ever see Ninneburky again, it'll be a miracle.

CHAPTER 41

A Message from the Thunder King

There was a celebration at the castle in the forest. Helki had won a great victory, another mardar was dead, and two more outlaw chiefs had come in to offer their submission to King Ryons.

"The oligarchs, the Temple—they're just thieves like we are," said one of the outlaw chiefs. "But a king, now—that's something different. Like something in the Scriptures."

Ryons had never in his life seen a book, much less read one. Obst promised to teach him, someday, how to read. "I have a Book of Holy Scripture," he said. "It's in my little cottage, unless someone has taken it. One of these days I'll go back and fetch it. A king ought to be able to read the Scriptures. Indeed, a king ought to know them better than anyone."

Helki returned from his battle with several dozen prisoners—prisoners no more, but men who'd freely chosen to serve the king who'd conquered them and spared their lives. Most notable among them were four brothers, black-skinned Hosa from the south, whose like had never been seen west of the mountains. Their language, full of pops and clicks, could be understood only by Obst, who had the gift of tongues.

"King Thunder sent his mardar to our country, and the mardar made our cattle die. He would have killed them all, and we would have starved, if our chiefs hadn't agreed to give him warriors," said the eldest of the brothers. They all had names, of course, but no one at the castle could pronounce them. This man's name meant Hawk, so that was what they called him. "We did not think a mardar could be killed, but now we have seen it. We want to see it again! And again, until there are no more left alive!"

Ryons mourned the loss of Szugetai. The horse-chief's men piled up a pyre of wood and burned the body, loudly singing from deep down in their throats until the old stone walls of the castle rang with it. Then they joined in the general celebration. By Helki's advice, this was to go on for three whole days.

"It's a good idea," Obst agreed. "You can see how hard some of the people have been working on the castle, clearing land, and putting up cabins. They need a holiday."

"The Lord be thanked we have nothing here that answers for strong drink," Helki said. "I've heard tall tales of what Abnaks can get up to when they're drunk."

"The Wallekki never drink," said Ryons. "Sometimes they let their slaves drink, and then they mock them when they're drunk."

"Never mind, Your Highness," Helki said. "There are no slaves in Lintum Forest. Most of us don't even pay our taxes."

Ryons didn't mind his people making merry, but he found it hard to share in their glee. He had to sup with his chieftains and award prizes to the winners of contests of archery, wrestling, and sheer strength; and he was cheerful then, because it was expected of him. But much of the time he preferred to spend with Jandra, Abgayle, and Obst. Having seen one live battle, he wasn't looking forward to the many that were sure to come.

"I know it must be hard for you," said Obst, "but it won't be quite so hard once you've learned to pray. God will give you strength, my boy."

At noontime on the final day of celebration, Abnak scouts came to the castle with a messenger. It was a tall Wallekki of the Wal-Kallut, demanding to see the King of Lintum Forest. And so the chieftains had to gather to receive him, and Ryons had to put on his finery and sit on his throne.

This man glared evilly at Shaffur, and Shaffur glared back.

"Beware this fellow, my brothers," Shaffur said. "My people have had dealings with his. They've not been pleasant dealings."

"And they are likely to be even more unpleasant, before the vultures feast on you," answered the Wal-Kallut.

"That'll do!" Helki said. "Let no one bicker in the presence of the king. What's your name, mister, and what's your errand?"

"I am Kayl, son of Eeb, son of Masur, who was the prince of the Bana-Sarr clan of the Wal-Kallut," the messenger said. "I command a thousand horsemen in the service of the Thunder King, master of the gods. I bring a message from him, the Great Man, to all the rebels who have run away to Lintum Forest."

One of Szugetai's men, who were now the king's sworn bodyguard, laughed raucously. Obst held up a hand to quiet him.

"We will hear the message, my lords and chieftains," he said. "But know this, Kayl—there is no man here who sees in your Thunder King anything but a wicked and deluded man. You would be wise to moderate your language."

Ryons agreed. He'd noticed a spreading grin on the face of old Chief Spider that should have spelled a warning to the messenger. And if Spider didn't strike him down, Shaffur would.

"I deliver the message as I was commanded by the mardar of my army: and it is this," Kayl said. "Know that the Great Man's armies now are marching into Obann in numbers beyond your reckoning. Their mission is to lay siege to the city of Obann, to destroy it, and to tear down the Temple to the god of Obann and carry him away as a prisoner. From this nothing shall deflect us.

"But the Great Man has not forgotten you! Once the city has been laid in ruins, his hosts shall march to Lintum Forest and hew it down with axes and burn it with fire. Not one of you shall be left alive. As for the slave whom you have styled a king, intending mockery, he shall be taken into captivity forever—after his eyes have been put out with hot iron. I have spoken."

Silence fell over the assembled chieftains—a silence that Helki broke with a loud whistle.

"Well! I reckon those words are like to give me nightmares for a month," he said; and the chieftains grinned.

"Anyone would think you were trying to ruin our celebration, mister."

But then Ryons stepped down from his throne. He didn't know what made him do it; he didn't know what he was going to say. The words just came.

"This is our answer to the Thunder King," he said. "Tell him this: the true God reigns in Heaven, but His eyes are on the earth. He knows your thoughts before you think them; His eyes find out the secrets of your heart. Whether I live or whether I die, the Lord is with me; He knows His people by their names. The wicked He sweeps away like dust, and they are seen no more."

Here the words stopped. Ryons felt as if he were standing alone atop the highest mountain in the world, and that the world was so far down below him that it didn't matter anymore.

He stood before the messenger; and Kayl the son of Eeb went pale under his swarthy skin, and some men saw him tremble. Without another word, he stepped back a step, and then another step; and then he turned and rushed out of Ryons' presence as fast as he could without running.

Suddenly Ryons was very tired, and his knees buckled. He groped behind him for his makeshift throne and sat down, hard. For a moment he wondered what had happened to the mardar's messenger; but it came back to him almost immediately.

"Praise God, who has remembered us in time of trouble!" Obst cried. The chieftains looked puzzled. Obst turned to Ryons and laid a hand on his shoulder. "Are you all right, King Ryons?"

"I think so."

"Do you know what you said to that messenger?"

"No, not really. Did I say something wrong?"

Obst laughed, and turned to the chieftains. "This boy spoke the Fortieth Sacred Song, composed by King Ozias under the inspiration of God's spirit—and he spoke it nearly word for word! This boy has never read the Scriptures. He doesn't know how to read, and I never taught him the words of that song. Can there be any doubt at all that he spoke the words God gave him? Can there be any doubt at all that he truly is a king, and the heir of King Ozias, who is to receive from God's own hand the throne of Obann?"

Ryons' bodyguards clashed their short swords on their round shields and bellowed their approval. Chief Spider threw back his head and guffawed. "Not a bit!" he roared. "Not the least little bit of doubt—and I'll split the skull of any man who says there is!"

"Looks like we've got another prophet in this army," Helki said.

The sun was up by the time they found their way out of the ruined city. Somewhere behind them, they knew, the First Prester's men were combing the place for them. How long would they keep at it before concluding that their prey wasn't in the city anymore?

"I wonder if Occus can lead them back to our camp," Jack said.

"I was surprised he found the river," Martis said. "But all he had to say was that we were camping in the Old Temple. Many men know where to find that." They had no way of knowing that Occus had lapsed into a delirium before he could tell them that. But it wouldn't take Reesh long, Martis knew, to decide that the Old Temple was the best place to look for scroll-seekers.

"We won't get far if they come after us on horseback," Ellayne said; and to that there was no answer.

Their only plan, as yet, was to put as much space as they could between themselves and the Old City, and avoid villages and farms. Beyond that, Martis had only a vague idea of staying well to the south of the river; and then they would have to go steadily eastward to get to Lintum Forest. Most of the journey would be on open, gently rolling plains.

"It can't be as bad as it looks," Jack said. "We've done what God wanted us to do. We've found the missing book. Not much point in finding it, if it's just going to be lost again!"

By noon they were too weary to go any farther without food and rest. They stopped under an isolated clump of undersized trees, with the blue vastness of the sky above them and the empty, uninhabited land around them as far as the eye could see. Because of the lay of the land, they couldn't see the ruined city; but they knew it wasn't very far away.

They didn't make a fire, only rested their bodies and munched on some biscuits. Ellayne cut a strip from one of the blankets and bandaged Martis' head. It needed washing, but that would have to wait until they came upon a stream. As Martis pointed out, they didn't know how long their drinking water would have to last.

"What do you say, Wytt?" Jack asked. "Is there any water in this country?"

The little hairy man sprang up onto Ham's back and sniffed the air.

"He says there's some good water, not far away," Ellayne said, as he chattered to her. "I guess he can smell it. What do you think, Martis? Can we get to Lintum Forest?"

He shrugged. "Who can say? If Reesh's men don't pick up our trail and ride us down; if a Heathen scouting party doesn't find us; if one of those giant birds, or some other deadly animal, doesn't make a meal of us; if we don't starve to death, or die of thirst—well, then, all we have to do is keep on trekking east, and eventually we'll get there. It'll be halfway through the summer by then; maybe even later."

In a little while they got up and went on, carrying with them the missing book of Holy Scripture, which none of them could read or understand.

CPSIA information can be obtained
at www.ICGtesting.com
Printed in the USA
FSHW011916150519
58179FS

9 781891 375552